& Fine

Big & Beautiful, Book Five

Mary E. Thompson

BluEyed
Press

For my brother, who's always encouraging me to be healthy, not skinny.

One

I still couldn't believe I'd been dumped. After spending two months with a guy I thought I knew him. I never imagined he would be such an asshole. He seemed sweet and considerate, kind, understanding, and decent. Little did I know he was none of those things.

I wiped the fresh tears from my cheeks and eyed myself in the mirror critically. My friends would pick up on the most subtle changes in my appearance so I had to camouflage my misery.

Or maybe it was just embarrassment.

Whatever it was, I wasn't going to rehash it all. Yeah, they'd want to lynch him as badly as I did, but it was just too painful to talk about. I mean, to think he said-

Nope, I wasn't going to get worked up again. I had to meet my friends in fifteen minutes. Every Tuesday we got together for a girls' night. What started out as one night a week to hang out with my three best friends from college had morphed into a night for six of us to get together, usually with at least one of the four men that had paired off with my friends.

Ever since the first time Mandy had brought her fiancé, Xander, to a girls' night I was jealous. Not in an I-want-him way, but in an I-want-my-own way. I'd always been popular, even though I was a full figured size 20. My 40D breasts were a big selling point with most men. They were for Cade. He loved my breasts.

Damn it! There I went again. Nope, I was done crying over men who weren't good enough for me. Especially ones who were first class assholes.

I yanked off my red framed glasses so I could focus on my red-rimmed eyes. It wasn't as bad as it could be, but it was still noticeable. Fuck. Addi would see right through me. Lexi probably would, too. I had to get a grip.

I rushed from my bedroom to the kitchen. I loved my two bedroom house, but it was quiet since Addi moved out. She and I were roommates freshman year of college at Erie University in Winterville, NY, where we still lived. After growing up in the city, Buffalo that is, going to college in a small town seemed crazy, but I fell in love with the place. Mandy and Claire were high school friends with a room across the hall from us. The four of us became friends quickly, and after 11 years of friendship there were some things you couldn't hide.

Like eyes that had clearly spent most of the day crying.

I knew crying over someone I'd only been with for two months seemed ridiculous. If any of my friends had done the same I'd call her out for being ridiculous, then take her out drinking and introduce her to a new guy. I fully expected similar treatment.

Although with most of them paired off our days of drinking were few and far between. Not to mention the fact that we were all getting *old* in a hurry. Twenty-nine wasn't really old, but after hitting that mark just a month earlier and realizing it was my last birthday before I turned 30, I started to feel my age. It didn't help that I was home, alone, by nine most nights. Even weekends.

When you can recite the cable line-up on Friday *and* Saturday night, you're old.

I threw a spoon into the freezer then rushed back to my bedroom. All day I'd been in the same clothes and I could go for something fresh. Being a photographer wasn't a grueling job, something my mother reminded me of regularly, but after working all day I felt a little stale in the same thing.

Oh, hell, who was I kidding. I just wanted to look cute when I went out. Normally I'd say because you never knew when you'd meet someone, but that night, well, I just wanted to make sure no one picked up on my mood.

God, if there was ever a night for all the guys to show up, it was that one.

The weather in Winterville was beautiful since it was mid-June. My favorite time of year, even though it was my busiest. Everyone wanted to be a June bride for some unknown reason. So far none of my friends got married in June, but Mandy and Xander were getting married in July. I knew I'd never be a June bride. Hell, I didn't think I'd be an any month bride.

After the day I'd had I wasn't even sure I'd date again.

I tugged on a pair of jean capris and found a loose fitting light grey top. Back in the kitchen I retrieved my frozen spoon and held it over my puffy eyes to reduce the swelling, and prayed it worked.

A few seconds later I was back in front of the mirror. The redness wasn't completely gone but that could have been from the cold. Why did I try this stuff when it really mattered? I should have tested that stupid theory when I wasn't about to go out.

Oh, well. I lined my eyes and dusted on eye shadow. A few swipes of mascara and I almost looked normal. Lip gloss and a bit of blush and I could pass for my usual carefree self.

With five minutes to spare I jumped in my car and drove over to Bite Me!, Charlie's bakery and our meeting site for the last year. If I had any desire to go the other way I'd be after a woman like Charlie... she could cook like a dream, she had this beautiful twinkling laugh, and she was the sweetest person ever.

Of course, she was also fat, like me.

We all were, but the others didn't like me using the 'f' word. No, not fuck. They didn't care about that one. I meant fat. They all said it was offensive to women like us. They preferred words like chubby or lush or fluffy. I just told it like it was. I was fat. No sugar-coating would change that.

But me saying it about myself and someone else calling me fat... it didn't work that way. When Cade said-

Nope, still not going there. Not with fresh make-up. I could have another melt-down later. Tonight was all about recon. I had a mission in mind. Cade was going to regret his every move, his every word. And next time it would be me telling him it was over.

If I gave him a second chance in the first place.

I threw my slightly used Honda CR-V in park and headed in to Bite Me! determined to make the night a success. Even if that only meant forgetting about that asshole for a couple of hours.

My phone rang when I was halfway to the door, and I pulled it out, ready to tell Addi I was about to walk in. Damn. It was my mother. She'd called earlier, when I was working, and I basically blew her off. She hated my job, called it a hobby, so she had no problems interrupting me at work. I guess she didn't get enough though if she was calling back.

I hit ignore and shoved the phone back in my purse. I'd pay for that one later, but I wasn't in the mood for her. My mom and I were close, in the sense of we talked every day, or close to it, but not in the sense of we ever had real conversations. Most of the time my mom was telling me how badly I was screwing up my life and giving me instructions on how to fix it. I wasn't in the mood for that.

Charlie was heading to our table when I finally walked in the door. She nodded me over and lifted her hand, showing me a plate with my cupcakes already on it. I hated when Charlie didn't let us pay. We were there every week, sometimes more, and about once a month she gave us all free cupcakes. Of course we snuck money into her tip jar when she wasn't looking, but still.

She set the plate with my raspberry lemonade cupcakes down next to Addi then went back to get her own salted caramel one before joining us. Mandy wasn't there yet, but that was nothing new. She was late for everything, but we loved her anyway.

"Hey Ads, what's up?" I asked as I took my seat. Joey was on the other side of my best friend and I nodded at him. He was a good guy, but I felt territorial toward Addi. They'd only been together about six months and the fact that they weren't engaged, or married, was a shock amongst our friends. Claire eloped with Aidan after about a month, Mandy and Xander were engaged after six months, and Lexi and Mike, well they were friends with benefits for a while, but they still got engaged two months after they made their relationship official.

Joey was good to Addi, but he still took my best friend away from me. She'd moved in with him and left me alone in our rental house. It was nice to have the space, but I missed my best friend. I went from seeing her every day to seeing her once or twice a week.

But she was happy, which made missing her worthwhile. That's what I kept telling myself.

"Hey, Sam, any crazy brides today?" she asked teasing me.

Addi was a teacher, high school chemistry, and while she was off for the summer I was working my ass off. In Winterville, NY, the weather was only nice for about two months. My two busiest months.

And my best friend was rubbing it in.

"Just watch it. I'll start telling them you're my assistant and giving out your number instead of mine."

Addi laughed knowing I'd never do it, but damn. All summer it was one crisis after another. None of which were actually important. I hated working with brides, but since they paid better, I did it.

Just don't tell my mother. She'd have me locked in a room doing career aptitude tests forever if she found out there was any part of photography I didn't love.

What I did love though, was doing shoots for families, capturing the sweetness of kids and the love of the parents. Even if it was just for a few minutes, I loved seeing the perfect imperfection of a family. The mess of families were just part of what made them wonderful.

"How many more days?" I asked Addi, directing attention away from my troubles and back to her. After years of working with people I found it was easy to distract them by asking about the things they were excited about. As much as Addi loved her job, she lived for summer break. Since this would be her first with Joey I knew they were planning a few trips and way more fun than I would get to have over the summer.

"Six more days," Addi breathed as though it took effort. "But they're exam days so I don't have much going on. I'll have to grade all my exams, but I only have five classes. I'll proctor a few exams and spend the rest of the time in my classroom getting ready to leave for ten weeks."

She leaned into Joey as she spoke and I could tell they'd already planned something big. Wondering what it was, I found myself jealous again... and thinking I'd never have what she had. I wasn't strong enough to get hurt again.

"What are you guys planning?"

I directed the question at Joey so he wouldn't feel left out, but I didn't think he would feel included for a while. It was hard to break into our circle, not because we weren't nice, but because we had so much history. Addi and I had lived together for 11 years until Joey came along.

"Since some of us still have work, we're only doing a few trips. I think we're going to head up to Niagara on the Lake one weekend, maybe down to the Finger Lakes, and we might even head out to New York City. It'll be fun."

Joey was beaming at her and I knew he would pop the question soon.

Addi was lucky to have him. And yeah, I encouraged her to date him. Addi met Joey when she was trying out casual sex for the first time ever. Joey was the lucky guy who stumbled into her path when she was on the hunt. Addi didn't want to fall for him, but everyone except Addi knew she'd never survive a relationship that was based purely on sex. Their road was a little rocky, but there was no denying they were great together.

"That sounds like a great summer," Lexi chimed in. She knew my reservations about Joey, but after getting married to Mike she had more in common with Addi's situation than with me. I knew she was trying to be supportive.

"Claire, you're hosting Mandy's shower, right?" Charlie asked.

Claire nodded. "Yep, everything is all set. It's a couples shower so the men are coming too. It's going to be at my house though so Mandy and Xander don't have to worry about clean-up."

"And we can't tell you how much we appreciate that," Mandy said, dropping into the seat next to Claire. "It's going to be so much fun. But no games or stuff like that. Basically just a chance for everyone to hang out and give us presents."

We all laughed at Mandy knowing she was being totally serious. Mandy loved presents, something Xander had picked up on quickly and took care of regularly.

Xander was right behind Mandy with their cupcakes and drinks. He took the seat next to her and passed her red velvet cupcakes and hot chocolate over. I didn't understand how Mandy could drink hot chocolate, even in the summer, but I lived on coffee some days and knew it wasn't that different.

Mandy was the bubbly one among us most of the time. Working in customer service had given her that outgoing personality. Claire was usually relatively quiet, although since she got together with Aidan she'd come out of the shell she hid in for the first decade I knew her. It helped that she'd started an organization helping prevent rape and was now a paid public speaker. She couldn't hide with so much of her personal history being public knowledge.

Between the two of them they carried most of the conversation for rest of the night. Everyone was making summer plans, even though all of us except Addi had regular jobs. Mandy and Xander had a trip to Cape Cod planned, Claire and Aidan were going to Mackinac Island in Michigan, and Lexi and Mike were going to Washington DC. Charlie even said she might get away for a few days since she'd just hired Addi's student, Kendall, and she was working full time for the summer.

I was the only one stuck in Winterville, working like a slave, for ten weeks.

No, I was going to be changing myself. Improving myself. I would be a whole new Sam by the end of summer.

When we all finished our cupcakes and the couples made it known they were ready to head home we cleaned up and said our goodbyes. I walked out with my arm through Addi's and asked if we could talk for a minute. Joey took the hint and said he'd wait for her in the car.

"I know you don't like him," Addi began.

"This has nothing to do with Joey. And I don't not like him. I just miss my best friend. I know he's good to you and you love him. Anyone can see he's completely devoted to you. You're lucky, I'm just jealous of him."

"Ooh, Sam. I never knew you went that way," Addi teased me.

I rolled my eyes but grinned. "You know if I did I'd go for Charlie so she could cook for me. I'd never marry someone who had the whole summer off and rubbed it in."

Addi threw her head back and laughed. She knew I hated it when she reminded me of her career, but she did it anyway. She also knew I loved my job and would never become a teacher no matter how great the hours were.

"Okay, then if it's not to tell me to leave Joey, what did you want?"

"I was wondering if you'd tell me about your gym. I think I'm going to start exercising."

Addi eyed me carefully. She knew I'd never shown an interest in exercise before. I'd often criticized her for bothering with it, claiming it was a torture tactic invented by skinny people.

I waited for her to ask why the change of heart and to jump on me for giving in. To tease me and say she knew eventually I'd cave. Or to just question why I'd care.

But she didn't.

Addi just nodded. "Sure. It's called Dave's Gym. It's sort of a hole in the wall, but inside is pretty great. They have trainers on staff that are included in your membership and all the exercise machines you could imagine plus weights. They offer a few aerobic classes, but not too many. Mostly it's men, but there are always women around. I've never felt out of place even though I'm heavy. I think you'll like it there."

I catalogued the information as she spoke, knowing I'd go check it out before I committed. If they had a website I'd look that over too just to get a feel for the place. It sounded decent though, like someplace I'd be okay going to, especially if Addi liked it.

"I can go with you tomorrow after school if you want."

"Oh, no, that's okay. I think I'd rather exercise in the morning when everyone else is at work. You know, fewer people to scare off with my fatness."

Addi cringed at the f word but didn't correct me. "Okay. Well, let me know what you think.

And if you need anything there just ask one of the trainers. They're great."

"Any one in particular I should ask for?"

Addi shook her head after thinking for a second. "Nah. They're all pretty good. The ones I've worked with at least. They do have female trainers too so if you're not into having one of the guys you can ask for a woman. They really work hard to make sure everyone is comfortable there."

"Sounds like a good place. Thanks."

Addi looked like she wanted to ask more, but she clamped her mouth shut. We said good night and I told her to say bye to Joey for me. I could at least try to be nice, right?

Two

I wasn't ready to join the gym just yet. I knew I needed to. Or at least if I wanted to make Cade regret being an asshole I needed to, but I wasn't quite ready.

Plus, I had work to do. That took precedence, right?

The perfect antidote to my shitty mood since I found out Cade was such an ass was a sweet family to spend the day with. Thankfully that was exactly what was on my schedule for the day. It was a new client, a family I'd never met before, and I was excited to get to know them. There was something about spending an hour or so with people and taking their pictures that always let you into their world. Especially when that world involved kids.

Winterville Park, near the center of town was a great back drop for pictures. In the nicer months of the year, all three of them, I used the park as much as possible for sessions. Occasionally I headed to the beach at Lake Erie, but the park was my favorite since there was such variety there, and it was closer.

I pulled into the lot and threw my bags over my shoulder. The family, the Alexanders, were supposed to meet me at the edge of the lot on the trail that led toward the bridge. No one was there yet, but I was early, as always. It was a cardinal rule of mine to never leave a client waiting so I was always at least 15 minutes early.

While waiting for them to arrive I mentally took stock of the park. Bright green grass covered almost all the area, with massive trees offering shade and bolts of light that made pictures come to life. A bridge crossed a small stream that ran through the entire area and led to a small pond at one end. A butterfly garden and wildflower garden brought in color to the otherwise monochromatic space.

People walked, biked, and skateboarded through the park on a daily basis. Kids loved the playground the town installed a few years ago, near the pond, to give the little kids something fun to do. My favorite was the gazebo.

An oversized gazebo anchored one of the edges of the park. Many a June bride dreamed of saying I do under the light wooden structure. It could easily hold just about any size wedding party, up to twenty could stand under it comfortably, and the surrounding open space gave guests of the lucky brides a 360 view of the ceremony.

To say I wanted to get married there was a bit of an understatement. That site was what inspired me to become a photographer. In college I went wandering one day and ended up finding the park. It was early spring and flowers were just starting to bloom. I'd always loved photography and was studying it at school, along with my business major since my parents refused to pay for my degree if I didn't have something marketable. Until that moment though, I never thought I could truly make photography a career.

There was a wedding going on that day. The edges of the bride's dress were muddy due to the overnight rain storm. The tips of the groom's shoes were caked with the same mud, but they only had eyes for each other. I stood in the back where I could see them both and knew I wanted to capture those moments forever.

Voices from the parking lot broke up my trip into the past and I turned with a smile to watch the family piling out of the SUV parked near mine. The mom looked ragged, the dad was grinning at something one of the kids said, and both kids looked ready to run, in opposite directions.

I had no doubt they were the Alexanders.

Maddie, the mom, walked over to me while Dad, Johnny, wrangled the boys.

"Are you Samantha?" Maddie asked tentatively.

"I am. It's nice to meet you Maddie."

"You, too," she said as we shook hands. "I just hope these guys aren't too much for you. I told my husband I wanted family pictures taken before Ben started kindergarten. The boys are a bit wild today though."

I smiled what I hoped was a reassuring smile and told her everything would be okay. Johnny walked up with one boy under each arm, all three smiling, and introduced himself.

"I'd shake your hand but I'm not sure I can lift mine."

I laughed and agreed. "No worries. You seem to have your hands full, literally. Should we head into the park?"

Maddie nodded and fell into step beside me while Johnny carried the boys behind us. The peals of their laughter scared a few birds from the nearby trees. More than one squirrel darted up a tree as we got closer. It sounded wonderful to me.

Once we made it to the bridge I slid my camera out of my bag and pointed it at Johnny and the boys. Before they had a chance to react I snapped a few shots of the three of them giggling like teenagers looking at their first PlayBoy.

During my conversations with Maddie I knew she wanted some posed family shots, on the bridge, in the gazebo, near the stream, but getting those shots would be dependent on how well I could keep the boys interested in what we were doing.

The family didn't opt for the matchy-matchy khakis and white button down shirts option, but they all had a cohesive look. Maddie was wearing a light pink a-line dress with a brown belt just under her chest. Johnny was in khakis but paired it with a light blue Polo shirt the same color as the sky. The boys were both wearing khaki shorts, Ben with an olive green Polo and Nick with a yellow Polo. All four of them were wearing flip flops.

"Dad, why don't you put the boys down for a minute while I get set up?" The boys kicking and wiggling had to be testing the strength in Johnny's arms, but more than that, I wanted the boys to get out some of their energy before I asked them to pose for their mom's pictures.

Johnny let them go and they immediately ran to the edge of the water. I caught a few shots of them crouched low and looking at something in the stream then turned my camera toward Maddie and Johnny who were watching their rambunctious boys with love clearly in their eyes. They weren't paying attention to me so I took pictures as I pleased, smiling as I caught them in a sweet kiss.

"Maddie and Johnny, can I get you two on the bridge for a minute?" They wandered over to the bridge and looked down at the boys who were yelling up to them. I caught the family moment then asked the boys to join their parents. They took off running and leapt into their parents arms.

Once I'd taken a few shots of them without their knowledge I asked everyone to look at me. I was poised over the stream, praying I wouldn't fall in while I shot. The four pairs of matching brown eyes looked over the edge at me and grinned. Within seconds the boys were squirming and I moved up the bank to get the last of the shots.

"Let's go to the gazebo next. It should be free this time of day." Maddie nodded and pointed in the direction we were headed so the boys could run ahead of the adults. I hung back to catch Maddie and Johnny holding hands with the boys running in the distance.

The gazebo was empty like I'd assumed. Ben and Nick ran circles around it but Maddie and Johnny headed right up the steps to stand inside. I took pictures as I approached, catching the boys bright smiles and flushed cheeks as well as Maddie's adoration for her husband and his blatant love for her. That was why I took pictures. Behind the camera I could become invisible and capture moments that the families didn't even know were right in front of them.

Johnny called the boys up to them once he noticed me standing there. Each boy stood in front of a parent with the parents' arms wrapped around the boy's neck, hands resting on their chest. It was one of the poses Maddie really wanted. They looked like the perfect little family and I felt just the slightest twinge of envy. They had something I wanted. I'd never been one of those girls who sat around imagining every aspect of my dream wedding, but I'd be lying if I said I'd never thought about it.

More than the wedding though, I'd imagined the marriage. The idea of having someone to share my life with, someone who loved me for me and didn't constantly tell me everything I needed to change about my life. That's not the family I wanted, unfortunately it was the family I had.

Speaking of which, my phone rang from deep in my bag. I knew it was my mom based on the ringtone. Not that I'd ever tell her I used Katy Perry's Roar for her to remind myself to be strong when she called.

I ignored the call and focused on my clients. The boys started moving again and we all went toward the pond. On the way we paused to smell the flowers, literally, and the boys tried, unsuccessfully, to catch a butterfly. A few more photos they didn't know I was taking and we made it to the pond.

The muddy bank drew the boys in right away and I knew their clothes would be ruined in seconds if I didn't get their attention. "Hey guys, want to go down the slides?"

Slides had always been my favorite as a kid. I loved the feeling of the fresh air whipping around me and the freedom associated with letting go and trusting I would be able to catch myself at the end. As an adult I didn't get that feeling much, even though it was only a few seconds long. To be able to let go of everything and not feel the pressure to succeed, to get married, to have kids, to lose weight, to be perfect... I could dream.

Right on cue my phone rang again. My mother believed nothing else mattered except her. If I didn't drop everything and answer her call she'd keep calling until I either answered or my dad convinced her to drop it. Usually the first one.

The boys took the bait and headed for the playground. I poised at the end of the slides and caught that look of freedom plastered on their little faces. They moved to the swings, Nick needing to be pushed by someone and Ben pumping his legs like a champ. They climbed the playhouse and even got their parents up there with them. I had them all look over the side and snapped a few shots of them, four pairs of flushed cheeks and giant smiles.

Back at the edge of the pond a few minutes later Maddie and Johnny kissed while the boys stood in front of them. At first they were looking at me, but once they realized what their parents were doing, the boys made faces and chorused, "Eewwwwww!"

I kept taking pictures.

Maddie and Johnny split apart with a laugh and Johnny snatched both boys up again. He ran up and down the bank with the kids screaming and laughing. Maddie looked on, love pouring out of her. They couldn't have been happier if they tried.

That's what I loved about taking pictures. You can't hide how you feel from a camera. It captures the emotions we wear, the honesty we might not want to show others. And I get to be a part of that for the families I work with. My job was awesome.

Katy Perry sung Roar again as I was packing up my stuff. The Alexanders were going to stay and play for a while and I agreed to meet with Maddie in a few days to go over the pictures.

Back at my studio I set about editing the photos. Some didn't turn out well when one of the boys moved as I shot, others had someone with eyes crossed or a tongue darting out to lick lips. I moved all the less than stellar shots to another folder and concentrated on making sure the best shots were perfect, no red-eye, no random glares, no imperfections.

Once I was satisfied with the results, I heard my phone ringing. Again. "Hi Mom," I said without any enthusiasm.

"Samantha! I've been trying to reach you for two days. I thought you were dead!"

My mother, the drama queen. If I didn't answer I must be dead. Not busy. Busy wasn't an option. Dead was.

"I don't know why you do that to me. You had me so worried!"

Yep, the guilt trip. If we'd gone on half as many vacations as my mother led me on guilt trips I'd have seen the world. Twice.

"Mom, I was working."

"Oh, good. You got a real job. Why didn't you tell me?" The hurt was back. It was all about her.

"Yes, Mom, I got a real job. Years ago when I opened my own photography studio."

She groaned. "That is not a real job, Samantha. It is a hobby. But not to worry. That's why I called you. Rose told me her daughter's company is hiring. You just need a college degree, any one will do, and since your father and I were smart enough to make sure you had a good one, you should be okay. I'm not sure what the job will entail, but I have her daughter's phone number so you can call and talk to her about the job. Rose said something about sending a resume but I don't have the address."

It was my turn to groan. She was constantly sending me on wild goose chases trying to get me a 'real job.' I hated it. I was happy with my situation. I loved working with families and I was not interested in living by someone else's rules. Not that my mother cared how I felt or what I wanted. She was just 'trying to help' she always said.

Like I needed it.

I dutifully wrote down the number even though I would never apply for the job. She made me promise to call Rose's daughter, not that I had a clue who Rose was, and I regretfully agreed. I wanted to call the woman as much as I wanted to go to the gym.

Well, maybe not even that much. At least going to the gym would lead to something good. All that phone call could lead to was me getting more frustrated with my mother.

"The job pays well and has benefits. Plus, they even offer membership to a gym, isn't that wonderful?"

I rolled my eyes. The only digs she didn't manage to get in was the fact that I was still single and hadn't procreated yet. If my mother didn't insult me at least twice a day I was pretty sure she wasn't happy.

God knew I wasn't happy, but that didn't matter.

"Sounds delightful, Mom."

She huffed. "You don't have to be so rude Samantha. I'm trying to help you."

"Mom," I began slowly, "I have a job. I work full time. Sometimes more. I love what I do and I make a decent living."

"Samantha, your job is just-"

"A hobby," I finished with her. "I know you feel that way, but it's not for me. I'm sorry you don't agree, but all the job offers in the world aren't going to turn me into a lawyer like Heather."

"Oh, I know, honey. You'll never be like Heather. You two are too different."

In other words, she was smart, beautiful, married, and had kids. I couldn't even get one of those right. Oh, yeah, and she had the right job. Oh for five. Can you guess who the favorite was?

"Thanks, Mom," I said dryly.

"Call Rose's daughter, honey. You'll feel better once you have a good job. And answer the phone next time I call you. I'll end up in an early grave if I think you're dead in a ditch somewhere."

"Yes, Mom."

We hung up, and I had the sudden urge to hit something.

Three

The next day I woke up still in a shitty mood. I hadn't called Rose's daughter yet, and didn't know if I ever would, but I needed to do something to stop feeling so off.

It was time. I had to do it eventually, and like ripping off a band-aid, I was going to get it over with. Between Cade's words echoing in my head and my mother's constant badgering, I figured it was time. Not that I'd admit it to her. She wasn't going to know a thing about me joining a gym. Ever.

Thankfully Dave's Gym wasn't far from my studio so if I decided to join I could exercise in the morning before starting work. I groaned. Just the thought of exercising daily made me feel sick, but I knew I had to do it if I wanted to make Cade sorry.

After fixing a bagel with only a little cream cheese for breakfast and chugging a cup of coffee, I was ready to go. I threw an outfit into a bag, hoping they had a locker room where I could shower before work, and left. I decided on fitted shorts and an old t-shirt to work out in and prayed I wasn't out of place. I tied my long hair into a thick braid to keep it out of my face and left.

The parking lot outside was busier than I expected for a Thursday morning. Pushing aside my fears and insecurities I grabbed my bag and headed in.

The first thing I saw when I walked in was light. I was shocked by how bright the place was. I expected dim lighting and a shabbiness that came with most gyms. A woman behind the front desk smiled pleasantly at me. "Can I help you?"

I guess it was pretty obvious I was new. "Uh, yeah. My friend works out here and suggested it. I was thinking about joining."

"Oh, excellent. I'm Jennie. If I can get you to fill out this paperwork I'll take you for a tour. We give you two weeks to try the place out for free before you have to actually join. They like to make sure you want to be here and not feel like you have to because you joined. Oh, you can sit over there to fill out the paperwork and I'll tell you all about the place while we walk around."

She pointed to a comfortable looking chair with a table right next to it. I smiled at the too-perky Jennie and walked over to the table. The front room was large, two story height, with tons of windows up high. From the outside the place looked like an old warehouse, and inside it looked the same, but not worn down like I'd imagined.

Off the front room I could see different rooms that appeared to be focused on different activities. One room held lots of spinning cardio equipment, from another came the clang of weights, and the last boasted loud music that had to be the classes Addi mentioned. Two doors behind me had 'Men' and 'Women' on them so at least I knew there were locker rooms.

I filled out enough paperwork to purchase a new house and went back to Jennie for my tour. "I think I'm all set."

"Great!" she said. "Let me get someone up here and I'll walk you around."

A voice from behind me said, "I'll take her, Jennie."

I turned and saw the most beautiful man I'd ever laid eyes on. He was coming from a hallway I hadn't noticed before, but he fit the part of gym rat. In a t-shirt that looked like it would fit a normal person just fine, his shoulders, chest, and arms threatened the seams. The shirt floated around his middle just enough to let me know he was lean, but not so much to make me think he was small there.

His legs were covered in shorts that also looked like they could use some extra space, and he had the bulkiest calves I'd ever seen.

If I ran into the guy in the street I'd run for my life, but in the gym he fit. If I did an ad for the place, he'd be the cover model, easily. His shaved head, sharp hazel eyes, and chiseled jaw took his incredible physique straight to holy damn. Even with the scars across his right eyebrow and chin, he was stunning.

And exactly the kind of guy I'd sworn off. Forever.

"Brady!" Jennie exclaimed, clearly surprised to see him. "Are you sure?"

She looked at him with an edge of something that I couldn't tell if it was fear or embarrassment. If she was afraid of the guy I wasn't sure I wanted to be alone with him. Then again, it was a gym. He wouldn't risk his job.

"I'm sure, Jennie. Thanks."

Brady nodded at me and let his eyes drift over me just briefly. He didn't look me in the eyes but he nodded in my direction before taking off toward the first of the rooms.

"Did Jennie tell you we give you two free weeks before you have to join?"

"Yeah," I answered, trying to clear my head. This guy was intense. He looked like he could crush me with his bare hands and that he was barely reigning in his desire to do just that.

"Good. Well, this is the cardio room. We keep all the equipment up to date and have someone come in every week to make sure things are running well. If you notice any problems with one of the machines just let anyone know and we'll make sure it gets on the schedule."

"Okay," I said, not really sure what else I could say.

"If there's an empty machine you're welcome to jump on. If not, we ask that you use the board. When people are waiting we also ask that you're only on a machine for thirty minutes. If the place is dead, like now, you can stay on as long as you'd like."

I looked around the crowded room and wondered what busy looked like if that was dead. There were people on three quarters of the machines. So much for not scaring too many off.

"The next room is the weight room," Brady said as he walked away. "We have free weights, kettlebells, medicine balls, and weight machines. The trainers' offices are in here, and they can help you with whatever you need. If you're not sure how to use a machine or want some help with a certain area, just ask."

"Are you a trainer?" I asked, hoping I wouldn't end up with him training me. He was a little too intense for me. Like he never had any fun. Although he was nice to look at.

"No, I'm not," he said without explaining. "We don't want people getting hurt so the trainers are paid staff, not here to get extra pay for what they already do. Usually there are two trainers available for sessions and one who will work the floor. If no sessions are booked, the others will be on the floor, too. We always have three here so there's no reason to get hurt."

"I won't," I shook my head, feeling like a child being chastised for playing around.

Brady looked at me again. His intense stare made me want to fidget, but I stood my ground. He leaned into me, almost like he was going to kiss me, then someone slammed weights together. Brady backed up so fast I thought I'd imagined his movement.

Hell, maybe I did.

Brady blinked once, then twice, and turned away from me. He walked to the third room. "In here we do aerobics classes. The schedule is posted every month and you can take home a copy plus we keep it updated on the website. We try to keep a variety of classes so sometimes we'll drop a class that isn't as popular and pick up a new class. You should be able to find just about anything at some point during the month."

I nodded and looked over the schedule posted on the wall. Spinning, yoga, pilates, zumba, kick-boxing… yeah, that wasn't going to happen. Getting my fat ass to the gym was going to be painful enough. Showing my uncoordinated skills in a room full of other people was something akin to torture in my book.

"Thanks," I mumbled, not willing to tell him it wouldn't happen.

"Can I ask you something?" he blurted out.

I looked up and found him studying me. He was close, too close. At that distance I could see the hints of green in his eyes and smell the cool, fresh scent that seemed to seep out of him. More scars were visible, not only on his face, but on his arms and one down his leg. His nose kicked to the side like it'd been broken more than once too.

All that, combined with the way he towered over my 5'9" body by six or seven inches, I should have been running from him. For some unknown reason I couldn't though. It was like he had me under some sort of spell. I couldn't turn from him and I didn't want to. I wanted to know what he wanted.

I finally nodded and Brady sucked in a breath. He turned away, like all of a sudden he didn't want to ask. I saw the struggle on his face and wondered what could be so bad.

Closing his eyes he shook his head then said, "Why did you want to join Dave's Gym? We ask everyone."

I knew that wasn't what he wanted to ask me, but I didn't push it. After that day I knew I'd likely never see him again. Even if I did join I'd make sure I didn't work with Brady. And I definitely wasn't going to be alone with him again.

He stirred up way too much that I was trying to run from. He was too good-looking for my own good and I wasn't getting involved with another jerk who would ditch me as soon as someone thinner came along.

"I just figured it's about time I get in shape. My friend is a member and likes it here."

Brady nodded as though my answer was perfectly acceptable. Only I knew it wasn't really the truth, but I'd never share the truth with him. I'd rather announce it at one of the weddings I had coming up than tell Mr. Perfect the real reason I wanted to join a gym.

"Is there anything I can answer for you?" he asked, his attitude changing as though he flipped a switch. He was still cold and distant, but he seemed eager to get away from me also.

"No, thanks," I mumbled.

Brady focused on me for a few seconds then reached out and clasped my hand in his. Sparks flew from our joined hands through me, but I forced myself not to react. There was no way in hell a guy that looked like him would be attracted to a woman like me. It didn't matter how many sparks flew, they were figments of my imagination.

Brady's eyes met mine and something that looked dangerously close to desire flashed across them. I pulled my hand from his to break the connection and thanked him for his time, then walked back over to where Jennie was sitting at the desk.

"How was the tour?"

I glanced back to where Brady was, but he disappeared. "Um, it was fine. I guess. I mean... who was he?"

"Brady?" Jennie asked as though I could be talking about any number of men.

"Yeah, Brady. He said he's not a trainer. He's a bit intense."

Jennie laughed softly. "Yeah, Brady's intense, but he's great. And no, he's not a trainer. He owns this place."

Shock dropped my jaw to my chest, and I had to force it back into place. "Owns it? How?"

Jennie shrugged. "I don't know. He's always owned it since I worked here."

I glanced behind me to make sure Brady wasn't there and leaned over the edge of the desk. "Can I ask you a question? I need you to tell me the truth."

Jennie cocked her head to the side and looked up at me. "Yeah, sure."

"How in the world is a man who's so frightening able to hold on to employees?"

Jennie laughed, a loud, gut-busting laugh. Tears leaked from the corners of her eyes and she struggled to catch her breath. "Oh, that was funny. Brady is intense, yes, but he's not frightening. He's great to work for. He really cares about the people he employs and he loves his clients. The turnover here is almost non-existent."

I pondered her words and wanted to believe she was lying, but something about her told me she wouldn't. She adored Brady. He chafed the hell out of me, but not her, and apparently not anyone else.

"Why were you scared when he said he'd give me a tour?"

"Scared? No. Shocked is more like it. Brady is big on everyone doing their job and no one stepping over the borders. He likes order. For him to show you around was more of a surprise than anything. I've never seen him show a new client around."

"Never?" I asked, wondering why in the world he'd take time out for me.

"Never. He usually hides in his office most of the day. I guess he had some free time.

Every once in a while he gets out here and associates with the rest of us, but he's always pretty quiet. Most people think he's a client because he doesn't usually take an active role that people see. He's really in touch with what's going on though. Best boss I've ever had."

Judging Jennie's age she hadn't had many bosses. She was easily five years younger than me, putting her around 24. Still, if she thought Brady was okay then there wasn't a reason for me to worry.

"So what did you think of the place?" she asked, drawing me from my mental assessment.

"Oh, it looks good. Basic, but I don't want fancy. What do I need to do to start my two weeks?"

"Great. Well, you'll get a temporary pass that will expire two weeks from today. After that you'll have to decide if you want to stay or not. I'd suggest trying out a little of everything in that time. You know, talk with a few trainers, take a few classes. See if we have what you like."

"Sounds good. I'll think about it," I told her, knowing I'd never step foot in the aerobics room. I smiled as Jennie took a picture for my pass and waited for it to print. She pointed out the locker room and suggested bringing a lock if I wanted to lock up my stuff next time, then waved as I walked away.

As someone who'd never really done any exercise, I had no idea what to do. I didn't want to get hurt, but I needed to make changes. Fast. Checking the time I decided to start with some cardio and go from there.

Thirty minutes later I peeled myself off the exercise bike I'd been using. I wiped it down then trudged to the locker room. The water was hot, which I was grateful for, and helped relieve some of the ache already settling into my muscles. I knew I'd overdone it, but no pain, no gain, right?

Or in my case, no pain, no loss.

Either way, I was going to lose weight if it killed me. And I was going to make Cade regret the day he dumped me.

Except as I showered and dressed then drove to work it wasn't Cade I couldn't stop thinking about. It was the stoney faced, heavily built, hazel-eyed hottie who owned my new gym.

And I couldn't stop from wondering what he'd look like if the cloud of intensity following him dissipated.

Or if I'd be able to resist.

Four

The next day I could barely walk. My legs burned when I tried to crawl out of bed and my stomach protested everything. I half wondered if I was coming down with the flu, but I knew it was just my exercise program. If I was going to be able to walk after going to the gym I needed to break down and talk to one of the trainers about the best way to lose weight. I also knew I needed to start learning something about eating healthier, not that I was looking forward to that either.

I had a couple of easy days with work, mostly editing shots, so I could work from home without having to go into my studio, although I didn't really like doing that. When Addi moved out I made her old bedroom into a home office. I never did photo shoots at home, but I could do my editing and contact clients from there. One day I'd have a studio at my home, but for now I was okay separating my work from my home life.

Once I finished my work for the day I headed out to the bookstore. I had a wedding over the weekend, but it wasn't one of the brides who demanded my attendance at her rehearsal dinner, so I had my Friday night free. And absolutely no plans. I figured picking up a new book, or a few, was as good of a plan as anything.

READ was a small bookstore close to my studio. I'd passed by it plenty of times but never actually went in. I knew the bigger bookstores would have a better selection, but as a small business owner I always supported small, local businesses when I could.

The smell of fresh books mixed with coffee met me at the door. Shelves and shelves of books filled the space. It was bigger than it looked from the outside and was well organized. "Welcome to READ, can I help you?" drifted over the books.

A woman came around the last shelf with a large grin on her face. She looked so friendly that I was immediately put at ease. Going into a bookstore and asking a skinny person for a book about eating healthy was like asking them for a cookie recommendation... useless. Most likely they had never been on a diet in their lives and wouldn't know the first thing about a good one, same with cookies.

But this woman... she was someone I could relate to. With her wide set hips and and fleshy body I could tell she had more rolls than a bakery. I loved her on sight.

"Hi, yes. I need help. I'm looking for a book about weight loss. Or dieting. Something like that."

Her chocolate brown eyes appraised me and she cocked an eyebrow at me. "Seriously? Why?"

I huffed a breath, and shook my head. The anxiety and anger I'd felt toward Cade came back to me in a rush. I knew I shouldn't unload on this poor unsuspecting stranger, but she got to me. Only someone as big as me, or bigger like she was, could understand the utter humiliation of being dumped the way I was.

So I told her. "I was dumped because I'm fat. I want him to regret it so I joined a gym. I figured I should try to eat healthier too instead of just exercising."

"What an asshole!" she exclaimed. "Oops, sorry. I'm not supposed to swear at customers. I'm Riley, by the way." I shook her hand and introduced myself. "Well, Sam, I think the guy who dumped you is a fool but I'll help you. Mostly I just think men suck. It's problematic though because I love men."

I laughed and nodded, knowing exactly what she meant.

"The bad thing is it's the hot ones that are the worst. It's like they think because we're plump that they can treat us anyway they want and we'll be okay with it, simply because no one else would bother. It sucks."

"Yep," I agreed. "That's what I'm going through. But I'm determined to make him eat his words. No one's going to get away with the things he said to me. He's going to regret it."

Riley rubbed her hands together and grinned an evil grin. "Let's get started then. Our health section is back here. My boss said something about the people who want to be healthy aren't going to have a problem walking to the back of the store for it."

I laughed, enjoying talking to Riley. She would fit into our group well. Maybe I should invite her to our next girls' night.

"Okay, here we go. Now you've got your restrictive books where you give up carbs or sugar or everything except vegetables. I have a feeling you're going to need a more balanced meal plan, something that let you eat whatever you want once in a while. I'd recommend this one or this one."

Riley handed me two books. Both sounded reasonable from the description on the back and could potentially help me. "Both?" I asked, wondering what she thought.

"Both works. They have slightly different philosophies so incorporating them together could help you faster. Then you'll be able to torture your asshole ex even earlier."

I laughed when Riley clapped her hand over her mouth for swearing again. "It's fine. Besides I agree. He is an asshole. The sooner I can show him what he missed out on the better."

"Awesome. Let's get you rung up."

Riley led me back to the front of the store and scanned the books. I handed over my credit card. "Samantha Reed? Are you the photographer?"

I nodded. "Yeah, my studio isn't far from here."

"Really? My best friend's boss used you for her website photos."

"Oh yeah? What's her name?"

"The boss is Beth, I don't know her last name, but my friend is Carrie Taylor."

"Oh, I remember Carrie. We only spoke on the phone to set things up, but she was great. Sorry to say this, but why is someone so sweet working for that bitch?"

Riley laughed loudly like it was the funniest thing she'd ever heard. "Carrie calls her Beth the Bitch. That's why I don't know her last name. It's really funny that you picked up on that, too. I keep telling Carrie to find a new job, but she hasn't had any luck."

I wrinkled my nose. "That sucks. Hopefully she can find something soon. Thanks for the help today."

"Good luck, Sam."

I waved to Riley and headed out, feeling better already about my mission.

~*~

The wedding went well that weekend, but I avoided the gym like the plague. I read through the books I'd picked up from Riley and was less than enamored with the idea of giving up junk food. There was no way I'd give up Charlie's cupcakes, but I could cut back on the rest.

Maybe.

I kicked myself for not inviting Riley, and Carrie, to girls' night. I'd have to find some reason to go back into READ so I could ask her if she wanted to join us. Without seeming weird or creepy about it. I just knew they'd fit into our group, and we could always use more friends.

I decided to brave the gym again on Monday, with a trip to the trainers first. I went in mid-morning thinking it would be even quieter. When I'd been leaving the first time the place was nearly deserted and I figured that would be the best time for me to go.

When I pulled in I remembered Brady saying the trainers took on scheduled clients and wondered if I should have called ahead. Even with one on the floor they might be busy and not able to really help me.

Jennie was at the front desk again and waved as I went through the gate. I waved back then headed straight to the weight room to find a trainer.

Two well built men were on opposite ends of the room, each talking intently with a client. Damn, I thought, there was only one left. In the back of the room was what looked like a small office so I headed there, hoping to find the last trainer.

Inside a man was sitting at the computer. I cleared my throat and he looked up. His smile was beautiful with perfect white teeth and soft pink lips. His jaw was rough and sexy and his eyes were a soft brown that reminded me of a puppy.

I was a sucker for dogs.

"Can I help you?" he asked in a deep voice.

"Yeah, I hope so. This is my second trip here and I was hoping to get some help with a plan, I guess. Maybe some tips."

He grinned as he stood. "Of course. We're here to help out so you can ask any of us if I'm not here next time. I'm Greg, by the way."

He extended his hand and I shook it. No sparks, but a warm, friendly grip. "Sam. It's nice to meet you."

"You too. So, first question is what are you trying to accomplish being here?"

I stared at him, trying to figure out if he was joking. It was obvious, right? "Um, what do you mean?"

"Well, some people come to increase strength, some are here to increase flexibility, some want to lose weight and improve their overall health. The way you work out should match your goals, otherwise why do it."

I nodded. It made sense, at least I thought it did. "I need to lose weight and improve my overall health. I want to be skinny." I didn't need to add that I wanted my ex to regret the day he dumped me, but I'm fairly certain he picked up on that need.

He smiled. "That's a great goal. You're a beautiful woman but being healthy is always a good thing to work toward. Having a healthy diet is the first part of that, but we don't offer nutrition coaching. You should pick up some books to get a feel for a healthy lifestyle that you can enjoy. I like anything that doesn't restrict what you eat, but encourages you to eat more healthy foods."

"I actually picked up a few books over the weekend. That's what I went for too. I need to be able to eat cupcakes once in a while."

"I totally understand," Greg laughed, patting his perfectly flat stomach. "So, first, we like to make exercise fun. If you don't enjoy it, you won't stick with it. What do you like to do?"

I cocked an eyebrow at him and said, "Sit on my ass and eat ice cream? But that's sort of what got me into this mess."

Greg laughed like I'd intended for him to. "Yeah, I get that. Is there any exercise that you do enjoy?"

I was pretty sure sex wasn't what he wanted to hear but that was the only exercise I'd ever enjoyed.

"I used to like swimming," I said, knowing I needed to come up with something.

Greg nodded. "Well, we don't have a pool, but tell me what you liked about swimming."

I shrugged and tried to think back to when I would swim a lot. "It was fun, relaxing. I didn't feel like I was doing exercise. I could go at my own pace without feeling out of breath. I don't know. It was just... like play instead of work."

Greg smiled and said, "That's what we want you to feel like here. Okay, so if you want to lose weight you'll need to do some cardio. Along with that I'd recommend some lifting. I know a lot of women don't like lifting but you can do it so you're toned instead of overly muscular. Why don't we go through the cardio room then we'll come back in here and I can show you a routine that will be good for you?"

I nodded and followed Greg from the weight room to the cardio room. Only a few people were there so Greg could walk me through all the machines and help me understand the benefits of each. We agreed a rotating routine would be for the best so my muscles didn't get used to the same machine and slow their progress. He also suggested it would keep me from getting bored and starting to view it as work.

Greg led me back to the weight room. He walked straight to the corner where the machines started and had me sit down. "All the machines have instructions on the wall. Since most of your cardio will be working your legs fairly well, I'd recommend most of your weights be with your arms. This group of machines uses the different muscles in your arms. Once we get your weight down a little then we can talk about adding in some ab exercises, too."

I sat back and let Greg direct and help me. I could feel my long dormant muscles aching with the new strain, but it felt strangely good. So good I didn't notice Brady approaching until he was right in front of us.

"Greg, the client in the corner looks like she could use some help. How about I take over here for you?"

Greg glanced at me then nodded at Brady. "Uh, yeah, sure. It was nice meeting you Sam."

"You too. Thanks for your help Greg."

He walked away with a smirk on his face that I couldn't interpret.

"What can I help you with?" Brady asked me.

I shook my head. "Oh, I think I'm good. Greg showed me some good stuff."

Brady's jaw clenched and I caught a hint of his fresh scent. My eyes drifted closed and a flash of Brady's arms around me made me gasp. When I opened my eyes he was watching me in that careful, intense way of his.

"Are you alright?"

"Yeah," I breathed, immediately embarrassed by the breathy, needy sound of my voice. "I mean, yes. I'm fine."

"Yes, you are."

"Excuse me?"

"Nothing. Well, there must be something I can help you with. Did he help you work out a plan?"

"Yes, we did that first."

"What is his plan?"

I narrowed my eyes at him as I stood up. He was close, too close, but he didn't back up as I stood. Our bodies were barely separated, and I could feel the heat radiating off him. Heat I wanted to burrow into and find comfort in.

But no, I couldn't do that. Brady was exactly the sort of guy I'd been telling myself I had to avoid. The kind of guy who made me forget everything except him. A guy who was so gorgeous that I couldn't look past his hotness to see the man underneath. And underneath this guy, with his intense stares and his strong and silent vibes, was sure to be more trouble than I'd ever known before.

My heart would be his and crushed before I ever knew what happened.

"Do you not trust your employees?" I asked.

The muscles in his jaw worked overtime as he ground his teeth together. "Of course I trust them," he growled. "I just thought maybe I could help you out. I do own the place. I hired Greg and taught him everything he knows."

"And it seems like you did a good job. He was very helpful. I'm not sure what else you could help me with."

"Humor me," he requested, ironically without any humor in his voice.

I rolled my eyes and huffed at him. "Fine. I want to lose weight so Greg recommended a variety of cardio, like changing what I do every day so I don't get bored and my muscles don't get used to it. Then he said to lift with my arms since the cardio will strengthen my legs more than my arms. He was showing me how to use these machines when you interrupted us."

"Why would you want to lose weight?" he asked as though it wasn't obvious.

I cocked an eyebrow at him and turned away. Flattery was always the first step. They butter you up with sweet words so you don't even look for the flaws underneath. But I was onto his game. I didn't even bother with an answer.

"Is there something else you think I should know? Since you clearly don't trust Greg, you must have another opinion."

Brady shook his head and growled. "I trust him. It's fine. Enjoy your workout."

He stalked away without looking back. Instead of feeling relieved, I was a little hurt. I had no reason to be, but he made me feel like I was doing something wrong by talking to his trainer. Like I'd crossed a line I didn't even know existed.

Maybe this wasn't the right gym for me. At least not if Brady was going to pop up every time I was trying to mind my own business. I'd been there twice and he'd barged in on both of his employees that were helping me. Maybe Jennie lied about how great it was to work for him just to make sure I joined.

Aw, hell, I didn't know. None of it made sense. At the end it didn't matter though. Brady was not, and never would be, a part of my life.

Five

I went back to the gym the next day and managed not to see Brady at all. I tried to convince myself I was okay with that. He would break my heart if I let him in and I knew it, but he was nice to look at. He'd certainly fueled enough fantasies since I'd met him.

Tuesday evening I was feeling slighted by Brady after two ambushes then nothing. I pushed him out of my head and tried to look forward to girls' night, even though I hadn't made it back to READ to invite Riley.

My mom called while I was getting ready to go. "Hi, Mom," I said into the phone without much enthusiasm.

"Samantha, I'm so glad I caught you before you went off to your little gathering."

My mom made everything I did sound unimportant and ridiculous.

"What's going on?"

"Brian and Heather are coming over Saturday for lunch and we want you to join us."

I rolled my eyes and huffed out a sigh. She never paid attention to me. "Mom, I'm working Saturday. This is my busiest season and I have a wedding."

"Samantha Jane Reed. You do not speak to me that way."

"I'm sorry, Mom," I said, sounding but not really feeling it. "I hope you have a good lunch, but unfortunately I have to work."

"Samantha, when are you going to get a real job? No one should have to work weekends. Plus, this silly hobby of yours isn't worth it."

It was the same argument all the time. My job was stupid. I needed to get a real one. I was wasting my talents. Blah, blah, blah.

"You are too smart to be standing behind a camera and working for peanuts. You should be out there doing more with yourself."

"Mom, I like my job. I'm not getting another one."

She huffed out a breath of indignation. "I don't know where we went wrong with you."

There it was. The self-pity that was supposed to evoke feelings of guilt. Of course they hadn't gone wrong, but my mother believed that if she acted like I was making her feel bad then it would make me feel bad and I'd do what she said.

It hadn't happened yet.

"Well, if you can't get out of your little wedding, then maybe we should have lunch without you."

God, please, yes! I would never be happier at a wedding in June than when it prevented me from an afternoon of guilt trips led by my mother.

"I'm sorry, Mom. Maybe you should," I said sadly, hoping she would think I was upset to miss the lunch.

"Or we could try to move it to Sunday. Brian and Heather are so busy though."

My brother and sister were the perfect children. Brian the doctor and Heather the lawyer were both married with kids. You'd think it'd be enough for my mother so she would leave me alone, but no, it just served to remind her that she had one child she couldn't fix. One who was so beyond help that I needed her guidance.

I was screwed.

"Brian and Heather probably rearranged a lot to make lunch Saturday. I'll be working some on Sunday anyway so I wouldn't be able to make it then either. Just have lunch and you can tell me all about it afterward. Tell them I said hello and I'm sorry I couldn't make it."

My mom blathered on a few more minutes about what my nieces and nephew were up to then graciously let me hang up the phone. I shook my head to clear the clutter she created and went to Bite Me!

Addi was already there when I arrived, as usual. Claire and Lexi were talking to Charlie at the counter so I sat down with Addi, figuring I'd get my cupcakes in a few minutes.

"No Joey tonight?" I asked when I sat down.

Addi shook her head. "No, he said he felt weird coming. Plus he's got something to do, meeting a friend or something. I just wish everyone liked him better."

My heart sunk. It was all my fault. Everyone picked up on my reservations about Joey and was treating him like an outsider. He was a part of our group whether I liked it or not and if I wanted Addi to stay then I needed Joey to like me.

"I think we all just need to get to know him better. He's sort of quiet and we're pretty loud. He gets lost in the shuffle. Maybe the three of us can get together this weekend. The more I get to know him the more I can drag him into our conversations."

"Really? Are you sure?" Addi sounded surprised and excited. I was a shitty friend. She'd been dating him for months and I didn't know the guy well. That right there said I wasn't putting Addi first. She was the one who mattered. I needed to change that.

"Yeah, of course. I've got a wedding Saturday, but how about late Sunday? Dinner?"

"That would be great, Sam. Thanks. I think you'll really like Joey once you get to know him."

I nodded, still trying to accept that someone else came first in my best friend's life. It was a strange feeling, knowing the person I'd counted on for years was no longer really there. Sure, I knew I could call Addi if I needed anything, but she would forever have to check with Joey. Well, maybe not forever, but for now at least. If they got married it would be forever.

"How's work going?" Addi asked, making me even sadder. She rarely asked about my job when we were living together. Granted I always told her anyway, but the fact that she had to ask, and had nothing else to talk to me about, indicated just how distant we'd gotten from each other.

"Work's fine. I had this great family last week. Two little boys with super sweet parents."

"You love working with families."

I nodded. "Yep. It reminded me of why I do this."

"Another shitty bride?" Addi asked, tilting her head to the side waiting for my explanation.

I shook my head but Mandy joined us before I could say anything. "You're not talking about me, are you?"

"Why do you ask?"

"Because you said something about a shitty bride. I'm hoping that wasn't a dig toward me."

I laughed and Addi looked back and forth between us. Claire, Lexi, and Charlie joined us while I was laughing. "What's so funny?" Claire asked.

"Addi asked if I was dealing with a shitty bride and Mandy thought we were talking about her."

They all exchanged glances. "Were you?" Lexi asked.

I smirked and shook my head. "No. Mandy's a dream bride, just like you were Lex."

"So what were you talking about?"

I shook my head. "My mom's driving me nuts. She thinks I should get a 'real job' and give up my little hobby taking pictures."

Mandy scoffed, Claire rolled her eyes, Addi shook her head, Charlie tightened her grip on the chair in front of her, and Lexi said, "Does she have any idea how good you are? You took the best wedding pictures I've ever seen. The way you're able to capture every little thing going on is amazing to me. You saw things at our wedding I never would have noticed."

I shrugged. "That's my job."

"Yeah, but not everyone can do it as well as you do," Mandy argued. "You're insanely talented Sam. I know you hate shooting weddings, but I'm really glad you're doing mine."

"If it weren't for the income I'd give up the weddings altogether. I was thinking about it, but with the added rent I just can't make it work right now."

"Oh, Sam, I'm so sorry. I knew it was going to be hard, but I had no idea I was making you give up your dream."

I focused on my best friend. Her brown eyes were sad and kind. She felt so guilty, and I hated it for her. "Ads, it's okay. How could I hold you back from moving in with Joey? That wouldn't be fair to you. I'm thinking about getting a new place, but I haven't had a chance to look anywhere yet. I could do with a studio apartment or something like that. I don't really need much. We don't have a garage, I mean, I don't have a garage so it's not like I have to rent a house. Going to an apartment might not be that bad."

My friends looked at me. With the exception of Charlie, they all lived in their own homes.

Mandy moved in with Xander when they were dating, but she'd added her own touches to make it just as much hers as it was his. Claire and Aidan bought a house together just after they got married. Lexi and Mike did the same. With Addi in Joey's house, they were all settled. Charlie lived upstairs from Bite Me!, but it was a studio apartment just like I was thinking of getting.

It was the rest of them who thought I was crazy.

"I can't imagine going back to an apartment now. Brownie loves having a backyard," Claire said, mentioning her dog.

"Well, Zada is happy inside our house, but I love having the space that we have. I'd struggle with an apartment too," Mandy agreed, subtly arguing that cats were better than dogs. It was an ongoing discussion we had.

"I think you're both nuts," Lexi chimed in. "I just like having more places to have sex."

Everyone laughed and agreed. None of them knew Cade and I had broken up, or that I'd given up men, so they chatted away, oblivious to my silence. Usually I was happy to join in the conversation, adding my own experience to the mix, but when my latest sexual experience was with a man who was repulsed by me, I wasn't excited about talking about sex.

"What's one fantasy you haven't had yet?" Claire asked. "One thing you want to do, but haven't yet?"

Smirks slid over faces across the table. I saw them all, lost in their imaginations. Me, though, I just wanted to have a man look at me and not see horror in his face. A man who wanted me for all of my body, and my mind.

"I can't wait to have married sex," Mandy said. "Xander and I haven't held back on a whole lot of variety, but everyone keeps talking about how different married sex is. I'm excited for that."

"Married sex is different," Lexi chimed in. "Mike and I had lots of sex before we got married, especially when we were just friends with benefits, but as our relationship changed so did the sex."

"Aidan and I didn't have a whole lot of sex before we were married, but yeah, I think it changed for us too."

I knew I had nothing to add to that conversation. Fantasies, yes, I had those, but married sex? I was pretty sure I'd never know what that felt like.

"Sex in a bed is a totally different experience for Joey and I," Addi said, blushing. "After we got past our casual sex phase-"

"And your insistence that you needed to be like your crazy sister," Claire interrupted.

"Yes, that, too," Addi agreed. "Sex changed for us though, once we had a commitment. Even moving in together things changed between us. It's been more tender, more passionate, more... amazing. I can't imagine going back to something else, not that there was a whole lot of anything else before Joey. Hopefully I won't have to find out if this is a once in a lifetime chance or if I might find it again. I don't want to look."

"Are you having trouble with Joey?" I asked, immediately concerned. I thought everything was going well with Addi and Joey, but if it was, why was she worried things might fall apart?"

"Everything's fine," Addi said quickly. "I just wonder if he's ever going to propose. I moved in with him, and it's only been a little while, but with everyone else racing down the aisle it makes me wonder."

"I know exactly how you feel," Mandy said, her soft red hair falling over her shoulders and her green eyes brightening with sympathy. "When Claire and Aidan got married I felt the exact same way. Xander and I were talking about moving in together, but we weren't technically living together yet. Claire and Aidan had just started dating and immediately got married. All of a sudden I started looking at my relationship in comparison to theirs. It made me nuts."

"But I reminded her that every relationship is different. And that still applies to you. Your relationship with Joey is not like mine and Aidan's or Lexi and Mike's or Mandy and Xander's. Mandy and Xander didn't get engaged until they'd been together about six months. Did that make their love any less significant than mine? No, of course not. We all do what we need to do to to make our relationships work."

"So you're saying Joey not proposing doesn't mean he doesn't love me, just that our relationship is moving at the speed it's supposed to move?"

"Exactly," Mandy jumped back in. "You and Joey didn't know each other before you started sleeping together, just like me and Xander. Lexi and Mike and Claire and Aidan had relationships, in one form or another, long before they got together, or at least got serious. For us, it takes a little longer to get to know each other. Moving a relationship forward and getting to know a person all at the same time takes a little more time than just one or the other. Our relationships moving slowly is not saying there's anything wrong with us, or the men we love."

I was glad Mandy could ease Addi's mind. I had no idea she'd been so concerned about her relationship. Again, I was a shitty best friend. One who had been so wrapped up in my own shit that I didn't realize anything was off with my best friend.

"Thank you," Addi said, squeezing Mandy's hand. "I needed to hear that." She visibly shook herself. "Okay, enough of this moody shit. Back to the question at hand. What's your sex fantasy?"

I smiled as the conversation continued. I sat back and quietly wished I had something, anything, to add to the discussion. But as my throat closed up and the emotions that had been filling me for a week welled up inside, I knew I needed to remain quiet, for fear of spilling the secrets I didn't want to share with my friends. The people closest to me, the women who'd been there for me through everything. Because I knew how they would feel if they heard the truth, and I couldn't subject them to the same pain I'd felt for a week.

Six

"Hey, you're new here, right?"

I was at the gym a few days later. I still hadn't seen Brady again, at least not while I was awake. He was starring in my dreams every night, which was highly inconvenient since I didn't want him. At least that's what I told myself.

I looked up at the voice into the most beautiful blue eyes I'd ever seen. He was stunning. Exactly the guy you think of when you imagine a hot guy in a gym. His dark blonde hair was a bit long and the tips were damp with his sweat. He wore a sleeveless shirt which would have looked horrible anywhere else, but I loved how it showed off his thickly muscled arms.

Sweat soaked his shirt and it clung to him, outlining every last muscle over his chest and abs and I nearly drooled right there looking at him. I could see, from the quick glance I allowed myself, that he was hung like a horse. His thighs were big enough to press against the material of his basketball shorts and his calves were hard and tight.

I wanted to lick the sweat right off him. He looked almost as good as one of Charlie's cupcakes, and that was almost impossible to beat. What I couldn't figure out was why he was talking to me.

"Yeah, I've been here about a week."

"It's a good gym. Some friends and I work out here after work. You should join us."

I flicked my gaze behind him to where his friends were working out. It was like an ad for Sports Illustrated. They were all sexy as hell and hotter than it. I knew I'd be tripping over my tongue if I stepped into a conversation with all of them. Just one of them was hard enough.

"I couldn't keep up with you. I'm okay by myself."

"Then maybe I could work out with you for a while."

I blushed, I could feel it. He was cute and he was hitting on me. It was the kind of stuff that only happened in my dreams, usually the daytime ones, not the nighttime ones. The nighttime ones weren't nearly this much fun, at least not until Brady showed up.

"Yeah, I guess that would be okay," I mumbled, trying not to be embarrassed by how gorgeous he was. Other women in the area were watching us and I knew they were wondering why a hottie like him would give a fat girl like me the time of day. I wondered myself, but I pushed it from my mind and enjoyed his company.

"I'm Blaine by the way. You're cute."

Another blush crept over my cheeks. Holy shit, he really was flirting with me. And he said I'm cute. What was I supposed to say to that? Oh, right...

"I'm Sam. And you're not so bad yourself."

There, I flirted back. Phew.

He smiled so it must have been okay. God, he was gorgeous. I wanted to melt into a puddle at his feet, but I figured if he was forward enough to come over and flirt with me, especially with his friends right there, then I would flirt right back. It felt good to have a cute guy look at me like he was, especially after everything with Cade.

Blaine, though, he seemed different. He came over to me, he flirted with me, he gave me back just a little of the confidence Cade stole from me.

"Do you live in town?" Blaine asked, bringing me back to our workout. He picked up a free weight, one of the biggest ones on the rack, and curled it like it was nothing. Blaine looked down at his bicep then up at me, making sure my eyes followed his movements. He was… shit, he was the sexiest thing I'd ever seen.

"Yeah, I have a photography studio not far from here and rent a house close by."

"Your own place, huh? That's convenient," he drawled in a sexy, bedroom voice. My eyes snapped to his and I nearly fell over at the blatant desire in his. He wanted me. I couldn't believe it. This sexy, stunning man wanted me. When he could get any woman he wanted.

"Maybe you could come over some time," I said coyly. I was feeling bold. He brought it out in me. Any man who was so open with his attraction gave me the courage to be open right back. Even though I'd sworn off hot guys, he was too yummy to pass up. He was the first guy I'd taken a chance on flirting with since Cade, and sure it was like shooting for the stars, but you didn't pass up an opportunity like him.

He leaned in close and looked me up and down, a lion appraising his prey. I trembled under his look, feeling naked for him. My body clenched, my nipples standing on end and my panties dampening at the possessive look in his eyes. It felt like he was going to take me right there, and I was so turned on I almost thought I'd let him.

"I don't think that's a good idea. See, I don't fuck fat chicks. And I don't like to see them in my gym bouncing their flabby asses all over the place. So why don't you pack up your shit and find another place to hang out," he snarled at me, a grin perfectly in place the whole time.

It took a few seconds for his words to sink in. When they did, tears rushed to my eyes and a lump filled my throat. I couldn't breathe or move. His face, the one I thought was so beautiful seconds ago, was feral and dangerous. He was ten times worse than Cade because he never gave me a chance, just toyed with me so he could insult me.

I heard the laughter and turned to see his friends watching us. They all knew exactly what was going on, I knew they did. My tears started falling, and I forced my feet to move, needing to escape them.

I didn't make it out of the weight room before arms closed around me, strong arms. I fought, thinking it was Blaine back for another round, until I heard the voice, angry and threatening. I'd never heard his voice like that, but I knew it was Brady. He tucked my head against his chest and held me tight, one hand stroking my back and the other holding my head to him, not letting me see Blaine and his friends.

"Get out. Now. All of you. I don't want to see a single one of you back in my gym ever again. I'd tell you to apologize to her, but you don't deserve the chance. You're not people I want here."

"You can't kick us out," one of them argued.

"Actually, I own this place, I can do whatever the fuck I want. Turn in your passes and get the hell out now. Or I can call the cops and have you all escorted out. Your choice."

I heard voices and a bunch of swearing but eventually they drifted away. I tried to pick my head up and push away from Brady, but he still held me tight. "Come with me," he whispered in my ear. It wasn't a question, but it wasn't a command either. I knew if I shook my head he would let me go, but I didn't want him to. Brady just kicked out paying customers who were helping his business. For me.

I nodded against his chest and he let go of me long enough to wrap an arm around my waist and guide me quickly from the weight room past the locker rooms and down the hallway into his office. He closed the door behind us but didn't let me go. Instead he pulled me against him again, wrapping me into a hug.

I tried to break free, knowing the longer he held me the more likely it was that I would start to cry. Brady didn't let go, he only held me tighter. He hand drifted up and down my back and he shushed me, like you would do for a baby.

My body reacted to his kindness and tears welled up again, falling freely down my cheeks and soaking through his shirt. I wrapped my arms around him and held on, clinging to him as if my life depended on it. At that moment I felt as though it did. He was the only thing holding me up, supporting my ample weight with ease as I let out all the anger and pain I'd been holding in for weeks.

I cried for the pain Cade caused me, for the jealousy I felt watching my best friends find love when all I found was assholes. I cried for being stupid enough to fall for someone like Blaine's trick. I cried for the hole I felt inside me when I thought about my future and men.

I liked men, I always had. And men usually liked me, too. I'd had my fair share of boyfriends, and most of the relationships ended well, but recently it seemed they just ended like fireworks. All flash, a big boom, and then nothing.

Brady held me as I cried and when I finally started to feel my breathing return to normal I was afraid to face him. It was obvious he overheard what Blaine said, and the fact that he jumped in to defend me so quickly and so firmly meant the world to me, but I knew Brady wasn't anything other than a conscientious business owner. Women like me were his bread and butter, fat girls who came back every year saying they were going to lose weight only to stop going but keep paying their membership fees because one day we'd get back into it.

Brady didn't really care about me. I knew that.

I finally managed to push away from him only to have him clamp down on my arms. He ducked down to look me in the eyes and I tried to wipe my tears before he could see them. Yeah, I'd just snotted all over the front of his shirt, but that didn't mean I wanted him to see me all blotchy and hideous.

"I'm sorry about those assholes. Are you okay?"

"Yeah, I'm great." I shrugged. I couldn't tell him the truth. He didn't really want to hear it. He was just being nice.

"You don't seem fine, Sam. Those guys were jerks and not all men feel the same way they do. I want you here. I hope you'll keep coming back."

"It's okay, Brady. You don't have to be nice to me. I know I'm just another customer, one you'll probably make a bunch of money off of if I actually keep coming here. But those guys are right, I'm just a fat chick and they don't want to see me. They want to see the ones in the skimpy clothes that are perfect. The ones who don't jiggle with every-"

"Stop!" he yelled. "Just stop, Sam. I'm not being nice to you because you're a paying customer. I'm nice to you because I like you. Jesus, Sam, all I wanted to do when I heard those guys was beat the shit out of them. I hate that they made you feel anything less than beautiful."

"I'm not beautiful, Brady. I know that, I've accepted it. I've been told enough lately that I'm horrible to look at and it's sinking in-"

"No!" Brady yelled again. "God dammit it's not true. When I look at you I see your curves, yes, but I love your curves. But there's so much more to you than your looks. You have gorgeous eyes and a laugh that lights up the room. Those guys are stupid fucking assholes who've never bothered to know you. You're amazing, Sam, and I want you to keep coming here because I like seeing you. I don't want to miss out on a chance to share even a few minutes with you."

My head was spinning. It was only a few minutes after I'd fallen for another guy flirting with me only to tell me he was disgusted by me. Could I believe anything Brady was saying?

"Please, Sam, believe me. I know it's hard to trust someone, especially right now after what those assholes said to you, but it's the truth. Jesus, I need to… fuck, I can't stop."

Before I could ask him what he was talking about his lips were on mine. He pressed me against his closed door and pinned me in with both hands on either side of my head. He leaned into me, his firm body pressing against my soft one. I felt his desire for me in his kiss, on his lips, in the pressure of his tongue against my lips, silently seeking passage into my mouth.

My lips fell apart, letting him in. His tongue dove into my mouth as though he was afraid I'd close it again. He tasted like sweat and heat and something fresh. It was something I knew I'd never forget, a taste that would be with me forever, long after Brady decided I was just another fat girl when he needed a skinny one.

Our tongues played together, learning each other's mouths, where the other reacted, how the other felt. I wanted to kiss him forever, feel his body against mine forever.

My hands drifted up his shirt, over his muscles. I felt the skin twitch beneath the thin cotton. I loved feeling a man come undone, losing control of his muscles and his grip on himself. Brady trembled against me, leaning his hips against me and letting me feel how much he wanted me. I moaned at the feeling of him, as though I didn't believe he could want me until I felt the proof of it against my stomach.

Brady broke our kiss and drug his lips down my sweaty neck. "Jesus, Sam, you taste amazing," Brady whispered against my skin. "I can't get enough of you, baby."

"Are you for real? Because I've had about enough of hot guys toying with me."

Brady jumped back from me as though I'd burned him. His rich hazel eyes bore into mine, and he almost looked angry. "I would never treat a woman that way, Sam. Especially you. I care about you. And I've been wanting to kiss you since the first time I saw you. Please don't lump me in with those fuckers just because I have a cock because I promise you that's the only similarity between us."

I looked at him for a silent beat before I burst out laughing. I couldn't explain why if I tried, but all of a sudden the situation was insanely hilarious to me. I laughed harder, clutching my side and doubling over. Tears ran down my cheeks and I fell to the floor. I clamped my legs shut so I didn't accidentally pee on the floor and finally braved a look up at Brady.

He was standing above me, hands on his hips. I could tell he was trying to look mad, or at least confused, but the corners of his lips kept pulling up into a smile. "You know you want to laugh. Go ahead, let it out," I told him.

Brady stared at me, fighting even harder not to laugh. I saw the moment he gave up and started laughing. He shook his head and collapsed to the floor with me, pulling me to him as we both laughed.

"You know what's so bad about this? I don't even know why we're laughing."

I laughed harder at his confession. I really thought I was going to pee my pants, but I managed to hold it together. "I'm laughing because you said cock. I'm pretty sure it was the funniest thing I've ever heard in my life. A big, sexy guy like you talking about another man's cock. I just couldn't stop laughing."

Another bubble of laughter rose up before I could squash it and we started laughing all over again. Brady finally pulled me onto his lap and shut me up with a quick kiss. "So, you think I'm sexy?" he smirked.

I rolled my eyes. "Fishing for compliments, big guy?"

"I think I need to fish with you. You don't give 'em out too easy."

"Yeah, well, back at ya."

"Hey, I told you how beautiful you are. But if you want to hear it again, I'll tell you as many times as you want how fine you are."

"Fine? Really? Is this the 90's?"

"Oh, just shut up and kiss me, gorgeous."

"Now that just might work."

It totally did.

Seven

I let Brady kiss me, enjoying the feel of his hard body against mine, the hard ridge of his erection pressing into my hip. For a few minutes I fooled myself into thinking it was all okay. That there wasn't any reason I shouldn't be kissing him.

Then reality sunk in.

The hands that were wrapped around his neck slid to his shoulders, and I pushed him back gently. His mouth hung open for a second before he figured out that I wasn't there anymore. He looked down at me, his eyes hazy with desire. I wanted it to be easy. To just believe his words and everything would be fine, but I knew I couldn't do that. I trusted too quickly with Cade, and again with Blaine, and it wasn't going to happen with Brady.

"I can't do this. I'm sorry," I told him, crawling off his lap carefully. I had no idea how he would react and if he was going to get violent I needed to be as far away from him as possible.

Brady hung his head and leaned his back against the door, blocking me in. I glanced quickly around his office for another way out. There was a door behind his desk that could have led to anything from a closet to the outside. If he flipped out it was my only chance though.

"You have nothing to be sorry for. I shouldn't have kissed you. You're right to be afraid of me."

I laughed gently, hoping I wouldn't scare him, and wondering why he thought I should be scared.

"It's okay. I just got carried away."

"No, Sam, you did nothing wrong. I'm the meathead who dragged you in here like a caveman then attacked you like I had a right to you. I hope you'll still join the gym, but I promise not to bother you again. Those guys will never come back here, but you won't have to worry about me either."

Brady jumped to his feet then pulled the door open. He walked to the other side of the office away from me. He didn't look at me, but I could see fear and frustration in his eyes. It made me want to know more about him.

He was apologizing to me like he'd done something wrong. I'd encouraged him. I wanted him. So why was he acting like he was the only one who'd started something?

"Brady," I began softly.

"Sam, don't. It's okay. I know I scared you and I don't blame you. Please, just go."

I didn't know what to say to him so I left. I was barely out of the office when I heard the telltale click of the lock. It felt like my heart was breaking in my chest. I wondered when my instincts had gotten so fucked up. Blaine and Cade I trusted without a second thought. Two guys who hurt me for no reason. But Brady...

Brady defended me, comforted me, and told me he wanted me, and I couldn't believe him.

There was something seriously wrong with me.

I was too upset to finish my workout so I gathered my stuff and decided on working from home for the day. I went outside into the bright sunshine and was halfway to my car when I wanted to kick myself. I stopped in the parking lot to decide what to do but shook my head and went to my car.

I wasn't ready to go home and face the silence alone, but I didn't really have anywhere I could go. Claire was giving a presentation at Addi's school, an end of year thing, Mandy and Lexi were working, and there was no privacy at Bite Me! to talk to Charlie. On top of that, none of them would understand why I was so upset about Brady.

There was only one person who knew what happened with Cade.

I pulled into the small parking lot next to READ and shook my head. I was seeking out advice from a basic stranger instead of talking to my closest friends. But I knew she'd listen and understand. She'd sympathize.

The bells on the door clanged when I pushed through. I caught a whiff of my sweaty smell and nearly turned right back around, but then I heard Riley's voice. "You're back already?"

I smiled. "Yeah. I'm a little sweaty though. I should have taken a shower first."

Riley cocked her head at me, seeing far more than any stranger should be able to see. "I have a feeling you weren't thinking clearly when you came here. What happened?"

I almost started crying when I heard the concern in her voice. She'd met me once and she was concerned with how I was feeling, gave a shit about me. It was something I hadn't heard in a while.

"These assholes at the gym were really mean to me," I told her, sighing in defeat.

"What did they say?"

I rolled my eyes at my own stupidity. "The one guy hit on me and when I asked him out he told me he didn't date fat chicks and didn't like seeing them in his gym either."

"His gym? Is he the owner?"

I shook my head. "No, but the owner heard it and threw them out."

Riley's eyes narrowed. "There's more to this story. What happened with the owner? Did he tell them they were right?"

"Brady? No. He defended me and tossed them out, threatening to call the cops if they didn't go on their own. Then he took me to his office so I could calm down. I cried all over his damn shirt."

Riley walked me over to a section off to the side that had a few plush chairs positioned together for people to sit and read. She gestured to one of the chairs and took the seat next to me. "You like him, don't you?"

I bit my lip and nodded.

"But you don't trust yourself. After that asshole ex of yours and now the dick at the gym, you don't know who's telling you the truth and who isn't. Especially with hot guys."

I nodded. "Exactly. I want to believe Brady is a good guy, but my radar is all fucked up. I have no clue who's a nice guy and who's a complete douchebag. Obviously since I trusted the two men who treated me like garbage and ran from the one who protected me and couldn't stop himself from kissing me."

"Whoa, he kissed you?"

"Yeah."

"Like, I'm sorry those guys were dicks kind of kiss, or I want you so bad I can barely keep it in my pants kind of kiss."

"Um, the second one?"

"Damn. Okay, so I have a tough question for you."

She hesitated and I started to get worried.

"What the hell are you doing here with me when you could be making out with the sexy owner of your gym?"

I laughed. "How do you know he's sexy?"

Riley cocked an eyebrow at me. "He. Owns. A. Gym. You don't open a gym unless you look like you belong in one constantly. That's why I work at a bookstore. I don't have a gym body. But I'd be willing to bet Brady's the hottest guy there."

I smiled at her affirmation. She was right, of course. I hadn't seen any other guy that came close to Brady, but I might have been a little biased.

"That's why I came here. Somehow I knew you would be able to help me. Oh, and I read those books you recommended. Losing weight sucks. But it'll be worth it when I can show my worthless ex what he missed out on."

"And show Brady what he's getting," Riley teased. My cheeks heated, something that rarely happened with me. I couldn't stop the grin spreading across my face.

"Hey, listen, this may be weird, but a bunch of my friends get together every Tuesday night. Why don't you and Carrie join us? We all just hang out and chill. One of my friends owns the bakery Bite Me! and we go there."

"No, shit. That place is awesome. I'll talk to Carrie, but that sounds great."

"Excellent. I think you'll really get along with everyone. And thanks for the advice."

"Any time. Just make sure you ask if Brady has a hot brother."

I laughed. "Definitely."

When I left READ I went home and took a shower, then got pissed off at myself all over again. Riley was right. I didn't know Brady, but at some point I needed to try to trust someone again, and Brady was making it pretty clear that he was someone who would be there for me, someone who would protect me.

There was something in his eyes that made me want to know more about him. The fear in his eyes when he let me out of his office... I'll never forget that. He was scared, not of me, but for me. And I wanted to know why.

After spending the rest of the day thinking about Brady I had to go see him. I wanted him to know I wasn't afraid of him. His eyes told me he'd never hurt me, but my eyes worried he'd break my heart. He was too attractive for me.

But I couldn't let him think I was scared of him.

Telling myself I wasn't getting dressed up for him, I tugged on a pair of shorts, my favorite red top, and red sandals. As I drove I convinced myself it was just because I was going to join his gym that I wanted him to be comfortable around me. Not because I liked him.

Definitely not.

I parked again and headed into Dave's Gym feeling like an idiot. I wasn't dressed for the gym and everyone who saw me would know I was there for something else. Of course, they'd probably think it was for a booty call or something.

Damn. Why didn't I think it through?

Pushing past my fears I went inside and asked the lady at the front desk, a woman I hadn't met yet, if I could see Brady.

"Can I tell him who's here?"

I told her my name and showed my badge then waited as she picked up the phone. After a minute she told me I could go back to his office.

I knocked on the door and waited for Brady to tell me to come in, then opened the door.

Brady was pulling a shirt over his head, but I saw his bare chest before he covered it up. More scars shone on his skin. His chest was well-defined and stunning. His stomach looked like something out of a magazine. Six pack didn't come close. He had eight, maybe even ten, defined abs that left me drooling. A light trail of hair dipped from his belly button below the waistband of his shorts, leaving me wanting more.

"I didn't think you'd come back," he confessed, watching me closely with those intense eyes.

"What happened to you?" I blurted out.

Anger flashed in his eyes, but it was gone before he said anything. His jaw ticked as he worked to control his temper. "It's nothing. What can I do for you?"

I shook my head to clear the sight of his scars, but the image didn't go far. "I wanted to apologize for earlier. I wish..." I took a deep breath, not sure if I could tell him the truth.

"What do you wish, Sam?" he whispered as though he couldn't breathe either.

I closed my eyes and prayed for strength. "I wish I'd never stopped you. I wish I'd let you kiss me longer."

Brady exhaled a long breath. My eyes stayed closed, afraid to look at him. What did that breath mean? Was he already regretting touching me? Did I make a huge mistake going back there?

Brady didn't say anything to my confession. Without opening my eyes I spun to the door. "I'm sorry. I shouldn't have come."

"Sam, wait," he said.

"No, it's okay. I understand. Thank you for being nice to me," I said, fighting tears as I reached for the doorknob. Then Brady's hand was on the door in front of me. And his knuckles were scratched up and bloody.

"What happened to your hand?" I asked, again unable to stop myself.

Brady ignored my question and moved between me and the door. He cupped my chin and tilted my face up to him. "I didn't want to stop kissing you. And that scares the hell out of me."

"Why?"

Brady took a deep breath and searched my face, his eyes scanning my features. "I don't know what I'll do if I'm not in control. I don't trust myself to lose control, but with you I feel like I don't have any."

I reached up and rested my hand against his jaw. His eyes drifted closed, and he leaned into my hand like a greedy cat wanting more. I didn't want to stop touching him. "Is that why your jaw is always ticking when I'm around you?"

Brady smiled and turned his face to kiss my palm. "Yeah. I need to be in control."

"Why?" I asked him again, wondering if he'd answer my question.

"I won't be him," he whispered and I knew he was talking to himself more than he was to me. I wanted to ask who, but I didn't. It was too personal, too much.

"What happened to your hand, Brady?" I asked, bringing his hands to my lips. I kissed each of his knuckles softly, my eyes locked on his.

"I was pissed at myself for scaring you. I went a little nuts on the punching bag," he confessed as I kissed the last of his knuckles.

I brought his hand back to my face and let him caress my skin. He touched me with a reverence I'd never felt before. My hands ran up his arms, both of us watching as we explored each other carefully.

His hands went to my waist, and he pulled me tightly to him. My body responded instantly to his, fire mixed with ice, need mixed with want. I pressed against him, the feel of his hard body against my soft one made me want more.

Brady's lips came down over mine slowly, waiting for me to stop him. His kiss was tentative, but behind it was a desire he was barely holding back. If Brady ever lost that control he was holding so tightly to there was no telling what would happen. The thought excited me more than scared me, and I wondered what I would have to do to snap that control.

With his lips on mine we kissed softly, barely even a kiss. My hands drifted around his neck and pulled him tighter to me. I raised up on my toes to reach him better and traced the seem of his lips with my tongue, willing him to open for me.

When he did, his control slipped a little before he regained it. His tongue glided against mine, and he tasted fresh, just like he smelled. Our tongues explored instead of fought, both of us learning the other without wanting to dominate. It was sweet, it was beautiful.

It was boring.

I wriggled against him so I could feel his erection between us. He groaned into my mouth and his hands slid to my ass and lifted me. My legs wrapped around his waist on their own. One hand moved up my back slowly over all the bumps and valleys of my body to my shoulder.

His tongue thrust deep and strong into my mouth, sending jolts of desire through me. I imagined that same enthusiasm between my legs and burned with need.

Then he was gone.

Brady pulled back from me and lowered me to the ground carefully. His hands steadied my hips, but he took a large step away from me. My heart plummeted as I waited for another guy to say he couldn't be with me because I was too fat. Because I wasn't right for him.

That another man might not be bothered by my rolls, but he couldn't stomach it.

"I'm sorry. I'll go," I stammered, backing away from him.

"Please don't go, Sam," he pleaded. His fingers tightened on my hips before I could get out of his reach. His eyes were closed, but I saw the pain that I'd noticed before etched across his face.

I couldn't leave. Not until I understood the pain.

"Why?"

Brady took a deep breath and rested his forehead against mine. He held me tightly but at a distance. I didn't know what he was going through, but I needed an answer.

"I'm not myself when you're around, Sam. It scares the shit out of me. But what scares me more is watching you walk out that door and knowing you'll never come back. I want you, Sam. I want you more than I've ever wanted anyone or anything, but I don't know who I am if I'm not in control."

"Why do you have to be in control, Brady? What are you afraid of?"

He shook his head and let go of me, walking across the room. He rested his hands on his desk and leaned over. The muscles in his back bunched and made me want to run my hands all over him. I could see the pain in him, even from behind.

"It doesn't matter. I just can't lose control. I would never hurt you, Sam. You have to know that. I'd never do anything to hurt you."

I stepped closer, needing to touch him, to look at him. I touched his back and he jumped, then settled against my hand. "Brady, look at me. Please," I begged.

He hesitated then turned his head slowly. His body stayed in place and he peered over his shoulder at me. I glided my hand around his body and tugged to get him to turn. With a sigh he turned and sat on the edge of his desk, bringing us almost to eye level.

"Do I look afraid of you? Do I look like I want to run?" He shook his head. "I'm just as out of control as you are, except it doesn't scare me. What does scare me is how much I think about you and how bad I felt when I knew you thought I didn't want you. I didn't come back here for this, but I'm not going to lie and tell you I'm not enjoying it. I'm not afraid of you Brady."

His hands skimmed my waist, fingers reaching from my hips to just barely below my breasts. Large hands, strong hands, sexy hands.

"Maybe you should be. I'm afraid of me."

"Then we take this slow. Unless you don't want to-"

"No," he nearly shouted. "I want to. Jesus, I want to. Are you sure?"

I smiled and glided my hands up his chest then over his shoulders. "I'm sure. And one day I'm going to snap that control of yours and see what I get out of it."

"No, Sam. You can't," he said fearfully. "Please promise me you won't."

"Brady, I don't want you afraid to be yourself around me. If you're holding back then I'll wonder who's really there."

"This is me. If I lose control it won't be me. It'll be... someone else. I can't be him."

"Who, Brady?"

He shook his head. He wasn't going to tell me. It was too much for him.

"Please, Sam, just promise me."

I could see how much it mattered to him. How important it was that I didn't push him. As much as I didn't want to, I agreed.

Eight

Wedding weekends were crazy, but knowing I avoided a torture session with my mother made it a little easier to swallow. I loved my job, but working with brides, dealing with the emotions of weddings, and working all weekend was less than desirable.

The bride, Megan, asked me about attending the rehearsal and rehearsal dinner, but eventually decided she'd rather have me focus on the wedding day. I'd love to say I didn't encourage her in that direction, but I totally did. Having to work both Friday and Saturday night got old in a hurry. Plus, most people cared more about the wedding than the reception, made sense, so rehearsal photos usually got tossed in a photo album or worse, a box.

I enjoyed my day as much as I could with my limited mobility and soaked in a hot bath that night. I didn't think I'd worked out that hard, but the muscles screaming convinced me otherwise. By Saturday morning, with the help of a few of painkillers, I was ready for the wedding.

Megan was one of those brides I could see myself being friends with under different circumstances. She was relatively easy to work with, but she had the potential to be completely insane on her wedding day. I had my work cut out for me.

Aside from Megan, her soon-to-be mother-in-law was a nightmare. Bobby's mom, Sandra, thought she was the bride, or at least she acted that way. I was happy I wasn't the wedding planner with a mother-of-the-groom like her.

My first stop of the morning was Megan's mom's house. Debra was a hairdresser and recruited one of her coworkers to do the hair of the entire wedding party. Champagne was already flowing freely when I arrived, putting Megan on edge.

"They're all going to be too drunk to stand up! I don't know what my mother was thinking," she whined after she greeted me.

Two of the six bridesmaids were sitting at chairs in the kitchen, mimosas in hand and chatting happily. The other four bridesmaids, including Megan's best friend and maid of honor, Belinda, were digging into the fruit tray with one hand, the other holding mimosas.

"It'll be fine," I assured her. "How many bottles of champagne did she buy?"

"I don't know. Why?"

I shrugged as though the answer was simple. "If it's more than three, hide the rest. Chances are no one will get drunk on that much."

Megan beamed like I'd just handed her a million dollars. Without another word she turned to the fridge and studied it for a few minutes. She closed the door again and looked relieved. She came back to my side and said,

"Two bottles. Including the one we've already opened. We should be good."

I smiled. "Your mom wouldn't want to ruin your wedding day. Nothing to worry about."

Megan nodded and joined her closest friends for a drink and some breakfast. There was no way they would make it through the entire day on fruit and mimosas. Not unless they were the sort of women that didn't need to eat to function. As for me, I'd had eggs, frozen waffles, and a big cup of coffee for breakfast.

As the women laughed and traded stories of marriage and relationships I worked my way around the room, invisible in my black ballet flats, black dress pants, and seafoam green button down shirt. One by one their hair was twisted into complicated designs that left their backs exposed and their shoulders lightly covered by the tendrils that fell. Even without the dresses on I could tell the pictures would be beautiful. Debra was very talented.

By mid-day the women moved upstairs to start getting dressed. I followed behind them and caught Debra's tear-filled eyes when Megan stepped into her dress. Belinda zipped her up and everyone in the room fell silent.

"You look beautiful, honey," Debra broke the silence. "Bobby is a lucky man."

Everyone murmured their agreement except Sandra. It was pretty clear she thought Megan was the lucky one, not her son. I really hoped they'd worked out all those issues between the two of them. Overbearing in-laws was a tough obstacle to overcome.

So I heard.

Once all the women were dressed and ready to go I ducked out to capture the men. It really wasn't fair that Megan and the other women spent almost five hours getting ready and the men would probably spend ten minutes. It made my job a bit easier though.

Bobby's parents' house was close to Megan's parents'. I heard clanging glasses and loud voices once I let myself in and followed the noise to the kitchen. Bobby stood in the middle of the room with both fathers flanking him. His groomsmen flared out from there, all holding shot glasses raised in the air.

"To Bobby. A great man who loves my little girl enough to take over the bills. I have a chance at retirement thanks to you."

Everyone laughed and clinked glasses before downing the shot. I took pictures of them as they talked and laughed, groaning to myself about the ridiculousness of men thinking marriage was a death sentence. Not to mention Megan would flip out if she knew they were drinking.

Bobby's dad poured one more shot for everyone and raised his glass. "Son, I've taught you all I know about women. I've armed you as well as I was armed. Now it's your chance to go out there and figure out what the hell they're all about and teach me because I still don't have a clue."

I shook my head as they all laughed and drank. Bobby wasn't swaying and his eyes were alert so I knew two shots were okay, but if he had more than that, they were risking my job.

Thankfully Bobby was eager to get married. He led the men out of the house and into a variety of vehicles that would carry them to the church.

In my car I stuffed a sandwich in my mouth, praying I didn't drop anything on my clothes, and followed the men to the wedding. They took their time getting out, which I anticipated, so I got inside and set up before they'd even breached the doors.

When all the guests were seated and everyone was ready to go, Bobby and his groomsmen took their place with the priest in front of the altar. Like I always did when I was shooting a wedding I found myself getting wrapped up in it, wondering if I'd ever get my chance in the pretty white dress.

What shocked the hell out of me was when I looked up at the altar and imagined Brady there waiting for me. The vision of him in a black tux, his intense hazel eyes watching me, as I walked toward him in a stunning cream dress with red velvet accents was almost too much to take.

I shook my head to clear the image. Just because he'd had a starring role in my dreams since I met him didn't mean I wanted to marry him. Yes, his kisses could accelerate global warming, but we hadn't even been on a date yet. Maybe he chewed with his mouth open.

I rolled my eyes at myself. Brady was perfect. That was what scared me about him. He was too perfect. He set me on fire with just a look and a brush of his lips. Marrying him was not an option. I'd never get anything done.

Bringing myself back to my job, I watched as the mothers were seated then the bridesmaids filed in and stood opposite the men. I moved back into position as the doors opened and Megan emerged on her dad's arm.

I swung my camera to capture the look on Bobby's face when he first saw her. The look of love and gratitude on his face told me all their struggles with their parents would be okay. Megan and Bobby would be fine. Theirs would be a happy marriage.

After the ceremony I took one picture after another of the wedding party and close family and friends posed in the church. The guests were already enjoying hors d'oeuvres at the reception, and the wedding party was excited to join them, as always. I toed that fine line between getting all the pictures Megan and Bobby wanted and watching everyone roll their eyes for one more shot, then announced we were done.

While they piled into cars and the limo, I went to the reception to make sure I captured their arrival. The guests were happily chatting, and drinking, as I walked among them and took pictures. When the wedding party was ready to be announced I positioned myself to catch them all coming through the doors.

"Sam? Sam Reed? Is that you?"

I spun and found a face in the crowd waving at me. "Monica? Oh my God. How are you?"

The DJ's voice muffled mine and I turned back to the doors in time to catch Bobby's parents coming into the hall.

"I see you're busy, but we have to catch up. I'm at Table 21. Please come see me," Monica said above the noise surrounding us.

"I promise. You look great, by the way." She beamed at my compliment then went back to stand next to a tall man with short dark hair and kind eyes. He was cute, but no Brady.

Once the wedding party was inside and the food was served I had a few minutes to relax. I smiled at the other guests sharing my table and dug into my dinner quickly so I could capture more pictures for Megan and Bobby.

I could feel my energy, and desire to be there much longer, start to fade as I stood up after dinner. Wedding days were hard on me since they were usually close to 16 hour days. After about ten I was pretty much done, but I had no choice but to stay. That was when things started getting fun with the reception.

The thought slipped into my head before I could stop it, but once it was there I couldn't ignore it. Was my mom right? Should I get a regular job? One that didn't require 16 hour days, constant weekends, and emotional people? A job that could lead to meeting someone? Someone other than Cade.

I couldn't dwell on those thoughts while I was working. I didn't really want to think about it anyway because I loved my job most of the time. If I could get by without doing weddings I would, but it could get complicated if I removed that income stream.

I forced the thoughts from my head. The idea of giving up weddings was not one I needed to think about when I was actively shooting a wedding. Megan and Bobby weren't paying me to evaluate my life. They were paying me to capture their happiest day. And I was going to do just that.

While the other guests were finishing up dinner, Megan and Bobby stepped onto the dance floor for their first dance. The room filled with the opening lines from Wanted by Hunter Hayes. Tears sprung to my eyes as I took pictures, praying they were more clear than they looked through my tear-filled eyes.

That song defined what I wanted, no pun intended. I craved someone who would worship me like the song said. To have someone who would put me first, who would move heaven and earth for me, was what every woman wanted. The urge to run to the bathroom and cry my eyes out was almost too much, but I was there for a job. I just needed a distraction.

"Will it bother you if we talk while you shoot? I'm not sure how long we're going to be here," Monica said from next to me.

I blinked back my tears and looked at her, pasting on the brightest smile I could. She was watching Megan and Bobby with a wistful look in her eyes. Before I was caught blubbering like a fool I dabbed my eyes and focused on the camera again.

"No, it'll be nice to talk. Why are you heading out?" I cringed once the words were out. All too often I was reminded of my need to think first and speak second. It'd been years since I'd seen Monica. We were friends in high school but didn't keep in touch well after. It was none of my business why she was leaving early.

Hell, I didn't even know why she was there. At least I stopped myself from probing into that area of her life.

"My mom called. She's watching my girls and the younger one is giving her trouble going to sleep. She's never stayed with anyone else and is used to me or my husband being with her." Monica shrugged. "You know how it is with kids."

I mustered up a smile and turned back to the camera. "Actually I don't. I don't have kids. Or a husband."

"Really? I just assumed. You always had boyfriends when we were growing up. I figured you'd be the first one of us to be married."

I shook my head. "Never even close. I've been pretty focused on building my business though. I haven't had time for much dating," I lied. Even as I said the words my stomach churned. I had plenty of time, just not enough interest. It was hard meeting men when I was taking pictures for families and at weddings. And obviously I wasn't very good at choosing good ones if I'd fallen for a bastard like Cade.

Maybe Brady was different. Maybe he would be someone I could trust. Who wouldn't be an asshole. Or maybe I was being played again.

"Are you a full time photographer then? Wedding photographer?" Monica asked, breaking up my daydream about Brady.

"Um, yeah. I mean, I do weddings, but I enjoy family sessions the most. Weddings are a lot of pressure, long days, and a few too many emotions for me. I do it because it's good money. Although I probably shouldn't be saying that as I shoot a wedding."

Monica laughed. "Your secret is safe with me."

"What do you do?" I asked, feeling the need to steer the conversation away from myself and my shortcomings. I got enough of that when I talked to my mother.

"I'm a guidance counselor. I love it. Normal hours, I work while my girls are in school, I have summers off, and it's pretty low stress. I work with the middle school so I'm not doing any of that college prep stuff and aside from normal middle school angst, the kids that age are pretty independent."

"Wow, that's a really rewarding job, I'd imagine. I'm a little jealous of the hours as I stand here on a Saturday night working."

Monica laughed. "Most people feel the same way. Especially since I'm off for the summer and enjoying the nice weather while everyone else is working. My husband's a teacher so we both have the summers off. We take a lot of trips."

I failed to squash the green monster that was rearing up inside me. Addi having the summers off was almost enough of a reason to quit my job and become a teacher at times, but hearing it from Monica too, and knowing what life could be like if I married a teacher.

Damn, why did my mother put that shit into my head? I loved my job. No, not past tense. My job meant so much to me. I wasn't going to quit and become a teacher, or a guidance counselor, or a -

"Sam!" Sandra, Bobby's mom, bellowed from right in front of me. "What is wrong with you? We need you. They're about to cut the cake."

"Yes, of course, Mrs. Reece. I'll be right there."

With one more sharp look, Sandra turned and stalked off toward the cake table. I apologized to Monica. "Duty calls," she sang. "It was great catching up with you."

We hugged and I followed Sandra across the room, wondering again if I could make it work if I gave up weddings.

Nine

The uneasy feeling I'd had at the wedding followed me the rest of the night. When I got the final check from Megan's dad I knew I couldn't eliminate weddings from my offerings easily, but by the time I got home and fell into bed I was tossing around more and more ideas of how to do just that. There were parts of weddings that I loved, but for the most part I just wanted to be done with the whole thing.

I slept in Sunday morning, not willing to wake up before noon. I always turned off my ringer after a wedding because without fail my mother would call me early, and it never ended well.

As expected, I had three missed calls from her by the time I dragged myself out of bed. Knowing she'd call back soon I ignored the messages, no doubt asking if I was dead in a ditch somewhere, and padded toward the kitchen. Coffee called my name until it slid down my throat in a delicious burn. Then I could function, just a bit.

My bags were in the office, where I'd dropped them on my way to crash the night before. With a few hours before dinner with Addi and Joey, I had time to work on the wedding photos while the event was still fresh in my mind.

Four hours later I was cross-eyed and almost welcomed the interruption when my mom called.

"Samantha, did you forget about lunch today? Why weren't you here? I called you, but as usual, you didn't answer your phone."

What the hell was she talking about? "Mom, you told me lunch was yesterday and I had a wedding. You never said anything about lunch today."

She sighed like she always did when I argued. A deep, painful sound that let me know how frustrated she was without even speaking. Not that it stopped her though, she was still going to lay into me. "Samantha, I don't know how you maintain that business of yours. Maybe it's a good thing you don't have a real job if you can't even keep your days straight. Lunch was today. I told you we would change it for you. Your sister and brother rearranged their days and you didn't show up. Not that anyone was surprised."

I bit back the nasty retort on my tongue and took a deep breath. She never told me they'd changed the lunch to Sunday. I would have remembered so I could come up with a good excuse. Instead, she never told me, and I was the bad guy for missing lunch. Cue the guilt trip.

"I swear Samantha, sometimes I wonder if you even care about me at all. Everyone moves their world around so we can see you and you don't have the decency to call. Are you going to do the same thing for July 4th? We always spent it together. Are you going to forget that too?"

Damn, she was laying it on thick.

"I'll be there, Mom. I'm sorry about lunch. I was working today, too. If I'd known about lunch I would have been there, but you never told me you'd changed things around for me. Next time I'll do what I can to be there."

She huffed, the sound so loud it was like I could feel her breath in my ear. "I told you about lunch, Samantha. Hopefully if you ever have a family of your own they will be more important to you than that little hobby of yours. Well, now that I know you're not dead in a ditch somewhere I have to go."

I hung up shaking my head at my insane mother. I don't know what she thought she told me, but it didn't matter. I had to get ready to meet Addi and Joey for dinner. Unless they changed something and never told me too.

When I pulled into the parking lot at Roger's the smell of cooking hamburgers hit me. My mouth watered before I even made it inside. It was definitely a night to eat my feelings. I just hoped Joey didn't pick up on my shitty mood and think it was personal.

Addi and Joey walked in a few minutes after I did. I hugged them both and we all followed the hostess to a booth overlooking Lake Effect Lane. Once we'd placed our drink orders we sat there, looking at each other.

"How was the wedding, Sam?" Joey asked me, clearly prompted by Addi.

I shrugged. "It was okay. It's a long day and I'm not thrilled with shooting weddings to begin with so it makes the day extra long. What did you guys do yesterday?"

They exchanged a glance, one that was filled with love and a touch of apprehension. The hair on the back of my neck stood up and I wondered what I was in for. If it was bad they wouldn't be there, together especially, to have dinner with me. On the other hand, if it was good I wouldn't have had such a bad feeling.

"We had a pretty quiet day," Addi began. "Joey took me up to the mountain for a picnic and we hiked a little bit. It was nice."

There was more to it than that. The mountain was where Joey and Addi met, except during winter when she was chaperone for her school's ski club. Joey managed the ski slopes, taught classes, and made sure everything worked. He was basically the master of all things related to the mountain.

But something was off with their story. They never went up there. Since all the snow melted and the weather became warm enough for the snow machines to not work, they hadn't been back. Well, Addi hadn't. Joey was up there all the time maintaining the property, but he never took Addi.

I narrowed my eyes at my best friend and she avoided my gaze. Yep, something was up.

"What aren't you telling me?"

"Nothing," Addi said too quickly.

The waitress chose that moment to arrive with our drinks. We all rattled off our dinner orders and she left again. Too bad for Addi I wasn't so easily distracted.

"We've known each other eleven years. I know when you're hiding something. What is it?" I asked her, not letting her get away with half-truths. Addi and I never kept things from each other so it bugged me that she was. Not to mention it all seemed to circle Joey.

If he hurt her, I'd kill him. "Should we go outside and talk?" I asked, trying to telepathically indicate I would help her hide the body if we needed to get rid of Joey. That's what best friends did, right?

Addi finally looked me in the eye and started laughing. "Really, Sam? Are you serious?"

I raised my eyebrows at her, silently asking her to prove to me why I should be worried. Joey sat there looking more confused by the second.

"Sam thinks you did something you shouldn't have done and is plotting where we should bury you body," Addi told him with a laugh.

I was glad she could still read my mind, or at least read the looks I gave her, but why was it so funny?

Joey looked at me with a pained expression. Yep, I'd definitely made things worse between us. Before he thought I didn't like him, now he was worried I'd kill him in his sleep.

"Joey proposed. We're engaged," Addi said, drawing my attention away from Joey. She was holding out her left hand, complete with a sparkling ring on the correct finger. My jaw hit the table as I reached up to grasp her hand. I pulled her toward me, Addi's stomach pressing into the table that separated us, so I could look at the ring.

It was beautiful. A simple style, which suited Addi perfectly, with a large diamond in the center and tiny diamonds set within the band that circled her finger. "The wedding ring that goes with it sits under the diamond and ends up looking like two bands with the diamond. They fit together perfectly. Just like Joey and I do."

It was a good thing I hadn't started eating yet because it would have come back up with that comment. Seriously, gag me.

I released Addi's hand and swallowed the bile that was tickling the back of my throat and pasted on a smile. "Congratulations, guys. I'm so happy for you."

"Thanks," they said together, grinning at each other instead of acknowledging me. They kissed and I rolled my eyes. Damn it. I was jealous. That little green monster was getting bigger and bigger over the course of just a few days. First Monica and her perfect life, now Addi. She was my best friend. I wasn't supposed to be jealous. Especially because I didn't want Joey for myself. I just wanted someone who looked at me the way Joey looked at Addi.

Maybe with a touch more intensity. And a shaved head, hazel eyes. Someone I'd have to look up to be able to see his eyes. Who owned my gym and had me squirming in my seat without even being there.

I was going to have to face it. I wanted Brady in a bad way. Obviously it was bad enough that I'd agreed to take things slow, which meant starting a relationship with him, against my better judgement, but it was worse than that. I was starting to see my future with him in it. He was the groom at the wedding, the man kissing me after our engagement, the one I snuggled against on the couch during a movie, the guy holding my hand when our child was born.

Damn, I had it bad.

I'd never gotten anywhere close to that worked up over any other guy. Especially not before our first date. I needed to get a grip.

"How did you ask?" I forced myself to say, bring my focus back to Addi and Joey. Asking him instead of her brought him into the conversation, one that had been pretty two sided so far.

Addi smiled at me and Joey sat back in his chair, focusing his attention on me. His hand held Addi's, but he was looking straight at me. "I wanted to ask her where we'd first met, but that was a little tough since we'd met near the lodge where she'd nearly taken me out."

"It was an accident," Addi protested. She told me about it when it happened, but Joey teased her that she just couldn't come up with a reason to talk to him so she created one by slipping on the ice so he would catch her. Either way, it worked.

"I know, babe," he said with a smile. "Anyway, I didn't want to be that much in the open for a picnic since it's kind of a high traffic area. We went up to the top to eat then walked down. Thankfully it's dry so we didn't slip. When we got to the spot where we'd turn off to go into the woods, I covered the slope with rose petals and installed a sign that read, 'Beware of Falling Men.'"

Huh? I gave him one of those WTF looks.

"Yeah, Addi had the same look on her face when she turned around. I was on one knee and told her that was where I fell in love with her. Every time she ducked under those branches or raced me off the slope, I fell a little more for her. And I asked her to be my wife. Obviously she said yes."

It was cute, I had to admit it. It suited them. Addi liked cheesy, and for Joey to go cheesy for his proposal said how much he understood her. I wouldn't go for it. Not that I needed an elaborate proposal, but dammit, I wanted to be the center of attention for my proposal. Something different. Something unique.

"Have you set a date yet?"

Addi shook her head. "Not yet. We weren't going to tell you because I haven't been able to get to see my parents. Joey asked them, but until I can get over there and show them the ring we're trying to keep it quiet. Sorry we didn't want to tell you."

It hurt. Six months ago I would have been the first one Addi would have told something to. She had Joey now. I was relegated to second best, if that. I wasn't first for anyone anymore.

"No," I forced out, pushing the pain aside. "I understand completely. It makes perfect sense. I won't tell anyone."

I smiled at them before they turned back to each other. I felt like a third wheel. Waiting silently for my food to arrive while my best friend started her new life with her new best friend, the man who'd permanently take that role on. The man who'd stolen her from me.

Damn, I hated being jealous.

Ten

The next day Brady wanted to take me out. Since we were taking things slow, I wasn't really sure what to expect from our first date. He told me to be ready at seven and to dress casual which gave me no clue what was going on. Evenings were warm so I opted for a pair of khaki shorts and a blue top. I couldn't decide between sneakers and sandals but opted for sneakers in the end. Brady was a fitness buff. For all I knew he could be planning a run through the park or something.

That would kill the date in a hurry.

Brady knocked on my door right at seven. I took a deep breath, suddenly nervous, then opened the door.

Dear. God. The man was gorgeous.

"Hey," he said with a smile, looking me over appreciatively. My skin tingled, but I held back, remembering our agreement to take things slowly.

"Hi," I replied.

"Are you ready to go?"

I nodded then grabbed my keys from the table next to the door and followed Brady. He took my small hand in his and led me to his Jeep. It was old with faded paint, rust spots along the bottom, and more dents than I had rolls.

"You look great, by the way. Beautiful," Brady said when he opened the passenger door for me. He leaned down and gave me a quick kiss then guided me into the car and closed the door behind me. When he sat down next to me his clean, fresh scent washed over me and calmed me.

"I like the Jeep," I told him completely honestly. It matched him. Rough, abused, but still kicking.

Brady eyed me as though he thought I was joking. "It's a piece of junk," he declared as though that would change my mind.

"It runs. And it's a classic, not a piece of junk. The only reason I have a decent car is because I put so many miles on mine every year. Otherwise I'd have something like this."

"Are you for real?"

"Brady, your crappy Jeep isn't going to scare me off. If that was your plan, sorry, but you failed."

He sat for a moment, thinking, watching me, then shook his head. "I didn't plan it. This is the only vehicle I have. I barely drive so I never bothered to upgrade to something better."

Brady started the car and headed toward the center of town. "Do you live close to the gym?"

Brady glanced at me but kept his focus on the road. "I live in the gym, actually. I have an apartment attached. I'm not sure if you noticed, but there's a door in my office. It goes to my apartment."

I cocked my head and smirked. That was totally awesome. If I could have gotten a studio that had an apartment attached I probably would have done it. Charlie lived above Bite Me! and loved it. I was jealous.

"That's awesome. I would love to live in my studio."

"Studio? What do you do?"

"I'm a photographer. I have a studio close to your gym."

"How is it I don't know anything about you?" he asked, laughing.

"I think it's because most of the time we've spent together our mouths have been busy doing other things."

Brady laughed and nodded. "I guess that's true."

"So, where are we going?"

Brady gave me a sidelong glance and offered a half grin. "To the pound."

There's no way I heard him right. It had to be a joke. Who went to the pound for a date? And why were we going anyway?

Oh, God. He was playing a cruel joke on me. Dropping me off or something like that. I had to get out, get the hell away from him. I couldn't handle another joke at my expense.

My heart pounded and blood rushed through my ears. Sweat coated my palms.

"Excuse me?" I said softly, praying I was wrong.

He laughed softly and made another turn, not looking at me. "I've been wanting to get a dog but didn't want to pick one out alone. I figured you might be a good help. Dogs respond differently to men and women. I wanted to get one that won't be aggressive toward women. I hope you don't mind me using you."

He pulled into the parking lot of the local SPCA. I tried to suck in a deep breath, but it wouldn't come. My lungs were full of fear. I knew this wasn't going to end well. Too many men had seemed kind right before they crushed me. I wasn't sure I could handle it from Brady, or anyone, on the heels of Cade, and Blaine, and Addi's engagement, and Monica's perfect life, and my mother, and-

Brady got out of the car and came around to my door. He opened it and I sat there, unmoving. I couldn't get out and listen to Brady insult me. I had to hold on to my fantasy of him just a little longer.

He crouched down and looked at me. I couldn't face him so I stared straight ahead.

"Are you afraid of dogs, Sam?" he asked, concern filling his voice.

I shook my head, not giving him any more than that.

"What's wrong?" He reached up and tucked a strand of hair behind my ear and I lost it.

"I can't do this," I laughed mirthlessly. "I really thought you were different. But taking me to the pound? That's a new kind of low, a new version of nasty. Take the fat chick to the pound and drop her off? I'm not going in there, and you-"

Brady stopped my rant with a rough kiss. I felt his anger in the kiss. His lips were pressed so tight to mine it almost hurt. His tongue butted against my lips, demanding entry I was determined to refuse.

He unbuckled my seatbelt as he kissed me and turned my body toward his, pressing himself between my legs. An erection grew against me, making me moan even though I didn't want to.

Dammit. The asshole used my moan to his advantage and forced his tongue into my mouth. He stroked against my tongue, softening the kiss, asking instead of taking what he wanted. One hand caressed my cheek while the other held me tight against his body.

When I finally gave in and slid my hands around his neck, he pulled back. His eyes were dark and dangerous, angry. "Don't ever call yourself fat again," he growled at me. "At if you don't stop thinking I'm an asshole this will be over before it starts. I know what I am, but I'm not cruel. I would never treat a woman like that, I've told you this already. I want a dog. That's why we're here. But if you honestly believe I could do that to you. That I would bring you here as a joke? I'll take you home right now, and I'll never contact you again. What you feel between your legs is how I feel about you, not some imaginary bullshit you tell yourself because of the other fuckers you've known. This," he nudged against my sex, "is me. But the choice is yours. Who are you going to believe, them or me?"

I chewed on my lip, feeling like a scolded child, but also relieved. In the back of my head, the doubt lingered, but I pushed it aside and looked up at Brady. He was angry with me. Not at me, but because of what I'd been through and how it'd broken my trust in men. I could see it in his eyes, focused on me and not straying from my face.

"I'm sorry," I finally whispered, dropping my eyes from his face. "It's not fair to you. Maybe I'm not ready for this."

"Too fucking bad because we're in this. You're not getting away because of some other asshole. This is about you and me, not him. You're ready. You want me as much as I want you, and one day I'm going to worship your body and make you forget every word that's ever been spoken to you in anything but adoration."

Tingled erupted over my entire body at the conviction and passion in his voice. Dear. God. The man knew how to turn a woman on with just a few words. I wasn't sure I'd survive him not being there, but I would enjoy every minute we had together, for as long as it lasted. I'd face the end when it came.

I finally relented and followed Brady inside, my hand clamped within his. I loved dogs so shopping for one, even if I wasn't taking it home, would be kind of cool.

Brady greeted the woman inside as though he knew her well. They chatted about the dogs they had and what Brady was looking for. She took us back to see the dogs who were already excited and letting us know they wanted company. I breathed a small sigh of relief when he didn't turn and walk out the door, leaving me behind.

We walked down the aisle lined with cages on each side. Every dog you could imagine was there, all colors and breeds. I wasn't willing to offer an opinion since the dog would be Brady's and not mine, but he pulled me along with him.

"I don't want an aggressive dog," he told Barbara, the employee who was helping us. "I don't want a lazy dog either. I'll take it out on runs and will train it so I want one that you think will be a good fit."

Barbara nodded and led us to a handful of cages toward the back of the room. "The dogs over here seem to be pretty calm. None of them give me any trouble and we think they're young which helps them to learn easier and they'll run."

Brady stood back and looked at the dogs. There were five cages that he was focusing on. The dogs were medium to large sized but I couldn't identify a particular breed for any of them. One of the dogs was sitting, wagging its tail, and watching us.

But it was ugly.

I felt bad for the dog because I knew no one was likely to adopt it. His fur was a little long and a mix of brown and grey. He had a long snout and big floppy ears but a small head that made him look a little like Dumbo. With a long, shaggy tail and a larger size, he was an intimidating looking dog, except that smile.

I shit you not, he was fucking smiling at us.

If Brady didn't take that dog home I thought I might.

Brady looked into the cages of the other animals and asked Barbara to let him in. One by one he got down on the dirty floor and gave the dogs full body rubs. He talked to them like they were regular people. And one by one he put them back in their cages. Then he got to the ugly dog.

"What's his story?" he asked Barbara.

She shrugged. "We really don't know. He was tied up outside one morning when we got here. It was raining and he was soaked through, but once we got him inside and warm he was better. He could probably use a hair cut, but he's a healthy dog, even though he's not much to look at."

Brady nodded solemnly and let the dog out of the cage. The dog came out with his tail wagging slowly, tucked low to show he recognized Brady's dominance. He approached Brady cautiously enough that I wondered if he'd been abused.

Brady held his hand up and waited for the dog to sniff his fingers. He nuzzled Brady's hand and came closer, his tail wagging more and more until his entire butt was swaying from side to side. As he got closer to Brady he ducked his head, but kept moving toward Brady.

When his big hand moved down the dog's back he moved against him as though he craved the attention. The dog settled into Brady's lap and licked his jaw. I wondered if Brady would flip but instead he just laughed.

"You're a friendly one, aren't you?" he asked the dog. "A little shy though, huh?"

I watched as Brady bonded with the dog, petting his back and talking to him. The dog got more and more comfortable with Brady the longer the two sat together, licking his face and nudging his hand if he didn't pet him enough.

Brady finally looked up at me and asked, "Do you mind petting him? See if he's okay with you, too?"

I dropped to the floor and held out my hand for a sniff and coaxed the dog away from Brady. Once he was clear, Brady got to his feet and asked Barbara about the dog again.

"Is he good with different people?"

"Yeah," she told him. "None of the employees have had trouble with him. He's a sweet dog. He may have been abused though so you need to be careful with him, but I think he's a good dog. You two shouldn't have any trouble with him."

Brady didn't correct her assumption that we would own the dog together so I let it go as well. It didn't matter what she thought. She didn't need to know it was our first date.

I rubbed the dog's ears and enjoyed the feel of his head nuzzling against me. He was a sweet dog. I knew Brady was going to take him and I was a little jealous. Although as long as Brady let me snuggle with him once in a while it would be okay.

Brady talked through the specifics of adopting the dog while I continued petting him. He settled across my lap and rested his head on the hard concrete floor, his tail still wagging once in a while. Normally they gave the dog his shots and a bath overnight, but Brady requested everything be done immediately so we could take him home right away.

An hour later the three of us pulled into a parking space at the park. With a grin Brady grabbed a picnic basket I'd not noticed before and climbed out of his Jeep. With Lucky's leash in one hand and the picnic basket in the other he reached for me and we held the leash together.

It was getting late, but the park was quiet which was nice. Brady stretched out a blanket for us and pulled out sandwiches, fruit, bottles of water, and dessert that he wouldn't let me see. Lucky sat next to us patiently until Brady pulled out a small bag of dog food and set it in front of him.

"You knew you were getting a dog tonight, didn't you?" I asked, all the drama from earlier forgotten.

He nodded. "I was hoping. I've always wanted a dog and have been looking for just the right one."

"And you found Lucky."

"Yep. He looks like a good dog."

"Why him?"

Brady looked at me, his expression getting more and more intense with each passing second. He smiled just a bit and said, "I'm a fan of the underdog. He looked like a dog no one else would want, but he was easily the best fit for me. At least I think so."

I nodded. "Is that why you named him Lucky? Because he's lucky you picked him?"

Brady shrugged. "A little. I also think I'm lucky to have him."

"I've always been a dog person. Two of my best friends are cat people, but I'd rather have a dog than a cat any day."

"Do you have a dog? We should get them together."

I shook my head. "I don't have one. I work too much for a dog. Maybe if I had a job I could come home more often I'd be okay, but I feel like I wouldn't be good for a dog."

He looked at me closely. "I can't imagine you not being good for anyone," he said softly.

I smiled shyly and thanked him.

We ate our dinner in companionable silence, the sounds of Lucky's excited eating making a soothing background noise for us. Once we finished dinner Brady opened the container housing chocolate chip cookies that looked homemade.

"Did you bake these?" I asked, curious about a man who baked.

He nodded. "Yeah. I don't bake often but I have a weakness for chocolate chip cookies."

"Yeah, I can tell," I said dryly. "You're almost as fat as I am."

Brady's eyes snapped to mine and I saw anger and disappointment. "You are not fat."

"I know what I am," I argued. "It's okay."

"Sam, you can't talk about yourself that way."

"Are you sure you're not blind? You're dating the fattest woman at your gym and just adopted the ugliest dog in the shelter."

"If appearance is all that matters to you then maybe we shouldn't do this. I thought there was more to you than that," Brady said sounding disappointed.

"You're kidding, right? If I was all about appearance I certainly wouldn't look the way I do. I'm just being honest."

"No, Sam, you're being mean. It doesn't matter to me if you're overweight, as long as you're a good person. But if you can go on and on about how 'fat' you are then I'm not sure I want to be around you. I've had too many women wanting to sleep with me thinking I'll show them some secret method to getting thin. I thought we dealt with this already. Twice."

"You think I'm using you," I mumbled, shocked and hurt. "I've never used anyone in my life. I make my own way and I do my own thing. If you think so little of me then I think you're right. We shouldn't do this."

I stood up and pulled out my phone. It hurt that he thought so little of me but it wasn't worth it to try to change his mind. I scrolled quickly to Addi's number, even though I knew she'd be with Joey, and touched her name.

Voicemail.

I kept walking, scrolling through my numbers hoping for someone to come get me from the park. Darkness was settling in quickly and I didn't want to be out there alone. And there was no way in hell I would let Brady give me a ride home.

"I'm sorry," he said from right behind me. "I shouldn't have said that."

"It's fine," I ground out, swiping the tears from the edges of my eyelashes. I wasn't going to let him see how much it hurt me that he would think something so horrible of me.

"We've both made assumptions about each other based on people from our past. People that deserve to be in our past. Sam, give me another chance, please," Brady begged.

"I don't know how many chances we get before we implode. Every time we're together we're either kissing like horny teenagers or fighting. I'm just not sure I can take that kind of emotional upheaval."

"I know. And I'm sorry. I just hate that word. It pushes all the wrong buttons for me," Brady admitted.

"How? I know no one has ever been able to call you that. And it's the truth about me. Sure I could say something else, but in the end it all means the same thing."

"Not to me, it doesn't. You can use any word besides that, but I'd rather you didn't insult yourself. You're beautiful, Sam. You need to believe that."

I shook my head and wondered what game he was playing. Cade was an asshole, but he never told me I was beautiful. He never made me feel the things Brady made me feel after just a few hours. He never gave me so much hope.

"I've never been beautiful, Brady. I know that's not me. I'm meant to be behind the camera, not in front of it, that's why I'm a photographer and not a model."

"You should be. A model, I mean. Sam, you sell yourself short. And I'm sorry for what I said, but I'm right about this. I'm an asshole, but you're beautiful. I should be begging at your feet for one chance. Instead I'm stupid enough that I'm begging for a third chance."

I rolled my eyes. "You don't have to insult yourself to make me feel better. It's not working."

"It's not for your benefit. I'm just telling the truth," he mocked me.

I laughed. Somehow he made me feel better. If his intense looks didn't make me melt, his smile was disarming enough that I had no choice. He stepped closer, tentatively as though he didn't know what I'd do. One hand brushed my cheek and my eyes slipped closed. He made me feel beautiful. Like I was someone who deserved to be with him. Even if it was temporary.

Brady would never want to be with me forever, and when it ended I knew it would hurt worse than anything else ever had, but I wanted him for now. I would take whatever he wanted to give me. And when it was over I'd hold on to the memories of him like a lifeline to keep me from drowning.

When his lips touched mine softly, I was lost. I couldn't stop the moan that rose from my gut and slid past my lips. Brady kept one hand on my cheek and let the other roam my back, gently caressing my cotton covered skin. I wanted more, all of him if I could have him, but knew it wouldn't ever happen.

I'd never have all of Brady, even if he managed to possess all of me.

Eleven

Brady dropped me off after our date like a gentleman. I invited him in, but he declined because of Lucky. He told me he wanted to come in. For some reason I believed him.

The next night was girls' night. I was thrilled to feel like myself again, and even more excited that two new friends were joining us. I'd almost forgotten about inviting Riley and Carrie to join us until I pulled up in front of Bite Me!

Addi was already inside, as usual, but strangely no one else was there yet. "Have you talked to your parents yet?" I asked as I took the seat next to her, bypassing the busy counter for a chance to talk to Addi alone.

She nodded and grinned. "Yeah. They were thrilled. They want us to set a date, but we're still thinking. We can't do winter because of school and it being Joey's busy time, but summer is hard for him too. We're considering one of the fall breaks I get. Maybe October, or maybe Thanksgiving weekend. There's just so much to figure out."

"About what?" Lexi asked as she took the seat on Addi's other side. She winked at me then focused on Addi.

Addi chewed her lip and glanced at me. I raised my eyebrows and she smiled. "Joey and I got engaged over the weekend. I was complaining to Sam about figuring out the wedding."

"Wait, what?" Lexi shouted. "Seriously? You're supposed to be enjoying this part. Congratulations!"

Addi beamed. "Thanks. There's just so many people to talk to. I need to buy a book or something."

"Oh, perfect. I invited two new people to join us tonight. One of them runs that bookstore, READ. Do you think everyone else will mind?"

"Mind what?" Claire asked as she sat down.

"I was just telling Addi and Lexi I invited two people tonight. Riley, who I met at READ, and Carrie, her friend, who works for one of my former clients. Riley was cool at the bookstore and Carrie was always friendly over the phone. Is it okay?"

The others looked at each other and shrugged. "I don't see why not," Lexi said. "You guys welcomed Charlie and me into your group, why not two more."

I breathed a sigh of relief. I didn't think there would be a problem, but until I heard it from them I was a little uneasy.

"Oh, here they are now," I said when Riley walked inside with another woman with brown hair and the prettiest eyes I'd ever seen. She was the kind of woman I always wanted to look at through a camera. Her eyes spoke her emotions. Not to mention she was beautiful. Even better, she was my size, but a bit shorter.

Riley and Carrie approached our table with tentative smiles. "Hey guys. We're glad you could make it. This is Addi, Claire, and Lexi.

122

Charlie is behind the counter and Mandy is always late."

"Not always," Mandy said as she took a seat next to Claire. "Who's this?"

"Guys, this is Riley and Carrie. I invited them to join us tonight."

"Awesome. Nice to meet you. Are you going to get cupcakes? Charlie makes the best in town."

"Oh, yeah, we're going. Sam, no cupcakes?" Riley asked. "You're going to be able to rub your skinny ass in your loser ex's face in no time."

All eyes swung to me with questioning looks. "What ex? Did you and Cade break up?" Claire asked.

"Why does it matter if you have a skinny ass?" Mandy demanded.

"Is he why you joined the gym? What did he say?" Addi asked.

Riley's face paled and she looked like she was going to run. "Sam, I'm so sorry. I just assumed."

I shook my head. "It's fine, Riley. They were going to find out soon enough. Yes, Cade and I broke up. He said, among other things, that I was too fat for him."

"Son of a bitch," Lexi muttered while the others just gaped at me.

"It's fine. He's gone and I'm better off without him."

"Why the gym, Sam? Because of him?" Addi asked.

I couldn't lie to my best friend, but I didn't want to tell her the truth. Admitting that I was that pathetic, to still care what he thought, only made me worse, not better. Of course the gym was because of Cade, but that was my business.

"What other things?" Carrie asked, jumping right into the conversation.

"What do you mean?" I asked, buying time and hopefully getting out of the whole conversation.

"You said 'among other things' that you were too fat. What other things did he say?"

I shook my head and fought the tears that welled up in my eyes. My tears weren't for him. I was over him. Cade didn't matter anymore. But no one would believe me if I said that. Not unless I told them all of it. And I didn't think I was ready to confess those words.

"It doesn't matter. He's gone. Cade's out of my life. I had a date last night. I'm doing all this for me."

I shared a look with Riley and knew she understood not to say anything more. She didn't tell them to be mean, she just didn't know better. I wasn't mad at her, but I didn't want her arguing with me.

The others didn't look like they believed me, but they accepted it and changed the subject. I stood up and walked to the counter with Carrie and Riley.

"I am so sorry, Sam. I had no idea your friends didn't know," Riley apologized.

I waved her off. "It's not your fault. I should have told them when it happened, but I was embarrassed."

"That jackass is the one who should be embarrassed. You're gorgeous. He's the blind one," Carrie added.

I smiled at her. "Thanks. It's nice to meet you in person, by the way. I don't know if Riley told you, but I'm Samantha Reed, or Sam."

"Oh, damn, you are. I don't usually let the lines of work and home blur."

I laughed. "Neither do I. Since we didn't actually work together it's okay, right?"

I felt like I was begging for her to be my friend. Carrie seemed like someone I could get along with. I could see why she and Riley were close. Similar outbursts of anger on my behalf and swearing that made me feel less like a trucker and more like I wasn't alone. I could use friends like them.

"Oh, yeah, it's fine. Beth the Bitch would have a shit-fit, but she's not ever going to be invited somewhere I am, so we should be cool."

"I don't know how you work with her every day. She was a challenge and I only had to do it for a couple of hours."

Carrie let out a vicious laugh that I knew meant she felt the same way. "She's a challenge," was all she said though.

At the counter I introduced Carrie and Riley to Charlie, and we all ordered cupcakes. Back at the table everyone had mercifully moved on to another topic.

Sort of.

"I just don't see the point in going to the gym. You get all sweaty and gross and it doesn't ever do anything. I'd rather get sweaty in the bedroom," Mandy boasted.

Everyone laughed.

"Well, I would too, but I still enjoy the gym. I've even got Joey going with me now. He was like you, besides how much he does for his job, but he decided to come with me a few times and he's liking it. He says it'll make snowboarding easier to focus on some of those muscles," Addi argued.

"It's harder for women to lose weight than men," Claire pouted. "Aidan can eat anything he wants and never gain an ounce. If I even look at a piece of cake I'm up a pound. I never weigh myself after a night here."

"Yeah, it's our biology," Lexi agreed. "It's another one of those things that's just not fair. Men get all the easy stuff in life... no periods, no panty hose, no boobs, well some of them have that one."

We all cackled in agreement. Men with boobs was a definite no-no. I tried not to be shallow and judge men on their looks, but sometimes it was hard. Sort of like Brady and Greg at the gym. Both of them were attractive, but there was something about Brady that I couldn't get out of my head, even though Greg was probably the smarter choice since he wasn't full of pent up aggression.

"Some men have nice boobs. Firm and sexy, that just make you want to run your tongue all over them," Mandy said with a moan.

I snorted in laughter. Mandy was too much sometimes. She'd certainly gotten a dirtier mind since she and Xander got together. Once upon a time Mandy was almost chaste. Xander turned her into a sailor on leave.

"Those aren't boobs, Mand, those are pecs. And yeah, I'll agree with the licking part," Claire remarked. "There've got to be some hot guys at your gym, Sam. Have you met anyone yet?"

Sometimes it seemed my friends thought I was a slut. I dated a lot, yes, but I wasn't sleeping with everyone I'd ever dated. A fact I'd told them over and over again. Still, comments like that made me think they didn't believe I could ever get hurt, or get serious. Like I would jump from one guy to the next constantly.

"There are definitely some cute ones there," Addi chimed in before I could answer. "The trainers are all hot and so are a lot of the guys who work out there."

"Aren't you engaged?" I teased. "You shouldn't be looking at other men with Joey around."

Addi waved her hand. "Joey is oblivious. Besides I can look as long as I don't touch."

I rolled my eyes at her, but Claire hadn't forgotten her question. "Have you met them, Sam?"

Knowing I couldn't avoid her I admitted, "I've met one of the trainers, Greg. He was really nice. A few of the members are hot. And the owner is cute."

Addi narrowed her eyes at me. "The owner? Brady?"

"Yeah. Why?"

Addi tilted her head to the side and thought carefully before she said anything. The longer it took the more anxious I got. Both for more information about Brady and because I hoped for something that would help me stop thinking about him.

"I was there almost a year before I met Brady. I'm just surprised is all. Did someone point him out to you."

I shook my head, worried about where the conversation was going. "He gave me a tour and then helped me when I was with the trainer because Greg had to help someone else."

I purposely left out that Brady practically shoved Greg out of the way, then rescued me from Blaine and the other assholes he was with. Addi didn't need to know those things.

"Really? That's strange. Brady doesn't seem to socialize with anyone."

I shrugged, playing it off as no big deal even though my heart was pounding. I really needed to get my attraction to him under control. Just hearing his name had me tingling between my legs. Then again, if real life Brady was anything like fantasy Brady I'd have more than a tingle between my legs. And if his kisses on our first date were any indication, I was pretty sure real life Brady was even better than the fantasy version.

"It wasn't really socializing. He just offered to help his employees when they were busy. I'm sure it wasn't a big deal."

Even though I knew it was. Greg didn't come back to help me after Brady left, but I caught him smirking at me. Brady admitted he'd wanted me the first time he saw me, but they didn't all need to know what was going on with us. Not yet.

"Maybe," Addi said thoughtfully. "It just seems strange to me. What did you think of him?"

"He's fucking gorgeous," I said without thinking.

Addi laughed. "Yeah, he is. He's definitely one of those guys with the sexy pecs that Mandy's talking about."

"Maybe I should join the gym," Mandy said thoughtfully.

"Yeah, that sounds like a good idea. Where is this place?" Carrie teased.

I laughed but inside jealousy tore through me. If Brady saw Carrie he'd be all over her. She was beautiful where I was just a frumpy photographer. Carrie was one of those women I could see showing up to the gym with designer workout clothes and would look perfect even after she was done. Hell, she probably didn't even sweat.

I shook my head at myself. Brady was intent on making me understand he wanted me. If he did want Carrie, I'd accept it and move on. I knew eventually he would go for someone else. Sure, I hoped it wouldn't be one of my friends, but in the end I wouldn't be with Brady.

The conversation continued about men's bodies and what everyone liked about them, but I didn't have the energy to contribute. I kept flashing back to our date the night before. The desire I saw in his eyes and the way he spoke to me made me believe what he said about me, to me. But hearing Carrie joke about wanting him reminded me of how many women would be after a man like Brady. I was a fool if I thought I could hang on to him.

Of course I still didn't know much about him. The most open he'd been was when he told me about Lucky, but even then he didn't reveal anything about himself. Unfairly, when he looked at me I felt like he could see all the way through me to my soul. The parts that I kept hidden from everyone else.

And it made me want to run from him. Almost as much as it made me want him.

Twelve

Brady called me every day, but we didn't see each other again for over a week. I joined Dave's Gym and was going three or four days each week, and Brady caught up with me at the end of one of my workouts.

"Come with me?" he whispered in my ear, scaring me. I hadn't seen him approach me and the voice right behind me made my heart pound in fear.

When I spun and saw Brady my heart managed to calm down, but he saw through my panic. "I'm sorry. I shouldn't have snuck up on you. I hate it when people do that to me."

"It's okay, I just didn't expect it is all. What's up?"

"Come with me. You'll see."

I let him take my hand and lead me down the hallway to his office again. He closed the door behind us and flipped the lock the same time he pressed me against it. His mouth closed over mine as his hands wrapped around my waist.

He kissed me urgently with a force I hadn't seen much from him. His tongue pushed between my lips, not giving me the chance to let him in. His large body made me feel small beneath him. I inhaled deeply to catch his scent but only got mine. Embarrassed of how badly I smelled I pushed him off.

"God, I smell horrible. I know you don't want to kiss me when I stink this bad."

He chuckled softly. "I actually don't have a very good sense of smell. After the third time my nose got broken I sort of stopped being able to smell much of anything."

"Jeez, you had a rough childhood. How did you break your nose three times?" I teased.

Brady closed up faster than a clam. He turned away from me and mumbled something about being a stupid kid, but I could tell there was more to it than that. And that, again, he didn't want to talk about it. He was becoming more and more of a mystery to me.

"I didn't mean to say something wrong," I said, prying without trying to make it obvious I was fishing for information. Between Brady's intense looks and the scars on his body, not to mention the broken nose, I knew something had happened to him. My gut twisted at the thought of what it could have been, but I didn't want to go there.

"It's fine. I shouldn't have dragged you back here. I've just missed you. It kills me that you're so close all the time and I can't touch you or kiss you. Today it got to me and I couldn't let you walk out the doors again without getting you alone."

I stretched up onto my toes and kissed his jaw, letting my tongue run down the scar on his chin. He twitched before his hands reached around to cup my ass. He pulled me tight against him, his erection separating us, then brought his lips down over mine again.

His lips were soft but urgent, asking me for permission I was desperate to give. I slid my tongue out to meet his, a conversation we could only have without words. I ached for him, but I knew he wasn't ready. He'd only ever touched my ass and my waist, never anything else. And after kisses that left me feeling like I'd been hit by a meteor, I wanted more.

I didn't want to rush him, but the feel of him hard against my stomach made my body do things I had no control over. As my back arched to rub myself against him, my hands coaxed him closer. A moan slipped past my lips and I felt Brady's control drift.

One hand moved from my ass up my side, over my hip, and continued north. When he got to the edge of my breast, still encased in my heavy-duty sports bra, he paused. With his control firmly back in place I let out a sigh of disappointment. I didn't want to rush him, but I also didn't want to check into a convent any time soon.

Brady pulled back from our kiss, leaving me breathless and swirling with frustration. He looked down at me, his eyes blazing with the fire I felt shooting throughout my body. "Can I touch you, Sam?" he asked with a gentleness I didn't expect.

"Dear, God, please," I begged, letting him know how badly I wanted him.

"You'll stop me if it's too much?"

"Brady, I'm wound so tight right now nothing could be too much," I answered honestly. I'd been taking care of myself, sure, but there was no substitute for an old-fashioned man-made orgasm. And it'd been way too long since I'd had one of those.

Cade, the fucker, was never big on making it worth my while. He always finished before it got good for me. Of course, I understood why after we broke up, but it didn't change the fact that I was desperate for a little attention down there.

Brady's large hands danced under the edge of my t-shirt, his fingers brushing the bare skin on my sides. My middle was my biggest part so I was insanely self-conscious about him touching me there.

Even more since Cade.

Brady's eyes held mine, searching for signs that I wanted him to stop. I silently urged him on and sighed happily when his hands slid up. My shirt drifted with them and I tried to tug it down so he wouldn't see me. He stopped.

"What's wrong?" Brady asked, his hands wrapped around my ribcage.

"Nothing. I just don't want you to see me. Naked, I mean."

"I thought you said I could touch you?" he asked, confused.

"Yeah, but touch is different from sight. I just... I don't like how I look without clothes on. I know you won't like it either."

I ducked my head as I said the last part. Brady and I had been having fun, but that was all about to end. He would be horrified by my body and likely run away screaming. I'd been dreading letting him see me. Going slow seemed like the perfect solution, until I realized he'd eventually have to see me naked.

With the moment staring me in the face I wasn't too thrilled with my plan.

I couldn't look up into Brady's eyes, but I felt them on me. I squeezed mine shut to block the pain and tears that were both welling up. Brady's hands dropped from my ribcage and I knew it was done. Over. Finished.

Then with a whoosh my shirt was gone. It caught on my glasses for a second, rendering me blind, then dropped behind me. I opened my eyes in shock and found Brady looking at me, rolls and all.

I covered my face with my hands and tried to turn away so I wouldn't see the disgust in his eyes. Brady wasn't like the others. The men I'd slept with just because I was lonely. He wasn't someone that I'd jump into a relationship with and figure out if I liked him later. Brady was different. He was someone I liked from the start, even before I really knew him. He intimidated me, but he also intrigued me.

And when I opened my eyes I knew it was going to be over.

"Look at me, Sam."

I shook my head.

"Sam, please open your eyes."

I peeked through one eye and found Brady standing in front of me with his shirt off. I opened both of my eyes and looked at him.

Covered in pink lines, some darker than others, of scars.

"Brady, what happened to you?" I asked with tears forming in my eyes. The pain his body showed was heart breaking. I wanted to know what he'd been through, and at the same time I didn't want to know. I had fears, but I didn't want them confirmed.

"I never take my shirt off, Sam. I don't want anyone to see this. We both hide beneath our clothes. For different reasons. I've never shown anyone what I look like. I always insisted the lights were off before I took off my shirt. You are beautiful without your shirt. I am not."

My heart split wide open as his words sunk in. How did he not realize how stunning he was. The scars told the story of his pain, but also the story of his strength.

My eyes scanned his body, cataloguing every mark on him. Some were long and thin, others were shorter and wider. Some of his scars were jagged while others were smooth. No two were alike, but I knew they'd all come from the same thing.

"I'm sorry you went through this, Brady. But you're wrong. You are beautiful. Every last inch of you," I told him as I kissed his scars. I started with his shoulder and worked my way over his body, kissing each one of his scars. His breath grew shallow and his hands clenched at his sides while I worked across his body. When I brushed my lips over the last one, a curving scar that started at his hip and dipped below his waistband, Brady hauled me against him.

His tongue thrust into my mouth and we kissed as though he was a military hero home on leave. Skin touched skin, lips touched lips, souls touched souls. When Brady's hand cupped my breast I nearly lost it. My body arched into his touch, eager for more. His fingers brushed over my nipple, making it harden to a painful point under the unforgiving fabric of my sports bra.

Brady shoved my bra up, exposing my breasts in the cool air conditioned office. He broke our kiss and looked down at me. "Dear God, you're beautiful," he said with reverence. His hands overflowed with my flesh and his mouth dipped to help, one nipple disappearing between his soft pink lips.

I moaned and rocked against him, the warm, wet feel of his tongue mimicked between my legs. I wanted him there, everywhere. He tortured my neglected flesh with his tongue and his fingers, bringing me closer and closer to an orgasm with each movement. I began to wonder if I could come just from him touching my nipples when I felt a deep tingling heat between my legs.

"Oh, fuck, Brady," I moaned, urging him on.

Sensing what I needed, Brady lifted me, drew my legs around his waist, and leaned my back against the wall. With my body supported his attention returned to my nipples, and the pleasure that was ricocheting through me. With one flick and another nip, then a twist, and a pinch, I rocked hard against him. He met me stroke for stroke, the thin fabric of our clothes only dulling the sensation slightly.

Before long I felt the familiar tightening of my body. My head dropped back, hitting the wall, but I didn't care. I arched against him harder, my thighs doing more work than they'd ever done to leverage me onto him. His teeth closed around my nipples as he brought them together, both in his mouth at the same time.

And my body let go. I called out his name on a prayer, praising him for making me feel so good. He swallowed my repeated words with a devouring kiss, his hips still rocking into me and his tongue matching the rhythm.

When I went limp in his arms, a wet noodle unable to stay upright, Brady dropped to the floor with me. He cradled me against his chest and held me. My strength began to return and my breathing began to slow, but I noticed he was gulping down air like he couldn't get enough.

My first thought was I'd worn him out. He shouldn't have been holding me up so long. I'd nearly killed him with my fat ass.

I tried to get off him so he could breathe more easily, but he held on tight to me. "Don't go. Not yet," he begged.

"I'm too heavy for you. You can't breathe."

"It's not because of you," he spurted, barely getting the words out. "Please. Stay."

I maneuvered myself so I was sitting on the floor but didn't wiggle out of his arms. I pressed my head to his chest and listened to his heart pound against my ear. Absently I ran my fingers over his exposed chest. The thickly ridged muscles jumped at my touch. My hand drifted lower and his happy trail tickled my fingers. I had an insatiable urge to keep going lower, but his breath grew more ragged so I shifted away.

Brady's arms held me close, not letting me get away. I forced myself to be still and wait for him to calm down. His breathing finally slowed and returned to normal and his arms loosened around me.

"Are you okay?"

"I think you're going to kill me," he said, still breathless, but better.

"I told you I was too heavy."

He shook his head and kissed my hair, inhaling deeply. "Nowhere near too heavy. Perfect. Beautiful. That was the sexiest thing I've ever seen. I stopped breathing when I was watching you. By the time I realized it I was hyperventilating. I'm sorry."

"You scared the hell out of me."

He laughed softly. "Now you know how I feel every time I see you."

I turned in his lap and pressed against him, delighting in the feel of his smooth skin against my nipples. My panties were soaked through, and I smelled like an old gym sock, but my man made me forget all that. His hands rested low on my back and held me tight. I kissed him, softly to make sure he didn't relapse. My tongue danced across his lips and he opened for me on a sigh.

His tongue was soft and warm in my mouth. It was a lazy kiss, one to learn each other. Our tongues caressed with the same lack of urgency that our hands did. And even with the easy feel of it, my body was heating up all over again.

Before we got too out of hand I pulled back from Brady. His eyes were hazy with desire, and he looked confused. "I know we're not ready for more than this. I'd love to return the favor though," I offered seductively.

Brady smiled and pulled me in for another kiss. With our lips still touching he whispered, "Not ready. If I can't even breathe around you I'm not ready for more. Although I'd love to go there."

I nodded and got up. With his eyes on me I fixed my sports bra and reached for my shirt. Once I was dressed again I handed Brady his shirt and sighed as he pulled it back on.

"You give me six pack amnesia," I told him as he stood up.

"What's that?"

"It's where I forget all the reasons I should be staying away from you when your shirt is off. Or in your case, whenever I see you."

Brady narrowed his eyes and cocked his head to the side. "Why should you be staying away from me?"

Damn. I wasn't supposed to tell him that. Quick, brain, come up with something. "Oh, just... because you said you wanted to take things slow. I don't want to rush you."

Phew, that worked. I hoped.

"Okay," Brady said in a voice that told me he didn't really believe me. "Well, thanks for going slow. I don't want to hurt you."

I nodded knowing it was inevitable. Brady was the kind of guy who could crush a woman's heart and a man's arm without breaking a sweat. Probably all before breakfast. Brady Wright was trouble. And I was thick in it.

Thirteen

My mom called that evening as I was having dinner, alone. "Hi, Mom."

"Hello Samantha. How are you?"

Oh great, it was the throw her off so I can ambush her later tactic. I hated this one because I always fell for it.

"I'm good, Mom. It's been a good day," I blushed. She wouldn't be getting the details of my rendezvous with Brady, but I wouldn't lie.

"That's good to hear sweetheart. I worry about you. All those random people you work with. It would be so easy for someone to take advantage of you."

"Mmm hmm," I mumbled. It was an argument I'd heard plenty over the years. A friend of a friend had a cousin whose daughter said she heard about a photographer who was attacked when doing a photo shoot for someone. I needed to be more careful.

It was ridiculous, but it was Mom.

"Have you looked through the websites I sent you? Doris's daughter met someone on one of those online dating things and said it was great. She dated a bunch of men and then married the one she liked the best."

I rolled my eyes. If she wasn't trying to change my career she was trying to marry me off. Being single at 29 was an insult to her, not a testament to me. Not that I didn't want to get married, but I certainly wasn't going to end up with someone like Cade. Or Blaine.

"I read the email, Mom, but I'm not signing up for online dating. I get plenty of dates on my own."

"Now, really Samantha, I thought you wouldn't lie to me about something like that."

I scoffed, borderline pissed that she would intimate that I couldn't get a date. "I'm not lying. I'm seeing someone now."

"You are? I didn't know that," she said, sounding like the cat that ate the canary.

Damn. The trap. I'd walked right into it.

"Well, you should bring him out to the house for July 4th. We'll have a cookout and Dad got sparklers for the kids. We're going to watch the fireworks too, of course."

I hesitated. I loved July 4th. It was inexplicably one of my favorite holidays. My family always got together and for some reason it was a peaceful holiday instead of one filled with drama. There was something about celebrating where we'd come from and the people who'd made it possible that we all loved.

And my mom knew how much it meant to me.

"Don't try to tell me you have to work because I know you never work on the 4th. Now what is your new friend's name?"

"Brady Wright," I confessed, knowing I had no choice.

"Okay, well, then, we'll see you and Brady around three. Please bring a salad to share. Bye."

I was dismissed. Mom hung up before I had a chance to argue. Brady might have plans. Maybe he was visiting with his family or didn't like the 4th. Maybe he wasn't ready to meet my family. We'd only been dating for a couple weeks. We'd had our share of heavy kissing sessions, but hadn't gone any further than that before that afternoon. And Brady said he wasn't ready for more.

How could I subject him to my family?

Two days later Brady joined me for a workout at the gym. His staff watched us with smirks on their faces, but no one said anything. "You don't do this much, do you?"

"Do what?" Brady asked, utterly confused.

"Work out with a client."

"Oh, uh, no. I never do."

"Never? Why never?"

He shrugged. "I keep to myself. If I do venture out here during the day it's rare that I talk to many people. My employees can handle things, but they know where to find me if they need something."

"Why did you buy the gym?" I asked, curious to know more about him.

He took a deep breath and blew it out slowly. "I liked it. The gym, I mean. I owned Dave's Gym when it was smaller, just a basement gym, but I wanted it to be more. When this space opened up I grabbed it."

He shrugged like it was no big deal, but I could tell there was more to the story. A lot more. Brady had lots of secrets, but he wasn't big on sharing them.

"What are you doing tomorrow?" he asked.

"Um, I'm busy actually," I stammered, not sure where we were going.

"Really? Are you working?"

I shook my head. "No. I'm off. I just have plans."

"Oh," he sounded disappointed. Damn, he thought I had a date.

"It's not like that. I'm just going to my parents' house."

"Oh," Brady sounded a little brighter, but not much.

"They always have a cookout for the 4th and we watch the fireworks from the neighborhood park. It's one of my favorite holidays so I like to go see fireworks and celebrate, dress up in flag clothes and be kind of silly."

"That sounds fun. I was going to see if you wanted to spend the day together, but it's okay."

Aw, crap. I wanted to see Brady, a hell of a lot more than I wanted to see my family. But I still didn't know if I could do that to him.

"You can come with me, if you want."

"Oh, I wouldn't want to impose. I'm sure your family doesn't want to meet me."

I sighed. "Actually, they do. I sort of mentioned you to my mom the other day and she's expecting you to come."

His intense gaze cut through my shit and went straight to the heart of the matter. So did his words. "Why didn't you want to tell me?"

I squeezed my eyes shut and willed myself to get through it. Brady rested a hand on my arm and let it drift down until he wound our fingers together. "What's going on, Sam?"

"I didn't know if you were ready to meet my family. We've only been seeing each other for a couple weeks and I worried you might think I was pushing you too fast. If you think that, it's okay. It's just my mom is sort of crazy about getting my life fixed up and she wanted me to sign up for online dating and I blurted out that I was seeing you without thinking about it and she latched onto it. So now she wants to meet you but she never bothered to ask if you were free or if I was ready to introduce you or anything and I'm sort of freaking out."

Brady laughed and tucked my head under his chin. "I can see that. It sounds like we've got ourselves a little problem. First, you need to decide if you want to spend time with me tomorrow. Second, if you do, you need to tell me if you're ready for me to meet your parents."

"Oh, it's not just my parents," I interrupted him. "It's my parents, my sister and her perfect family, and my brother and his perfect family. I'm the black sheep. The one without a decent job, without a spouse, without kids, and, according to my mother, without a real shot at a good future."

He cupped my cheeks in his hands and turned my face up to his. He kissed me softly, gently letting our lips touch until I felt the fight leaving me and desire seep in. Then he pulled back.

"I'd be more than happy to go with you tomorrow. I'd love to spend the day with you, and meeting this perfect family will be interesting. I don't know anything about those so it'll be good to see one in action."

"Brady, you don't have to do this. It's too soon."

"Not for me, Sam. I'd love to meet your family. But if you're not ready to introduce me, that's up to you."

I shook my head and knew the truth. "I want you to meet them. If you're sure."

Brady kissed me again, this time letting his tongue slip into my mouth. I held onto him tightly and tried to forget about everything except Brady. When he pulled back it was too soon, but just right. I could see the haze of desire in Brady's eyes and felt powerful knowing I'd put it there.

And with him by my side, even facing my mother for a day didn't seem too daunting.

~*~

I shouldn't have been so confident. My mother outdid herself. The second we walked in the door she sized Brady up and decided he was another project. One she wasn't willing to take on herself and wasn't possible for her daughter.

Thankfully Brady didn't seem phased by it at all. He laid on the charm for my mom anyway, not that she noticed. "Mrs. Reed, you have a beautiful home. It's clear you have impeccable taste."

"Yes, well, my husband has worked very hard for everything we have. He's a police officer for the city of Buffalo," Mom said proudly.

"That's impressive," Brady said as though he didn't know. He took me to lunch and I spent the last three hours briefing him on every detail of my family so he'd know what to say and what topics to skip. Not to mention who everyone was and how perfect they all were in comparison to me.

"Yes, it is. He's a strong man. Smart, too. What is it you do Brady?"

I bristled, knowing how Mom felt about entrepreneurship and self-employment. As soon as she found out Brady owned his own gym it would be over.

"I own Dave's Gym, where Sam and I met."

Mom laughed and swatted at an invisible fly. "Oh, you must be joking. Samantha thinks exercise is a form of torture invented by skinny people."

Yeah, I guess I'd said that a few too many times.

Brady chuckled good-naturedly and said, "No, I'm not joking. Sam's been coming to my gym for almost a month now. Not that she needs to lose any weight to be beautiful."

I smiled gratefully at Brady as I waited for Mom's next move. No doubt it would be-

"Samantha could stand to lose a good bit of weight. She's always been a fat one. Even when they were kids. She'd rather be inside watching TV than outside or doing anything athletic."

I felt Brady bristle beside me and squeezed his arm before he said anything he couldn't take back. He softened just slightly and looked down at me with pity I didn't want to see in his eyes. I raised my eyebrows and rolled my eyes so he knew I was used to it.

"I think Sam's beautiful. I'm all for being healthy, but not for losing weight just to look a certain way. Sam doesn't need that."

"I would think owning a gym that you would be all for making sure people want to lose a lot of weight."

"Mom, where's Dad?" I asked, attempting to interrupt the tension building between them I might think my mom was nuts, but Brady didn't need to be subjected to her. Which was why I didn't want to bring him in the first place.

Mom glared at me then rolled her eyes in Brady's direction. Finally she nodded toward the back of the house. "Everyone is outside."

I tugged Brady's arm down the hallway and away from my mom. "You weren't kidding about her," he whispered as I pushed through the door to the yard. "She's a bit intense."

I laughed. "Coming from you that's rich." He narrowed his eyes at me and cocked his head. "You're the most intense person I've ever met. I thought you hated me being at Dave's the first time I met you. Even the second time I thought you wanted to bite my head off."

He leaned down and nibbled on my neck. "More like bite the rest of you. I wanted to throw you over my shoulder and drag you back to my apartment and lock you up until I'd had my fill of you."

His words affected me more than he realized. My nipples hardened and between my legs ached and dampened. My arms surrounded his neck and I leaned into him, delighting in the erection I felt starting between us. A throat cleared behind us and I remembered where we were.

Damn. That could have gotten good.

I spun around and plastered a smile on my face. "Hi everyone. This is Brady Wright. Brady, my dad, Gary. My sister, Heather, and her husband, Mark. Brian, my brother, and his wife, Jane, and the assortment of kids."

Heather came over with her hand out, ever the professional. "It's nice to meet you Brady."

"Thanks, Heather. You as well. I hear you're a big time lawyer, working mom, and all around wonder woman. That's pretty awesome."

My sister blushed like a school girl. My hard ass, kick ass, lawyer of a sister was blushing.

"I'm sorry, you seem to have me at a disadvantage. My sister hasn't mentioned a word about you to anyone."

My mom picked that moment to come outside. She was carrying a glass of iced tea and looking every bit the elegant wife she pretended to be. She'd tied her hair back into a low bun. Her khaki capris were neatly pressed with a crease down the front and back, and her light blue blouse was a nod to the holiday, even if it was silk.

"Samantha has found someone who's as successful as herself. Apparently Brady owns a gym."

"I'll bet," Heather purred as she inched closer to him.

Seriously? My sister, who was married, was hitting on my boyfriend, with her husband ten feet away.

"Heather," I snapped, attempting to draw her out of her daydream about Brady. He chuckled softly beside me, but I did not find her funny.

"Sorry," she muttered, shaking her head. "So Brady, what gym do you own? I've been thinking about switching to a new one."

I rolled my eyes and sighed. She was ridiculous. It was like she'd never seen a hot guy before. Then again, Mark didn't look anything like Brady.

"I own Dave's Gym, in Winterville."

"Oh," Heather said, sounding disappointed. "We live in the city. That might be a bit too far to drive for the gym."

"Yeah, it's certainly too far to drive to visit your sister once in a while so I imagine it'd be hard to go daily just for the gym," I snarled at her, not hiding my general frustration with her.

Thankfully Mark came over and rescued us. Or maybe he was rescuing her. "Hi, I'm Mark," he said, extending his hand to Brady. Brady shook it with a nod that looked like a bit more than just a hello, but I didn't speak men.

"Nice to meet you. Heather here was just telling us you guys are thinking about a new gym."

Mark raised an eyebrow at my sister and she had the decency to flush. "I didn't know that, but okay. How did you get into owning a gym? It's got to be a pretty big responsibility."

Brady nodded and shrugged at the same time. "Owning any business is a big deal. Mine's a little different than Sam's since I have employees, but with any business the most important thing is treating people well. I hire people that I like, people that I know will treat everyone well. We don't tolerate judgement at Dave's Gym, that was the first thing I learned."

"Is that what your father taught you?" Heather asked. Mark wrapped an arm around her shoulders and pulled her against him. I tried to hide my snicker at his jealousy, and her infatuation. Then I looked at Brady.

His lips were drawn into a thin tight line. His entire body went rigid. He looked like he was going to punch something. "My father didn't teach me anything," he growled. "He's dead."

Fourteen

How did I not know that?

All our conversations and all the time we'd spent together he'd never mentioned anything about his father. Come to think of it, or his mother.

"What about your mom?" I asked, feeling like shit for not knowing anything about him.

"My mom died when I was two. I don't remember her. Apparently I'm her spitting image. That's what my dad always told me."

Heather and Mark drifted away, sensing our need to talk. I was grateful for their consideration and made a mental note to thank them later.

"When did your dad die?" I asked, wondering who raised him.

"When I was 18. I moved to Winterville after that and Dave took me in."

"Dave? Like Dave's Gym?"

Brady nodded. "I had no money, no skills. Dave and I sort of ran into each other and he offered me a studio apartment in his basement. He taught me everything I know about the gym. When he was ready to retire he gave me the gym."

"Wow, Brady I had no idea. I don't know how I didn't know all this, but I'm sorry I never asked."

He shook his head. "Don't worry. I don't talk about my past very much, especially my parents. Besides, your world is a whole lot more interesting."

I stepped into his arms and let him make me feel better about being so horrible. As he rubbed my back I realized how much I'd come to count on him in such a short amount of time. I'd barely thought about Addi or being so alone since I met Brady. Yet in the same time, I'd learned nearly nothing about him. He knew almost everything there was about me, and I didn't even know his parents were dead.

I was a self-centered person. I'd never thought that about myself before but it was hard to ignore as we stood in the middle of my parents backyard and Brady comforted me after I found out he'd lost both his parents.

What was wrong with me?

"I'm sorry about your parents. Were you close to your dad?"

"No," Brady stated with no emotion.

"Did he ever remarry?"

"No," Brady stated again, but I could feel tension seeping into him. "This is about your family today. Let's not ruin it with my past. It's behind me. We don't need to talk about it."

I nodded in agreement but couldn't help wondering why he was reluctant to talk about his past. Maybe it was just too painful. I thought about the scars on his body and worried I was right.

We joined my family again and Mom launched right back into her interrogation. "So, Brady, where did you go to college?"

College was, in my mother's mind, a determinant of whether or not you were a decent human being. Just because a lot of the criminals my dad locked up were high school drop-outs my mom thought if you didn't have a good college degree you were destined to end up behind bars.

"I didn't go to college."

Mom pursed her lips so tight they disappeared. At a table surrounded by people who were highly educated, a high school diploma was not good enough for my mom. I couldn't have cared less, but Brady may as well have told my mom he was a serial killer.

"What did you do instead?" she asked, like it mattered. She'd hate him no matter what.

"I started working at Dave's Gym. Dave gave me a place to live and taught me how to run a business, how to treat people, how to survive. Year after year he gave me more responsibility and eventually he turned the business over to me. In the five years since I've taken over we've tripled our membership and moved to the current location, which is more than twice the size of our old site."

Mom looked like she was going to pop. It was hilarious. I coughed to hide the laugh that started to bubble out of me. It never made sense to me why she hated self-employment so much.

"Well, isn't that nice," she ground out.

I rolled my eyes at Brady, and he squeezed my thigh under the table. He'd understand how my mom was eventually, at least as much as I did, as long as he wasn't offended by her.

"So, Brady are you into any sports?" my dad asked in an attempt to change the subject.

I shot him a grateful smile, and he winked at me. Brady answered, "Yes, sir. I grew up playing football and still enjoy watching the game. I've taken up boxing as well, although it's for fun and sport, not a career for me. Being around here I imagine everyone loves hockey, too."

My dad nodded his approval. At least someone liked Brady besides me. Oh, and my sexed up sister.

"You'll have to come with us to some football games this fall. The force supports the local schools and we go to a game each weekend to cheer them on. Sammy here gets really into the games."

Brady grinned at me with his eyes twinkling. "Oh, really. I didn't know you were such a sports fan."

I shrugged, feigning indifference, but I could tell I wasn't fooling him. "There are a few things you don't know about me."

"Mmm hmm," he said before turning back to my dad. "That sounds great, sir. I'd love to join you. What do you do on the force?"

My dad leaned back and rubbed his mostly flat stomach with a grin that was supposed to be bashful, but instead looked wolfish. Dad loved to tell people about his job and how hard he worked to stay in shape. He was proud to still be out on the streets and chasing down the bad guys instead of buried in paperwork behind a desk.

Heather leaned over to me as Dad started talking. "He's gorgeous. Where did you find him?"

I smiled, "He already told you, we met at his gym."

Heather shook her head. "I don't know what shocks me more... that you're going to the gym or that you brought home such a hottie. Not saying I ever thought you couldn't get a guy like him, but damn. He puts Channing Tatum to shame."

I laughed. Channing Tatum was a god in Heather's world. Saying Brady was hotter was the highest compliment she could give a man. Of course I agreed with her.

"When he first started talking to me I thought he hated me. He can be really intense. Then these jerks at the gym were nasty to me and Brady kicked them out then comforted me. He told me he'd wanted to kiss me since he first saw me. He's an amazing kisser."

Heather raised her eyebrows and glanced over at Brady. "I can totally see that. I bet he's spectacular in bed, too," she whispered conspiratorially.

"Actually, I wouldn't know," I confessed, feeling strange having the conversation with Heather. We'd never been overly close, although we loved each other. I couldn't recall any time we'd ever talked about sex. Although technically we weren't then either.

"How do you not know? I'd have jumped him on day one. What are you waiting for?"

I peeked at Brady, but he was still wrapped up in a conversation with my dad. "We're taking things slow. My last relationship ended pretty bad and Brady's cautious, too. We decided not to rush into anything and get to know each other first."

"Wow," Heather said with arched brows. "If Mom knew that she'd probably like him a bit more. Sorry about her. You know how she is."

I shrugged. "I'm used to it. She asks me at least once a week when I'm going to get a 'real' job. She thinks I just sit around all day and watch TV."

Heather laughed. "You would think someone who spent their life as a housewife would know how easy it is to be insanely busy without a job and would realize you have all that plus work. I couldn't survive without my housekeeper."

"Yeah," I argued, "but you have kids. If there's one thing Mom is even more disappointed in me for it's that I'm 29 and haven't brought any grandkids into the world yet. You'd think five would be enough."

Heather nodded. "I know I'm done. I think Brian is, too. It's up to you and Brady now."

"Whoa, we've been seeing each other for a few weeks. We're not walking down the aisle yet. We're not even sleeping together."

Heather shrugged. "Some people wait. Maybe he'll want to wait until he's married. Is he a virgin?"

I narrowed my eyes and thought back over our conversations. He'd never mentioned it either way. "I don't think so, but I haven't exactly asked for his list of past lovers. We're just not there yet. He hasn't said anything about waiting for marriage. We're just going slow."

Heather looked over at Brady again, staring just a little too long. Thankfully the men had turned their conversation to sports so Mark was oblivious to Heather's longing looks at my boyfriend. Thankfully I found it more entertaining than irritating.

"Would that be a deal-breaker for you? If he wanted to wait?"

My head tipped to the side while I thought about it. I glanced over at Brady and he winked at me then leaned close. His lips brushed my throat then ran up to my ear. He nibbled my ear lobe then whispered, "I'm not a virgin and I'm not waiting for marriage. Just waiting until I can control myself around all your sexiness. Hopefully that's not a deal-breaker."

His tongue darted into my ear, making my eyes slip closed. He nipped my ear again then sat back up as though nothing had happened and rejoined the conversation with my dad.

"What was that?" Heather whispered in my other ear.

Brady's hand squeezed my thigh and I grinned. "He heard everything we said," I told Heather. "And he said he's not a virgin and not waiting for marriage."

Heather's eyes danced over to Brady's and her cheeks pinked. "Oh, my God, I feel so high school right now. How embarrassing," she whispered.

Brady leaned over again, his lips tickling my ear as he spoke. "Tell Heather not to be embarrassed. I'm pretty fucking thrilled to put Channing Tatum to shame and it's nice to know she's on our side, not your mom's."

I grinned as he spoke and as soon as he moved away Heather yanked my arm over to her side. "What did he say?" she hissed.

I repeated his words and watched my cool, calm, and collected sister turn bright red. After a few seconds we collapsed into a heap of giggles like when we were kids. Mom's eyes narrowed on us and she demanded to know what was going on. "Nothing!" we chorused then fell against each other giggling again.

Once we ate dinner and the kids had been ordered off to the bathroom, we all headed down the street to watch the fireworks. As always the park was crowded but we were able to find a seat just outside the barriers where we could watch. We laid out four blankets to lie on. Mom pulled out glow-in-the-dark necklaces and bracelets for the kids and Mark bought them all fiber optic wands.

"This is the first time I've done this," Brady confessed as we sat down.

"Oh, the park is great. I know there are fireworks displays all over, but they do a great job here. Where did you go last year?"

"Nowhere. This is the first time I've ever gone to see fireworks on The Fourth. I've always sat home and enjoyed the day off."

I gawked at him. How was that possible? "Not even as a teenager or anything? You never took a girlfriend to make out under the fireworks. It's very romantic."

He pulled me between his legs so my back was to his chest. He lips brushed my ear. "It would be a bit more romantic without your mother giving us dirty looks, but no, I never took a girlfriend. You're the first."

He called me his girlfriend! Holy shit. I mean, I sort of thought of him as my boyfriend, but saying it was different than thinking it.

Although he didn't actually say it, just implied it. Does that count?

"What's wrong? You went still."

I shook my head. "Nothing. It's nothing."

Brady leaned around me so he could catch my eyes. He stared into them for a few seconds before he declared, "I don't believe you. What did I say, Sam?"

"It's stupid."

"Nothing is stupid. If it's bothering you, I want to know."

I sighed heavily. "You said you'd never even gone with a girlfriend and that I was the first. It sounded like you were saying I was your girlfriend, but you didn't actually say it. I got excited for a second then felt stupid because it was really nothing."

Brady stared at me, not speaking. I felt worse and worse with each passing second.

"See, I told you it was stupid. Just forget I said anything."

I turned my face away from his so I wouldn't have to watch him watching me. Brady cupped my chin and tried to turn me back to him, but I wouldn't. "Look at me, Sam, please." I couldn't deny him, I looked. "I don't really know what to say because I didn't realize you needed to hear the word. I've thought of you as my girlfriend since the first time I kissed you. I thought of you as mine before then, but I couldn't claim you. You are my girlfriend, you are my partner, you are my everything, and one day I hope you'll be my lover. I'm sorry I didn't clarify that before."

Damn he was good. "Thank you," I whispered.

"So," he began with a devious grin, "does that mean I'm your boyfriend, or do I have to fight for the title? Defend your honor? Tell off your mom?"

I laughed and shook my head. "No, you don't have to do any of that. You're my boyfriend, as far as I'm concerned, you have been since the moment your lips touch mine. I don't date more than one person at a time. You're it."

"Phew," Brady said dramatically. "That was a close one."

I laughed and tilted my chin up for a kiss. Brady obliged with one hand resting across my neck, his thumb caressing just under my jaw. He shifted to get a better angle just as the first of the fireworks lit up the sky.

"Just kissing you makes me see fireworks," Brady whispered against my ear as he pulled back.

I grinned at his line and snuggled against him. He dropped back to his elbows so he could look up without hurting his neck then rested a hand on my hip. My head rested against his chest, using him as a pillow, and I watched as the sky lit up with one color after another.

My nieces and nephew cuddled against their parents and grandparents during the show and squealed during the duds, oohed and aahed for the other ones. Brady's lips rested against my head more than once and everything about the night was overwhelming for me. I didn't tell Brady, but I'd never brought a guy to the fireworks. All the times I'd watched the show, I couldn't ever invite a guy that I knew wouldn't be around for the next year.

It was too special to me.

With Brady though, it was different. It'd only been two weeks since we first kissed, but I knew we were different. And I wondered as the finale electrified the night sky if I'd be lucky enough to share the experience with Brady again in a year.

Fifteen

When I talked to Addi the next day she asked about my Fourth. She knew it was one of the few days I enjoyed spending with my family. She'd gone with me a few times, but she and Joey had a fireworks show that night at Winter Ridge so I knew she wouldn't be able to come anymore.

It was okay though, because for one year I had Brady.

When I admitted to Addi that Brady went with me, she insisted I bring him to girls' night. I figured if he could survive my family, my friends would be a piece of cake.

But I was still anxious. I went to Dave's Gym early Monday so I could talk to him about it, giving him the option to say no if he didn't want to go.

He understood right away and said, "This is even more important to you than meeting your parents, isn't it?"

I nodded and bit my lip, feeling like I would pop if he didn't make a decision soon.

"You know I'll go, babe. Don't worry. It'll be fine," Brady insisted, then pulled me in for a kiss. His hard body brushed against mine as he kissed me, lazy, gentle, soft kisses as though he had all the time in the world. I wanted nothing more than to stay there in his arms, but I couldn't. I had a meeting.

"I'm sorry," I said, pushing back from him. "I've got a bride coming in thirty minutes. I need to run."

Brady nodded. "Of course. Show her how wonderful you can make her day."

I wrinkled my nose. "I'm not sure I really want to. I sort of hate shooting weddings."

"Then don't," he said simply, as if there was no other answer. "Life's too short to do something you don't enjoy, Sam."

"I wish it were that simple. Weddings bring in a lot of money for me. I'd have to move if I gave them up."

"Then I guess you have to decide what's more important, your house or your happiness."

When he put it like that, I knew what I had to do. I thanked Brady with another scorching kiss then ran off to the locker room to shower and change.

By the time I pulled into a parking space at my studio I knew what Brady said was true. I needed to just move forward and do what was right for me. I'd been holding on to the house in case Addi needed to come back, but they were getting married. She wasn't coming back. And I needed to move forward with my life, too.

The bride, Ann, walked in shortly after I did. On her arm was a man who barely looked old enough to vote, let alone get married. Not that Ann was any older.

"It's so nice to see you again," I told Ann, shaking her hand and gesturing to the seats in front of my desk. "You must be Lee."

The man nodded and shook my hand. "Nice to meet you. I've heard a lot about you from Ann."

I nodded my appreciation and took my seat on the other side of the desk. "So we need to talk about exactly what you guys want for the wedding day. What shots, what sort of time you need me there, everything."

We launched into a discussion I'd had countless times before, but my heart wasn't in it. When I first started shooting weddings I thought it would be a fun day. Sure, I expected stress, but I didn't expect the anxiety and anger from the brides. Ann was sweet and cute and easy to talk to, but I knew she was going to be a difficult bride when she started talking about all the shots she wanted me to take.

I took notes, marking down everything she wanted me to capture, noting special shots that weren't automatic ones, and thought of my afternoon appointment. I was meeting with a family, and I knew it was going to be a much easier session.

"My friends are all going to call you, Samantha. Two of them just got engaged and three others are pushing their boyfriends to propose. I've been showing them your website for months."

I forced a smile then said the words I desperately wanted to be true. "Actually, yours will be my last wedding. I'm not going to do any more after I finish yours."

A devious grin slid over Ann's face. "I'll be your last one. Ooh, they'll be so jealous. Why would you give it up? Weddings are so much fun!"

I tried not to cringe at the screech in her voice. "I'm focusing on other aspects of my career. Plus, it'll be nice to have a few weekends off here and there. With weddings I work basically all weekend, every weekend. It gets exhausting after a while."

"Oh, I can understand that," Ann said sympathetically. "Lee has to work one weekend every six months and it's just torture. We totally get what you're saying."

Really? Yep, they were totally the same thing. I didn't even answer.

"Okay, so we're good for the 28th?" I nodded. "Excellent. Well, thanks for making us your last wedding, Samantha. I know it's going to be a great one to end your career."

Ann and Lee led the way to the door. They said goodbye and stepped out into the sunshine, leaving me to figure out the rest of my life since I'd put it in motion.

~*~

A few hours later I had appointments lined up over the weekend to tour some apartments and a couple condos in my new budget. I was excited about moving forward with my life. I knew I wouldn't have a big place, but it would be mine. Not mine and used-to-be Addi's. I would make it work, and the family that walked through my door as I was closing my laptop reminded me of exactly what I had to look forward to.

The Coughlin family were all smiles when they walked in. Mom, Amy, was beautiful with long hair that nearly glowed it was so blonde. The little girl holding on to her leg had the same hair, but Dad's rich brown eyes. Dad, Eric, was carrying a tiny baby and holding hands with a little boy whose dark hair had the same red tint when the light hit.

They were an adorable family.

"Are we early?" Amy asked as she shook my hand.

"Of course not. You're right on time. Let's head back to the studio so you guys can get comfortable."

The baby was only two weeks old, which was why they were in for pictures. Amy wasn't comfortable having him outside in the grass and knew she wanted shots of him lying down. My studio was the perfect option for the family, another reason I loved what I did and paid the price for having my own studio.

If my plans actually went through and I was able to eliminate weddings my studio would become even more important. I'd have that many more sessions in the studio than I currently did. Maybe even one day a week with one hour mini sessions, back-to-back with families.

Ooh, I liked that idea.

The little boy squealed, drawing me back to the family before me. I smiled as Eric lifted his son high in the air and zoomed him around the room like he was an airplane. I rushed to grab my camera off the table and started snapping pictures of them being silly while Amy settled the baby on the blanket I'd laid out on the floor.

"What do you want to start with? The kids or everyone?"

"Um," Amy hesitated, looking at her family. "How about the kids first?"

I nodded. "Sounds good. I'd like to take a few shots of each kid alone, then get them together. Maybe you guys can each play with one kid while I take pictures of the third?"

Amy smiled and headed over to entertain the oldest, Gracie, and I focused on the baby, Tommy. He was curled up on the blanket sleeping, but was starting to stir. I took a few quick shots while he slept, changing position to capture all sides of the snoozing baby. When he stretched, I clicked quickly, catching him in a yawn looking absolutely adorable.

Tommy started to whine, drawing Amy's attention. She picked him up and cuddled him against her chest, looking down at him with pure love. I took a few candid shots of them before distracting Gracie.

"Do you want to see my special box of toys? It's only for girls who are really good for their parents. Are you one of those girls?"

Gracie nodded enthusiastically and followed me to the back of the studio. I'd learned over the years what sorts of toys would entertain the kids the most. I made sure I kept some of the latest toys on hand, but also some older favorites, including lots of stuffed animals.

"Mommy, mommy! Look what she has!" Gracie pulled a small unicorn from the box and grinned like she'd won a prize. I snapped some shots of her beautiful smile and bright eyes. When she ran over to Amy I caught the look of excitement mirrored on her face too, seeing pure joy at what her daughter had unearthed. While Gracie talked, Tommy watched his big sister with big curious eyes. He smiled widely when she spoke, recognizing her voice and loving her even at such a young age.

Eric and Bobby, their older son, joined in the discussion after a few minutes. Eric exclaimed the same happiness over what his daughter had found, thrilled for her.

Bobby watched me carefully, looking at me then back at his sister for a few minutes. I listened to them talking, Gracie telling Bobby she was able to see my special toy box because she was a good girl. He finally worked up the courage to approach me and said, "Miss Samantha? Mommy says I'm a good boy. Can I see your toys, too?"

My heart swelled over the sweet, polite little boy in front of me. I reached for his hand and said, "Of course you can. You seem like you're a wonderful boy. Maybe there's something in there that you'll like."

Bobby walked with me and kneeled on the ground next to the open toy box. He dug through little by little, methodically searching for that one special thing that would make him as happy as Gracie was. I watched him through the lens of my camera, preserving the determined look on his face as he rooted through the loot.

When his little fingers closed around something, I knew he'd found what he was looking for. A grin slowly formed on his lips until he squealed with delight when he lifted the truck free. It was from a show that was apparently popular, not that I knew anything about it, but my nephew had gone nuts over it last Christmas.

"Daddy!" Bobby yelled. "Daddy, look!" He held his truck up above his head to show it off. Eric grinned and rushed over, all excited about Bobby's new truck.

"Wow, dude! That's a cool truck. He's your favorite isn't he?"

"Yeah, Daddy, he is. This is so awesome. Can we come here every day so I can play with it?"

Eric laughed. "Well, I don't know about that, but it looks like Miss Samantha is going to let you play with it for a little while. Do you want to show Gracie and Tommy?"

"Yeah!" Bobby took off across the studio to show his new prize to his sister and brother. Bobby and Gracie traded toys, each inspecting the other's, then traded back. I shot the whole time, enjoying their excited faces.

"You have a beautiful family," I told Eric, who was standing next to me, watching them.

"I'm a lucky man," he said honestly. "It's hard to believe we were Bobby's age when we got together."

"Really?" I asked, incredulous.

"Yeah," he laughed. "We went to preschool together. We were best friends when we were four and ended up in the same elementary school. We've had our ups and downs, but no matter what we always leaned on each other as best friends. I've never imagined my life with anyone but her."

"That's amazing," I confessed, wishing I had someone I could consider my best friend, or someone I might share my life with. For so long it was Addi that I was lost without her at times. It was clear that Addi and I had drifted apart when I brought Brady home to meet my family before he met my friends.

"I've never been so scared as I was the day I asked her to marry me. I was sure she was going to say she hadn't explored enough, or dated enough, or traveled enough."

"Why did you ask her if you weren't sure what she was going to say?"

Eric shrugged. Amy caught his eye and looked at him with so much love I thought my heart was going to explode. I snapped a shot of the look that passed between them, still focused on the conversation with Eric.

"We weren't dating when I asked her. She'd just gotten out of a bad relationship. Well, maybe bad is making it sound worse than it was. It wasn't a great relationship because it wasn't right, but he wasn't horrible to her, they just didn't fit together. She came over to cry on my shoulder and we were watching slapstick comedy and sharing a carton of ice cream. I always kept her favorite, cookie dough, in my freezer for when she came over. She said she didn't think she'd ever find the right guy and I told her she was crazy. She brushed it off, but I pressed, insisting that she would be happy one day. I couldn't take her arguing so I finally told her I'd been in love with her forever and was just waiting for her to be done dating other guys so I could ask her to marry me. She was shocked, and she didn't believe me. So I got down on one knee and pulled out her grandmother's ring, the one her mom had given me when I asked her parents if they would be okay if we got married one day."

Tears welled in my eyes. I couldn't imagine anyone being that sweet. Amy was a lucky woman.

"I said yes once I knew he was serious," Amy said, stepping up to her husband with their three kids. "Until he pulled out that ring I honestly believed he was just trying to make me feel better. The truth was I was dating other guys to try to forget about him. Who meets their soulmate at age four, right?"

"The lucky ones," I assured her.

Amy tipped her chin up to Eric, who happily accepted her kiss. Tommy was nestled between them, Gracie and Bobby looking up at their parents. It was a perfect little moment that I was lucky enough to witness and save for them.

Eric and Amy told me about their wedding and finding out when she was pregnant with each of the kids as I continued taking pictures. As the afternoon wore on I knew I'd made the right choice to eliminate weddings from my business. Working with that family swelled my heart until it was too big for my chest. And that sort of work would make me so much happier than living in a house that no longer felt like home.

Sixteen

The next night Brady was meeting my friends for girls' night. He knew what my friends meant to me, and bringing him to meet them was a significant step for me.

"My friends are the family I chose," I told him when he asked why I was nervous. "I love my family, but they make me crazy a lot of the time, especially my mom, as you saw. With my friends though, they accept me for who I am. Oh, did I tell you Addi and Joey are members? That's how I learned about Dave's Gym."

He nodded and rubbed my thigh. "You told me, honey. You don't have to be nervous. I will do my best not to embarrass you."

I snorted. "It's not you I'm worried about. Chances are my friends are going to do their best to embarrass me and you'll never want to speak to me again after tonight. I'll make one of them take me home if you decide you're done."

I meant it as a joke, well mostly, but Brady looked genuinely concerned. He pulled into a parking space and unbuckled his seat belt. Instead of getting out he turned to face me. "Sam, I know you. Nothing your friends could say would change how I feel about you. But if they're really your best friends why would you worry about them? They don't sound that wonderful if you're worried they're going to scare me off."

I waved away his concerns. "I was just kidding. They like to joke and will likely tell you stories about me, but it's all just for fun. If you're scared off by them then I'll know you aren't the right guy for me."

"Did your ex meet them?"

I shook my head vehemently. "Not a chance. He wasn't ever anything more than for fun. I've never introduced my friends to anyone." Brady cringed as I shrugged an apology. "Sorry, I know you don't like hearing about him."

"You don't like talking about him any more than I like hearing about him."

He was right. I wasn't ready to tell Brady why Cade and I split or why I'd joined Dave's Gym. If I had my way he'd never know the truth about either of those things. Thankfully none of my friends knew the whole truth either so that was one secret that wouldn't come out.

"Let's go," Brady said gruffly before he climbed out of the Jeep. I followed him and paused behind the vehicle to calm myself. I could see everyone inside, boyfriends and husbands included, watching us. I finally knew what a fish in a fish tank felt like, being watched from a distance but unable to interact.

Except we were about to interact. Brady was about to meet my friends. Gulp.

He slipped his hand into mine and half dragged me across the parking lot. Aidan caught the corner of my eye and I thought about how I flirted with him the first time we'd met. I thought he was just a friend of Claire's until he practically fucked her against the counter while feeding her a cupcake. It was one of the most erotic things I'd ever witnessed, and a little disturbing.

Claire, above any of the others, had a reason to torture me with Brady. Hopefully she was her usual kind self though. She'd promised me she didn't hold a grudge for my behavior with Aidan and even admitted that she didn't blame me for reacting to him the way I did.

I just hoped no one reacted to Brady that way.

The familiar scent of sugar and deliciousness filled me once we were inside. Brady's hand rested lightly on my lower back and guided me toward the counter. Charlie was waiting for us instead of Kendall and flashed us a grin. She slid over my plate with my usual order of two raspberry lemonade cupcakes and a bottle of water before turning to Brady.

"It's nice to meet you, Brady. I'm Charlie. What can I get you?"

Brady flashed his own grin and I watched Charlie's smile slip. She was drawn to him too. Big shock.

"What do you recommend?"

"Well, that depends on what you like," Charlie flirted with my boyfriend. Damn, it was going to be a long night.

Brady shrugged as he glanced toward the case. His eyes landed on me again, heated and full of desire that made my pulse kick up. "I know one thing I like," he whispered in my ear. He turned back to Charlie and said, "I'm not too big on chocolate, but I like something other than plain old vanilla."

"Well, I've got a few fruit based cupcakes or some that are a little more decadent. My favorite is the salted caramel, but I've also got cherry coke, margarita, coffee or mocha, cinnamon roll, or s'mores. Sam's favorite is raspberry lemonade."

Brady gave her an appreciative glance then asked for one cherry coke and one salted caramel cupcake. Charlie waved off his money when he tried to pay and I pulled Brady away telling him we all slip money into the tip jar before we go anyway.

Two seats were available for us between Addi and Aidan. Brady held the chair next to Addi out for me then sat next to Aidan. "Guys, this is Brady. Brady, my friends." I went around the table introducing everyone knowing he'd never remember all their names.

Brady leaned past me and reached for Addi's hand once I'd completed introductions and said, "Addi, it seems I have you to thank. Sam said you're the one who told her about Dave's Gym. I hope you and Joey," Brady indicated Joey with a nod, "enjoy it there."

Addi nodded, looking a bit gobsmacked. "Yeah, we do. It's a great place. Not that I'm a poster child for any gym," Addi joked shyly. She'd always been fit and healthy but carried more weight than she'd like. Even going to the gym regularly and being active all the time, Addi was big like the rest of us.

"You're the perfect spokesperson for my gym. I want real people there, not super-sized muscle men and women who look like they've skipped too many meals. People should strive to be healthy, not to be skinny."

Twelve pairs of eyes gawked at the super-sized muscled man sitting beside me. Brady was exactly the man he described not wanting there, but it was obvious none of us were the women who skipped meals.

"So you'd turn away people who were too built?" Xander asked, clearly confused.

Brady shook his head. "No, of course not. I won't turn anyone away, but I don't want Dave's Gym to be a place where anyone feels uncomfortable. If I witness, or one of my staff witnesses, someone being cruel to another member, they're gone, no questions asked." Brady rested his arm on the back of my chair and his hand cupped my neck, caressing gently.

"Phew," Xander breathed, "as long as I know you wouldn't kick me out."

We all laughed. Xander was nearly as built as Brady, except he'd earned his muscles from his work as an electrical engineer and rebuilding old homes in his spare time. Brady's muscles were gym manufactured, but I had no doubt he knew how to use them.

"As long as you treat everyone with respect, I'd be happy to have you there. It doesn't really look like you need a gym though. What do you do?"

"I work in construction. Remodeling older homes. I'm an electrical engineer."

Brady nodded appreciatively. "Once upon a time I thought about being an engineer. Need a college degree for that sort of thing though. Owning a gym works for me."

"You're obviously very successful," Claire said. "From what Sam and Addi have said your gym does well."

"It's a good business. Dave had a great start when he turned it over to me. I just kept going with his vision."

"Don't sell yourself short," I argued. "You said it's three times the size it was when you took over. That sounds like you know what you're doing and are good at it."

Brady laughed. "I surround myself with the best people. My employees are phenomenal. I wouldn't have a place to work if it weren't for them."

"You're a smart man," Charlie said. "Any owner who can recognize the value of good employees is a great employer."

"Spoken like a true business woman," Brady complimented her. Charlie blushed.

"You're lucky too though," Riley said. "Owning a business can be expensive. It's awesome that Dave gave you the gym. He left it in good hands, clearly, but it helps a lot when you aren't starting from scratch."

"I agree completely," Charlie added. "Starting this place went a whole lot better than I expected, but I was prepared with a year's worth of income saved up just in case I couldn't make it work."

Riley groaned. "I think my bosses are going to retire within the next few years. I'm dying to take over the business, but I know when they retire they're going to sell it. I've been saving like crazy, but I just don't have enough right now."

"Have you looked into loans? I got one when I moved Dave's Gym to the new location. I couldn't maintain things any longer at our old place, but I didn't have the free cash to move. I got a good loan. I could give you a name if you want."

Riley nodded enthusiastically. "That would be great."

"Are you really that nice?" Mandy asked suddenly. She'd been silent so far, which was unlike her, but her question surprised me.

"Mandy!"

"It's okay, babe," Brady assured me. "What do you mean?" he asked Mandy.

"You come in here, out of nowhere, and you're dating Sam, talking about being a good business owner, and offering to help Riley get a loan. It all just seems a little too much."

"Mandy," Claire hissed.

Brady nodded his appreciation to Claire then focused on Mandy. "Well, I've been in Winterville for 15 years. For a long time I kept to myself, still pretty much do. I'm dating Sam, and I'm not sure what the issue is there. I am a good business owner and you can ask any of my employees how they feel about working for me. As for Riley's loan, I didn't say I'd help her, just that I could give her a name. I'm not in a position to be the bank for someone else."

"Why did you bring him?" Mandy asked me.

"Why are you being like this? What did he ever do to you?"

"It's been two weeks since you and Cade broke up. The guy who dumped you because you were too fat. And now you're in here with a man who looks as close to perfect as a guy can look. You've never brought a guy here. None of us ever brought a guy here if we weren't serious. I find it hard to believe you could be serious in less than two weeks."

Brady tensed beside me. His fingers tightened on my neck and I knew he picked out the words from Mandy's statement that I didn't want him to notice. "What is she talking about?" he growled at me.

"Nothing."

"He's why you came in, isn't he? He said you were too… Is he why you use that word?" Brady turned to face me, his hand slipping from my neck and running down my arm until he held my hand in his.

Everyone at the table sat in silence as Brady and I spoke.

"Yes and no."

"Which is it?"

"Yes, he's why I came in. I wanted to make him eat his words. I said that word long before he was around, but it's the truth. I'm f-"

"Don't. You. Dare. That word will not come out of that beautiful mouth again. Now that I understand where that comes from I will make sure I show you, even more, exactly what I think of you. As for the other part... Why do they think you were still dating that asshole two weeks ago?"

Everyone gasped.

"That's when they found out we broke up. I didn't go into details about when or how or anything else, just let them believe what they wanted to believe."

"When did you and Cade break up?" Mandy asked.

"Four weeks ago," Addi whispered. "When you first asked me about the gym. I knew there was something off with you that night, but I passed it off as my imagination. Dammit, Sam, why didn't you tell me?"

I closed my eyes and willed the pain away. I didn't want to think about that day. Ever. "It's no big deal. It's over. He's not in my life anymore."

"And he's not going to be ever again. That fucker doesn't deserve you," Brady said adamantly, pulling me toward him. My head fell to his shoulder and he pressed a kiss into my hair.

"Okay, he can stay," Mandy admitted, smiling. "I like him. Are you bringing him to the wedding?"

Shit. I'd forgotten Mandy and Xander's wedding was that Saturday. "Um, I hadn't thought about it."

"Well, I'm inviting him. Brady, we'd be honored if you would come to our wedding. Riley and Carrie, you guys too. I don't know if I already told you that."

Riley and Carrie exchanged a glance then nodded happily. Brady nodded too, tugging me tighter to him. My soft body melted into his hard one and I knew Brady was a much better choice for me than Cade had ever been. Even more so since he stood his ground against Mandy and won her over for it. Maybe I'd finally made a good choice.

Seventeen

"Do you want to come inside and see my place?" I asked quietly when Brady pulled up in front of my house. I'd met him on the front porch earlier so he never went inside, but I didn't care about him seeing my house. I just wasn't ready for the night to end.

"Sure."

Brady followed me out of the car. My anxiety over the evening trailed behind me, leaving me feeling better with each step. I wasn't sure why I expected so little of my friends, but they shocked me. Not only did they make Brady feel welcome, but they didn't embarrass me. Yeah, Mandy pushed him and questioned him, but that was mostly because she was being protective and didn't know the whole story. Overall it was a great night, especially since Brady didn't notice the looks of admiration from my friends behind his back.

I let him into the house and flipped on the lights, wondering what he thought of my home. I'd put a lot of work into making it mine since Addi moved out a few months before. The house was small, but I loved my cozy home. Giving it up was going to be a little bit of a challenge, but I knew it was just a house and I could make any place my home.

My couch was the most comfortable one I'd ever sat on and my TV was a little on the small side, but it was enough for me. They would help make my new place feel like home, too.

And somehow I knew Brady wouldn't judge me based on my house, this one or the next.

"Nice place. How long have you been here?"

I tossed my purse onto the table near the door. "Forever. Addi and I had an apartment when we finished college but wanted a yard so we moved here about four years ago."

"She lives with Joey now." It was more a statement than a question.

"Yeah. He had his own house up at Winter Ridge so it made sense for them to go there. I miss her, but I know she's happy."

Brady nodded like he understood. I wondered if he had a best friend or group of friends that he hung out with. I wasn't sure how I could ask without sounding like I needed to know everything about him. Instead I offered him a drink.

"Just some water is good."

He followed me to the kitchen as I teased, "Totally committed to the healthy lifestyle, I see. Do you ever give yourself a day off?"

"I ate two cupcakes tonight."

I laughed. "True. I guess next time we'll have to have a drink instead of a couple of cupcakes then. I wouldn't want you getting soft." I patted his flat stomach and found myself unable to remove my hand. His thin t-shirt wasn't enough to mask the rippling muscles I found. My hand moved on its own, tracing the lines and skimming over the skin that danced for me.

"I don't drink. At all," Brady ground out, sounding pained and something else. I looked up to question why he didn't drink. When my eyes met his all thoughts drifted away and were replaced by need. Raw, bare, powerful need. The same need I saw in his eyes.

"Brady," I whispered tentatively.

"Sam..." drifted past his lips as he moved closer. Then his lips were on mine.

The gentleness of his kiss shocked me. Our other kisses were passionate, aggressive. But this one, oh, this one was better. This one left me feeling loved, worshipped.

His hand cupped my cheek and kept me frozen under the delicious torture of his kiss. When his tongue brushed against my lips a sigh escaped me as I opened for him. My hands, still on his stomach, rubbed soft circles against his shirt. I lifted the fabric and continued my exploration on his bare skin, loving the feel of his heat and strength.

Brady yanked his shirt off, leaving his body exposed to me. I saw the scars on his chest, but they were only a part of the man in front of me.

Unable to stop myself I ran my tongue over one of his scars. He hissed in a breath, but I kept going, kissing and loving the scars that covered his chest and stomach. My hands rested on his hips, as much to steady myself as to feel him. I worked over his body, kissing, touching, enjoying him. He moaned and gripped my arms, pulling me up to kiss him.

His tongue pushed into my mouth in the needy, controlling way I'd come to equate to Brady. He held me close to him, his warmth heating me up from the outside while his kisses worked on the inside.

Brady's fingers toyed with the edge of my shirt, dancing along the bare skin hidden beneath. I arched into him, pressing my body into his warm hands. He ran his palm along my stomach to my back and held me to him. I moaned at the feel of his erection pressed to my stomach, aching between my thighs to feel him there.

Our interactions had been hot but limited. I wanted him. Kissing Brady turned me on in ways I'd only heard of existing. Having him touch me was something out of a fantasy. But I knew he was cautious, overly so in my opinion. Still, I didn't want to scare him off.

"Can I touch you, Brady?" I asked, pulling back from our kiss to taste his skin, trailing my tongue down his throat to circle his small, tight nipple. He hissed in a breath and tugged me tighter against him at the contact.

"Jesus, I'm not sure I can do this, Sam. I want to rip your clothes to shreds and pound into you."

"So do it," I begged, my panties soaking through with the thought of Brady taking me how he wanted. Hell, as long as we had sex I didn't really care how it happened.

"I can't, Sam. Not until I know I won't hurt you."

"I'm not made of glass, Brady," I argued, nipping at his skin.

Brady growled and pressed me against the counter. He tore at my shirt until it was gone, tossed behind him. His eyes dilated when he saw the red lace bra I wore. He closed his lips over the peaks of my nipples straining for his attention. Desperate to feel his lips on me, I fought with shaky hands to unclasp my bra. When I finally managed to remove it Brady brought my nipples together and circled both with the tip of his tongue.

My head fell back, cracking against the cabinets, but I didn't care. Brady lifted me onto the counter and positioned himself between my legs, grinding his erection against my core. "I need you Brady," I moaned, aching for him to touch me.

His fingers dipped beneath my shorts like a heat seeking missile headed straight for the target. When he brushed against me we both moaned. "I don't know if I can do this, Sam," Brady ground out, his voice laced with fear and desire. "I don't think I can stop."

"I want you, Brady. I don't want you to stop."

"We have to go slow," he said, dragging his thick fingers through my folds to my core. He inserted one slowly, then slid it back out. My eyes rolled back in my head and my core clenched.

"I'm not gonna last, Brady. Oh, fuck."

"Neither am I, baby. I can't take much more of watching you. Come for me, Sam. Don't hold back."

The slow, torturous glide on his fingers in and out of me created a slow burn deep inside. When his thumb rasped over the tight little nub that was throbbing for his attention, my body coiled and released faster than I thought was possible. I screamed, incoherent babbling falling from my lips as he carried me quickly from one orgasm straight into another. Each was bigger and stronger than the last, my hips moving on their own to work in tandem with his hand, and making me want more and more.

With the last rush, the fifth, maybe sixth, I knew I was done. My hips stopped pumping, my body slowed and stilled, Brady's hand following my lead. When my eyes were finally able to focus on him again he looked at me with such awe that I know I blushed.

"That was the most beautiful thing I've ever witnessed. Do you have any idea how gorgeous you are, Sam?"

Instead of answering I simply pulled Brady in for a kiss. His tongue thrust against mine the same way his hand had moved inside me. He was nearly as out of breath as I was, but neither of us wanted to stop.

Until I went for the button on his shorts.

"No, Sam. I can't have you touch me. I'll lose it."

"I trust you, Brady," I insisted. "I don't like know you make me feel so good and I can't return the favor."

"I didn't do it so you would feel obligated, baby. I wanted you to feel good, and I wanted to see you. I fucking loved watching you."

"And I want to make you feel good."

"I do, baby, I promise. I should probably go though. The gym opens early in the morning."

That stung. Sure, I knew Dave's Gym opened at five am, but I felt like there was more to it than just being responsible.

"Okay," I agreed reluctantly. "Are you okay with going to the wedding Saturday? Did you have other plans?"

"I'm not saying no forever, Sam. Just not yet," Brady answered, reading my mind. "And yes, I'm okay with the wedding Saturday. It'll be fun to watch you in action."

I snorted. "I don't think it's really that exciting."

"Everything with you is exciting, Sam."

I smiled even as Brady picked up his shirt and pulled it over his head. He wasn't a charmer like some guys, but he definitely knew the right thing to say to make me melt.

I walked him to the door and accepted the sweet kiss he left me with, then locked the door and went to bed, alone.

~*~

"Samantha, where have you been?" my mom asked when I answered her call the next day.

"Um, working?"

She sighed loudly. "I've been calling you for days. Why weren't you answering your calls?"

I finally cracked. "I didn't want to hear it Mom. I know why you're calling. You've got a job prospect for me, or a guy for me to date, or some criticism about my current job or about Brady. I wasn't in the mood, Mom."

She squeaked in indignation. "How dare you speak to me like that?"

"Mom, I'm not trying to be mean, but every time we talk you're criticizing one aspect of my life or another. I wasn't in the mood for it. I know how you feel about Brady. It was written all over your face the other day."

"I'm just trying to watch out for you Samantha. Your sister told me you were thinking about moving to a smaller place. I'm assuming that means things aren't going well with your hobby. I have some opportunities for you to consider. I've sent you an email so I know you get it all correct since last time you said you must have written the phone number down incorrectly."

I managed to stifle the laugh that threatened to bubble out. I'd forgotten about that one. She was so mad when I admitted I hadn't called Rose's daughter, or whoever it was, because the number I dialed was disconnected. Thankfully she was too embarrassed by my 'lack of professionalism' to call and get the number again.

"Thank you, Mom," I gritted. "I'm not looking for a new job though. I have a job, one I love. I'm simply making some changes."

"What changes?"

"I'm not going to shoot anymore weddings," I confessed. I knew she'd flip. The weddings were the only part of my business she had any respect for. They brought in the most money and being a wedding photographer was a respected position, in my mother's opinion.

"Oh, Samantha, why? You'll end up homeless and starving."

"Thanks for your confidence, Mom."

"Just make sure you don't turn to that Brady when you're out of a job. He doesn't seem like the kind of guy who would take care of a woman."

"I don't want to be taken care of, Mom. I'm taking care of myself."

"Yes, well, when things fall apart for you I'm sure Brady won't be around to help. He's not reliable, Samantha."

"You don't know anything about him," I argued, defending him even though I didn't know much more about Brady than my mother did.

"I know his type, Samantha. Your father has told me too many stories about men who are just like him."

"Stop right there, Mom. Brady is not one of Dad's prisoners. Don't group him into that category. And if you don't like Brady, that's your issue, not mine. I think he's a wonderful man, and I'm not going to let you destroy what we're building. For once in my life, Mom, I'd appreciate your support."

"I can't support you when I know you're making the wrong choice, Samantha."

I sighed heavily. "I'm sorry to hear that, Mom. I disagree with you, and if you aren't willing to respect the choices I make in my life, my career, and my relationships, then I'm not really interested in hearing what you have to say. I need to trust myself, and every conversation with you makes me question myself. That's not fair to me."

"Because you should be Samantha. You're not making wise choices-"

"Stop, Mom. I don't want to hear it. Until you're willing to accept my life, as is, without needing to correct it, I don't want to hear from you."

I hung up, not giving her another chance to argue. The phone rang again a few seconds later, and I declined her call. It rang again, and I declined that one. With the third call I just shoved my phone in my desk drawer, putting my mother out of my mind. I had more important things to worry about, like figuring out the set up for one of my best friends' wedding.

Eighteen

On Saturday I still hadn't talked to my mother. She'd called, but I sent every call to voicemail until I heard a message saying she was sorry and she was going to respect me. I hadn't gotten that yet.

So I got myself ready for the wedding. They were keeping it small, only family and close friends, so I wasn't in the wedding. I wasn't sure how I could shoot a wedding and be in it, so I was grateful I didn't have to juggle the two tasks, even though a part of me secretly hoped I'd have gotten the chance to be a bridesmaid by now. I was in Heather's wedding and Addi asked me to be her maid of honor, but I liked weddings a lot more when I was in the bridal party instead of just the hired help.

Brady was going to meet me there instead of following me all over town for the early shots. Part of me wished he could be there for all of it, but he had better things to do than wait around for me to work, even if he did say he was interested in it.

I got to Mandy's parents' house first. She and Claire were getting ready in Mandy's old bedroom. Her parents were somewhere in the house too, but it was pretty quiet. Thankfully Mandy was fairly low key so I wasn't there overly early.

"Wow," I whispered when I walked into the familiar room, seeing Mandy in her dress. Even though we didn't know each other in high school, being in college in Winterville we went to Mandy's parents' house a lot during our college years. They had great cookouts all summer and they invited us all over regularly.

"It's perfect, isn't it?" Claire asked.

"It really is. Xander is going to flip his shit when he sees you."

Mandy grinned and I knew that was exactly why she'd chosen the backless dress she was wearing. Triangle pieces fit over her chest with dainty straps that did not look strong enough to hold up her abundant breasts. A band wrapped around under her chest before giving way to a floor length skirt that floated to her feet, barely covering white heels with garnet rhinestones on the toes.

"I had to have this dress when I saw it. Of course I needed an industrial strength backless bra to go with it, but it's going to be totally worth it when he sees me. Sam, you've got to capture the look on his face."

I grinned. "I definitely will. I imagine it'll be a cross between wanting to drag you out of the church and absolute love."

"He really does love me, doesn't he?"

"Do you even need to ask?" Claire said. "He adores you."

"We're damn lucky," Mandy grinned. When she focused on me I was a little shocked by the conviction in her eyes. "And Brady is a lucky man. I think you picked a good one."

I laughed. "Brady and I are temporary. He's gonna wake up one day and realize he can get any woman he wants."

"Why would you say that? He adores you," Claire argued.

I shrugged. "I just know how men are. We haven't even slept together. I'm pretty sure he doesn't want to."

"Sam, you're wrong. I saw the way he was looking at you the other night," Mandy said.

"Was that before or after you interrogated him?" I smirked.

"Both. And during. He looked like he wanted to eat you alive. He had so much passion in his eyes whenever he looked at you that Xander and I had to go home and have sex for hours to get rid of the burning between my legs."

"Ew! I did not need to hear that!"

"You asked for it. Besides, it's the truth. That man wants you. I'd be willing to bet he'll be dragging you off to a quiet corner tonight."

Claire laughed. "It's usually the women who get horny at weddings, not men."

"True, but I just think Brady won't be able to stop himself when he sees Sam in this dress."

I rolled my eyes at my friend, but of course I'd been hoping the same thing. I'd carefully selected a black dress so I could blend into the background, but it was fitted over my chest with a super short and flirty skirt that started just below my chest, making my legs look long and my waist look small. I'd added a pair of red sandals that laced up my calf, dangling ruby earrings, and a black pearl and ruby necklace that dipped into my cleavage.

I knew I looked good.

And I really hoped Mandy was right.

"I think we're all getting lucky tonight," Claire grinned. I loved hearing Claire talk about sex. When we'd first met she wasn't a virgin, but after being raped by her high school boyfriend she gave up men and sex. Until Aidan came along and swept her off her feet. She was a completely different person with him, someone full of passion and love and joy. I loved seeing that in my friend.

"I can only hope," I murmured.

A knock on the door interrupted our conversation. Mandy's parents walked in, her mom tearing up when she looked at her beautiful daughter. "Oh, Mandy, you look so gorgeous."

"I don't think we can do this," her dad said.

"Why not?" Mandy asked, alarmed.

"I don't think he deserves my little girl," he said, his eyes misting.

I captured the moment without any of them knowing what I was doing. Mandy hugged both of her parents and thanked them for always being there for her. She touched up her make up, checking that none of it streaked with her tears, and we headed for the church.

Xander and his best friend, Drew, who we'd met at a Christmas party at Mandy and Xander's house a few months ago, were dressed and hanging out behind the altar at the church. I hugged them both and asked Xander if he was ready.

"He's been flipping out the whole day. He wants to see her so badly he can barely breathe," Drew answered for him.

"Well, I just saw her and I promise she's worth the wait."

"I know she is, but I'm starting to wish I hadn't waited so fucking long to marry her." Drew smacked his on the back of the head. "What the fuck was that for?"

"Dude, we're in a church. Stop saying fuck."

"He's right, you know," I added, earning a glare from Xander.

"I knew I liked you," Drew said, slinging his arm around my shoulder.

"Have you gotten rid of that horrible girlfriend yet?" I teased him.

"Nope, she's still hanging around."

"The dumbass even bought a new house and moved her in with him," Xander stage whispered, earning him another smack. "Ow, shit. What the fuck!"

"Language!" Drew yelled, raising his hand again. Xander backed away and slugged Drew on the shoulder, thankfully the one I wasn't pressed against.

"Dammit!" Drew yelled. "Sam, I might need a massage. Can we add best man massage to the list of your duties for the day."

"Hands off man," Xander warned. "She's taken."

I blushed as Drew looked down at me. "Really? Do I need to check him out? Make sure he's good enough for you?"

I laughed, imagining Drew trying to intimidate Brady. Xander answered before I could. "Mandy already did that. She tried to scare him off the other night, but he didn't back down. He's a good guy. He'll be here today though, if you're feeling frisky," he teased his friend.

"Is Brandi coming?"

Xander snorted. "Do you really think Mandy would allow her to be here?"

"You really need to find someone better if she's that horrible," I told him. "Mandy gets along with everyone."

Drew sighed. "I know. But Xander just said you're taken so I'm out of options."

I laughed and winked at him. "Lucky for you I met a couple new friends. Mandy invited them. Maybe you can hook up with one of them, they're both really nice."

Xander laughed at my pathetic matchmaking attempt. I knew Drew wouldn't actually go for it when he had a girlfriend, even if she did sound like a horrendous bitch.

"Thanks, but I think I'll just wait for you to realize we're destined to be together."

I laughed as the minister walked in the room. "Are you ready?"

Xander grinned. "Absolutely."

~*~

The wedding was short and sweet. Xander's eyes bugged out of his head when he saw Mandy in her dress. His hazel eyes, reminding me too much of Brady's, raked over her body, making Mandy flush. When she finally reached him at the altar he barely contained his desire to drag her into his arms. She just grinned knowingly.

When they were announced man and wife, Xander kissed her with more than his fair share of church tongue. I caught the kiss, all twenty-seven seconds of it. Yes, I counted. I always did because I snapped pictures continuously and I wondered how many I took of the first kiss. It was one of those magical moments that every couple loved to see.

The reception was at Winterville Park. Being mid-July the weather was warm but still comfortable enough to be outside. Mandy didn't care where the reception was as long as they got married at her parents' church, and Xander wanted to be outside. It worked for both of them.

A large tent was set up in the park, near the bridge where I'd photographed the Alexander family a month earlier. It was the perfect backdrop for more shots of Mandy and Xander and their families. I took advantage of their distraction, watching Mandy and Xander, and took picture after picture.

I was so focused on my job that I almost forgot about Brady being there. When he stepped up behind me and wrapped his arms around my waist I squeaked before relaxing into him. "You're amazing to watch," he whispered, kissing my neck.

I smiled and turned in his arms, letting my camera dangle around my neck so I could reach up and kiss him. "It's really not that exciting. I told you that."

"Oh, but you're wrong. See I get to sit back and watch you move, in this little dress, and it's amazing to watch. This dress is going to make me crazy."

I grinned and tickled the stubble along the back of his neck. "Maybe that's why I wore it," I teased.

Brady groaned. "Oh, you're evil." He leaned down and kissed me, hard and fast. His tongue plunged into my mouth and his hands squeezed my sides, pulling me to him. I gasped at the feel of him against me, heating my skin and making me wish we could duck into a private spot just like Mandy and Claire teased about earlier.

Brady pulled away abruptly and removed his hands from my side. "Shit, did I hurt you?"

"Huh?" I asked, genuinely confused and more than a little turned on.

His hands ghosted over my sides as though he could feel if I was in pain, then it clicked. "You didn't hurt me. Well, maybe a little when you pulled back, but that was just because I didn't want you to stop."

A smile drifted over his face, leaving him looking boyish and handsome. He had such a hard, serious look about him all the time that whenever he smiled he seemed so much younger, handsome instead of scorching.

"I don't ever want to stop kissing you, Sam, but I don't want to ruin Mandy's wedding. I think she might kick my ass if you miss a shot."

I threw my head back and laughed, but Brady was completely serious. He was scared of my beautiful, red-headed friend. Then again, she was probably the one most likely to kick his ass. Mandy earned her red hair.

"I think you'll be fine, but I do have to get a few more shots before I can relax. I'll be able to sit for dinner and can even dance a little, if you're up to it."

Brady nodded once then kissed me quickly. He disappeared into the crowd and I focused on my job.

Three hours later I was finally able to kick off my sandals and enjoy the night. Tea lights twinkled in mason jars strung all around the tent, giving off an ethereal feel. The dance floor was crowded and the tables were empty. All the food was packed up and the caterers were gone, leaving only Charlie's cupcakes for hungry guests.

I'd finished my duties. Mandy made sure to tell me after they'd cut the cake, had their first dance, and tossed the garter and bouquet that she wanted to me have some fun. I was grateful, but I was also exhausted. I was disappointed that Drew left shortly after dinner, but he said Brandi was having a fit and he needed to get home. I made sure to take a few shots of Drew with Xander and Mandy before he vanished, but I knew they'd always remember that he left early to get home to her.

I flexed my toes, digging them into the grass under the table, and wished I could massage my feet without flashing the entire reception. My other friends were on the dance floor, including Riley and Carrie who were fitting right in with everyone else. I wanted to be out there with them, but I needed a few minutes to stretch my toes, and maybe my back.

Strong hands came down on my shoulders, rubbing slow circles in my back. I moaned, half not caring who was standing behind me, and dropped my head forward. My hair fell over my shoulders and my glasses slid down my nose. It felt amazing, and I was pretty sure I was going to marry whoever was attached to those amazing hands.

"You looked like you needed to relax," Brady said softly in my ear.

"That feels so good."

I could hear the smile in his next words. "Your skin is so soft. I couldn't resist touching you. Your feet have got to be killing you."

I groaned. "You have no idea."

"What do you say we dance a little then head back to your place and I can give you a massage?"

I tilted my head back to look at him. "Really?" I asked, tears filling my eyes. He had no idea what he was saying, or why it would mean so much to me, but emotions choked me as I imagined his hands all over my body.

"I can't wait to get my hands on all of you, Sam. If it'll help you relax," he sounded unsure, like me questioning him meant he was doing something wrong.

I smiled up at him and said, "Thank you."

Nineteen

Since I met Brady at the wedding we had separate cars to leave. He followed me back to my house and grasped my hand as we headed up the walk to the front door. I let us in and tossed my keys and purse on the table then untied my sandals and tossed them in the closet.

"Let me put my camera up. I need to plug it in so I can start editing tomorrow."

"You work all the time, don't you?" Brady asked, following me through the living room, past the bathroom, and into my home office.

I shrugged. "Not all the time, but I like to go through pictures from an event or a shoot as quickly as possible so it's not hanging over me. I don't like having a long to do list."

I plugged in my camera so my computer would capture all the shots and I'd have a back-up to work from. When I turned, Brady was leaning against the door frame, looking more delectable than Charlie's cupcakes.

"You can't look at me like that, Sam," he growled.

"Why not?"

"I won't be able to control myself around you," he said simply, as if that would explain everything. "Come on, I owe you a massage."

"You don't have to, Brady. If you don't want to, it's okay."

Brady narrowed his eyes at me, trying to figure out the hidden meaning behind my words, but he didn't push. "I want to, Sam. More than you can imagine."

I nodded and let him lead me to my bedroom. My heart rate kicked up. We'd never been in either of our bedrooms before. Sure, he'd seen me half naked, but we were in his office. The other times we'd kissed we'd both been fully clothed. Being in my bedroom invoked a sense of intimacy that made me nervous. We were crossing a new line, one I wanted to run over, but one that I knew would change things.

Brady hadn't said anything about sex. The possibility was there, but I hadn't even gotten my hands on him. I knew he wasn't small if the bulge in his pants was any indication, but he wouldn't let me touch him, which worried me.

"Stop thinking, Sam. There's nothing to figure out here. I want to make you feel good. That's all that's going on. I'm not ready for more yet. I'm not sure I could handle more tonight. Not after seeing you in this dress all day."

"Then how about you help me out of it."

I walked toward him, feeling anxious and terrified. His eyes held mine as I moved closer to him, close enough that I could hear him swallow. When I stopped in front of him his eyes trailed over me. He gulped again then nodded. I turned so he could unzip me and pulled my long hair to the side.

Brady's fingers trembled against my bare skin. Slowly he slid the zipper down my back.

When it reached the end his lips touched my back, following the same path. "You taste like heaven," he murmured against my flesh, drawing out goosebumps.

Brady's hands went to my shoulders and slid the capped sleeves down, his hands following the fabric the length of my arms. He glided his palms back up then trailed them down my back to my waist where the dress got hung up. He gave it a gentle tug and it fell at my feet.

With my back to him, I couldn't see the expression on his face. Tension ramped up within me, unsure if he was going to continue or make a run for it now that he'd basically seen all of me. Sure I still had on my black bra and panties, but those didn't cover up the jiggly parts.

"You're absolutely gorgeous Sam. The sexiest woman I've ever seen. I'd say you're fine, but I know you don't like that word."

I laughed at his joke, letting the anxiety I'd been feeling slip away. He wasn't about to run. He wasn't teasing me. He wasn't leaving.

And just like that, I fell a little bit in love with Brady Wright.

"Do you want to take off the rest or stay like that?" he asked, his voice deep and husky. I could hear the desire in his tone, but I wanted to push him. Brady said he wasn't ready for sex, but I was. And I was starting to wonder how he could resist if he really liked me as much as he said he did.

It was time to test that resistance.

"I'd rather take it all off, if that's okay with you," I whispered, peering over my shoulder at him.

He gulped again, his Adam's apple bobbing in his throat. "You or me?" he asked.

Only one answer for that question. I smiled at him and said, "You."

His eyes held mine, passion firing through the hazel orbs. I knew he wanted me. But I wanted him unable to resist me.

His hands drifted over my back before settling at the strap that rested across the center. He fumbled for a minute before pulling the two sides apart. He ran the straps down my shoulders then lifted my breasts into his hands so my bra could fall to the floor.

Brady's mouth suckled at the skin on my neck. His hands supported my breasts, his fingers playing with my nipples. I tilted my head to the side, making sure he had enough room to kiss my neck, and he laughed softly against my overheated skin.

"You like that," he said, not asking, telling. "You skin is so soft and perfect. Makes me want to find out what other parts of you are this soft, this sweet."

I groaned and rolled my hips back against him, nudging my ass against his enormous erection. He hissed in a breath then closed his teeth over the tendon on my neck. His tongue darted out and soothed the bite before he asked, "Did I hurt you?"

"I told you, Brady, I'm not made of glass. I can take a whole lot more than that."

"Good," he said before spinning me in his arms and pulling me tight to him. In one move his lips came down on mine, his tongue pried my mouth open, and he searched my mouth. His hands grasped my ass, kneading my flesh beneath the black satin panties I'd been dripping into all day. I wanted him to move lower, work his fingers beneath the fabric, and touch me, skin to skin, but he didn't. Instead he tortured me with his tongue against mine, his fingers achingly close to where I needed them, but too far away.

Brady broke our kiss and trailed his lips down my neck, over my collarbone, and straight to my nipples. I clutched his head, holding him in place, the rasp of his shaved hair pricking my fingers. My head fell back as he moved to the other nipple.

Then his hands ran down my sides and paused at the edge of my panties. I could tell he was working up the nerve by the way he slowed his kisses on my nipples, going from devouring me to simply enjoying me. I cupped his chin and he looked up at me. With our eyes locked, he hooked his fingers around the waistband and slid my panties down my legs. He lifted each of my feet to slide them out from beneath me, then looked up at me from where he knelt on the floor in front of me.

"Finest woman ever," he said firmly, his eyes locked on mine.

When he finally released me, his eyes went straight between my legs. I wanted a few others things to go there, but I'd settle for his gaze.

"I think I promised you a massage," he forced out, his jaw twitching with the effort. "Why don't you lie down?"

I walked backward toward my bed, watching Brady the whole time. His eyes never left me and when I sat on the bed and pushed back to rest my head on a pillow he sucked in a breath that told me he'd gotten a peek as I'd shifted.

Not that it was on purpose. Of course not.

"On your stomach, Sam," Brady ordered as he stood and stalked toward me. "I need to get to your back."

I did as I was told, knowing Brady's control was slipping further and further from his grasp. When his palms brushed my skin I forgot all about Brady's control, and my desire to snap it, and melted into his touch. I groaned, reveling in the feel of him, eliminating the tension and aches in my back. Long, even strokes eased the soreness and direct contact obliterated the knots that littered my muscles.

He worked down to my legs once my back felt like he'd replaced my spine with jelly. He skated over my ass, palming the globes before continuing seamlessly down the length of my legs, relieving the same tension the coiled those muscles.

When he finally reached my feet I thought I was going to wake the dead with how loudly I moaned. Dear god the man was good with his hands. He tugged my toes, rubbed between each of them, dug his thumbs into the balls of my feet, and then used his thumbs to ease my arches and heels.

"That feels so good," I told him, wiping the drool from my chin. If Brady was going to stick around I was going to have to have him give me more massages.

I couldn't think about that though. The guy wouldn't even sleep with me. It was only a matter of time before he found someone he would be willing to jump into bed with on sight.

"I'm glad you're enjoying yourself," he said, sounding pained. I smirked to myself, knowing he was faltering, but I was too relaxed to do anything about it.

"I could enjoy myself a lot more if you'd crawl into bed with me," I teased, wondering what he would say.

I heard the rustle of fabric then felt the bed dip beside me. Holy fuck, he actually got in bed with me!

I rolled over to face him and looked up into the sexiest expression I'd ever seen. His lids were half-closed in that sexy, too much to take sort of way. His eyes were shining like he couldn't wait to get his hands back on me. His lips were plump and pink and wet. His breath throbbed out of him as though he was on the verge of hyperventilating.

And his shirt was gone.

Jesus, the man was beautiful. Scars and all.

My eyes ran over his naked torso, wishing he'd let me see the rest of him. His muscles stretched and bulged with every move he made. I couldn't stop myself from touching him, from tracing his muscles, his scars, my hands memorizing his every dip and curve for when he inevitably left.

"Can I touch you, Sam? Will you come for me?"

I throbbed at his words, heat and desire and need pooling between my legs. I bit my lip and nodded, suddenly feeling crazy shy. He was going to watch me. I could see it in his eyes. He wanted to see me. And I wanted him to do anything he wanted. Even if he wouldn't let me see him or touch him, he was going to do those things to me.

And I knew it was going to be the most amazing feeling in my entire life.

Brady's hand slid over me, heat licking a path over my skin as his fingertips trailed across me. He was propped up on one elbow, watching me, his eyes following his hand. He tweaked my nipples, circled my belly button, and tickled my inner thigh. Then he leaned forward and kissed me softly as his finger dipped between my legs.

My hips surged off the bed, needing more and needing him to stop. That one brush was too much. It wasn't enough. Dear god, Brady was going to kill me.

"I'm not gonna last, Brady. I'm about to come."

"Then come, baby. I want to watch you, hear you." Brady kissed my bare skin with each word, letting his tongue brush against me for just a second before his lips puckered against my flesh. The sensation of his lips and his fingers, one slow and sweet, one fast and lascivious, drove me faster and higher than I'd ever been. I knew when my body finally released that I was going to completely lose control.

It was rare that I let a man see me that mindless. Few had ever gotten me to where Brady held me. Somehow I knew it would change the way I felt about Brady. That it would push me over the imaginary edge of my feelings for him. I was already falling for him, even though I knew it wasn't the smartest thing to do. But I couldn't stop my feelings for him any more than I could stop the orgasm rushing toward me like a speeding train.

When it hit my body took over, leaving my consciousness to fend for itself. I thrashed, I bucked, I screamed, I may have even bit him. I didn't care. I was in free fall, loving every sensation that coursed through my body. I couldn't stop the endless waves of pleasure, and I didn't want to.

Brady's hand slowed, pulling me from the euphoria I had settled into. His lips danced over my skin, heating me as his fingers cooled me. I knew I couldn't handle more, but I was already aching for it. I reached for him, dragging his head toward mine so I could kiss him.

His tongue thrust deep into my mouth without hesitation. I felt his passion and control, tightly wound together as though they were one in the same. He wanted me to know how he felt, but only under his conditions. He had to be in control.

And God help me I still wanted to snap it.

Brady slowly pulled back, kissing me gently as he eased away from me. He brushed hair from my cheek and I looked up at him with slightly blurred vision. I wanted my glasses so I could see his expression clearly, but I didn't want to break the moment by reaching for them.

"That was the most amazing thing I've ever seen. You are insanely sexy. I hope you know that."

I tried to smile, but it fell flat. His words warmed me, but I struggled to accept them. I knew it was easy to be sexy when you were having an orgasm. It turned men on to see what they could do to a woman. It was everything else that I struggled with. Was I sexy outside the bedroom? Was it enough for him to want to have sex? Did he see me as more than a pair of boobs and a place to stick his cock?

Brady cupped my chin and gently drew my face back to his. "I'm not kidding, Sam. I want you so bad right now that it's killing me that I'm not already inside you."

"I wouldn't be opposed to that," I said softly, knowing what the answer would be before he even spoke.

"I can't, Sam. I'm sorry."

"I understand," I lied.

Brady kissed me again, softly, like he cherished me. I struggled with what it meant. I knew how I felt about him. I trusted him. Completely. It scared the shit out of me. After everything with Cade I wasn't sure I'd ever trust a man again, but I was lying in my bed, naked, after Brady gave me the most fabulous orgasm of my life.

I was falling for him.

But he didn't feel the same.

"I should go," he said against my lips. He was already pulling back. It tore at my heart, but I wasn't going to hold on to a man who didn't want me. I'd never been that woman, and I wasn't going to start with Brady. If he didn't want me, I'd let him go.

"Okay," I said, climbing out of bed. I pulled on a pair of sweatpants and a t-shirt so I could walk him to the door. When I turned to face him he already had his shirt on and he was watching me closely.

"I'm not rejecting you, Sam. I'm just not ready. This is all about me, not you."

Seriously? He was giving me the worst break-up line ever?

I resisted the urge to roll my eyes and forced a smile. "I know," I lied. "I'll walk you out."

Brady reached for my hand. I slid mine into his, wondering if it would be the last time I was able to touch him. I hoped not but wasn't sure of anything as we walked to my door.

I nearly laughed at how wrong Mandy and Claire had been earlier.

At the door Brady turned to me. He cupped my chin and leaned down to kiss me. It started out soft and sweet, but when I touched his lips with my tongue, he spun me, pressing my back to the door, and covered my body with his. He thrust his hips against me, heating my body all over again. His tongue searched my mouth, delving into every crevice he could find before caressing my tongue with his. His hips matched the rhythm set by his tongue, spiraling my body higher and higher until I was sure I could combust right there.

Then he pulled back.

"This is why I can't sleep with you yet. I'm sorry. I shouldn't have attacked you like that."

"Are you kidding me?" I asked, breathless and confused. "That's passion. That's sexy. That's not a bad thing, Brady. If you didn't make love to me the way you just kissed me I'd be pissed off."

"Make love?" he asked, rolling the words around on his tongue. I froze. Shit, I never should have said those words. What the hell was wrong with me? "I like it. That's exactly what I'm going to do one of these days, Sam. And when I do you're going to let go of all those questions you have in your head about me, about us, and accept how you feel."

I blushed. He knew me too well. Which was slightly terrifying.

"Okay," I whispered.

He kissed me again, hard and fast, then he was gone.

And I was alone.

Twenty

Finding an apartment was not as easy as I expected. I was familiar with Tree Brach Apartments, where Claire lived before Aidan, but I wasn't in love with them. Still, it fit my budget so it was a possibility. I checked out a few other apartments in town, but struggled to accept that I was basically moving backward. I'd been living in a house for years but going to an apartment felt like I'd failed. I was having a hard time with that.

I was also having a hard time with everything going on with Brady. He knew the right things to say, but it was hard to accept his words when his actions were telling me something different.

He still wanted to see me, so I decided that was a good thing, but he wouldn't let me touch him. Tuesday, after a disappointing day on the apartment hunt, Brady came to girls' night. We all rehashed Mandy and Xander's wedding, talking about how perfect it was. Addi was up next so everyone jumped on her planning train, asking what they were going to do and if they'd set a date yet.

They hadn't.

Brady claimed he had to be up early Wednesday morning so he didn't come over after girls' night, reminding me again that I didn't know much about him. I knew he had scars, not just the physical ones, and I worried those scars would split us up in the end.

I pushed all thoughts of Brady away as I entered the tiny house I'd found available for rent at the edge of town. It was in a decent area, only about five minutes from my studio. It was tiny, but it would work for me being by myself. The realtor, Stephanie, who managed the rental showed me around.

"It's small, but for one person it could be perfect. You said you're alone, right?"

Her unintentional words stung, but it was the truth. "Yes, I'm alone. My old roommate is getting married and I just can't keep up with our rent on my own."

"Well, this place is in your budget. I think it could work for you," Stephanie said. "Should we look around?"

I nodded and followed her through the space. "The kitchen is tiny, but all the appliances are updated and full size. There is a small pantry too, which is nice. You're tall, so these high cabinets won't be an issue for you."

"True. I don't think I have more than this anyway. Addi and I lived together for so long that we shared all our stuff. When she left I realized I was short some stuff, but with just me it isn't a big deal."

"Well, as long as everything else is that way, you'll be fine here."

Stephanie showed me the small dining area, which was the perfect size for a four person table. The living room would be big enough for my couch and maybe a chair, but not much else. The bedroom worked though.

My bed would fit and I could put a desk along one wall so I could work from home occasionally. The bathroom was tiny, like the kitchen, but with it just being me, it worked.

"What do you think?"

"I think it's perfect," I told her honestly. "When is it available?"

"It's available now, but we'll need to run a background check and a credit check. Once we get everything back, we can get you the keys. When would you like to move in?"

"As soon as possible. I'm on a month-to-month lease right now. If you think I can be in here within a month I'll give notice today."

Stephanie smiled. "As long as there isn't anything in your background check or credit check, I don't see why that would be a problem."

I nodded. It felt good to have it settled. I knew the sooner I moved the better it would be. I could save the extra income I still had coming in from the last few weddings. It wouldn't last long, but if I was smart I could make it work for me until things picked up on the other side of the business.

Stephanie and I walked out together and I agreed to stop by her office the next day to fill out all the paperwork I needed to complete. I wasn't sure how long Brady's meeting was going to last, but I wanted to tell someone about the new house I'd found so I headed over to READ.

"Hi Sam," Riley said as I walked in. "What are you doing here?"

"I just found a new house."

"Ooh, so exciting. Congratulations! Things much be going well then?"

I shrugged. "It's going okay. I officially cut weddings from the services I offer, but I still have a few left that had already been booked. Of course I'll do Addi's wedding if she wants, and any other friends and family, but I won't shoot weddings for my career anymore. I love working with families and even businesses and stuff like that. It's less stress, but more rewarding for me."

"What do you do for businesses?" Riley asked, crossing her arms over her chest. Riley was a bit bigger than the rest of us, but she was beautiful. She had a perfectly round face and rarely wore make-up. Her skin was soft and clear and I was totally jealous of her. She kept her hair pinned back most of the time, but the light brown color matched her eyes perfectly. She had a tattoo of a butterfly perched on an anchor on her left forearm and her lower lip was pierced.

She was totally unique right down to the tops she wore that she sewed herself.

"It depends what a business needs," I answered her, imagining how I could bring Riley's personality into the store a bit more. "Like with Beth, Carrie's boss, she just wanted updated head shots. Some businesses want pictures for their websites or promotional products. Some need help designing or improving their websites. Some want brochures to hand out, like florists and people having special events."

Riley nodded thoughtfully. "I think we could use some of that here. READ is a great business, but we need to improve the website and make it look a little more homey in here."

I glanced around the space. It was fairly bland. Bookshelves covered all the walls and filled every available space in the middle, except the one little corner with a seating area.

"What's your goal here? I know it's a bookstore, but do you want customers to sit and read or come and work or just stop in and buy books?"

Riley glanced around as if she was seeing the space for the first time. "Maybe all of it. I'm just not sure where we'd put all that."

We walked through the store. "I don't know much about bookstores, but aren't a lot of them going to online books now?"

Riley scrunched up her nose. "Yeah. I love the feel of a new book in my hands. I have one of those ereaders, but it's not the same for me."

"But that's what people are using now. You should consider having an affiliate program with the big sellers. Let your customers browse your website for the books, maybe just an online account of what's in the store, and then a link to order it electronically if they prefer that. Then you could accept online orders for people who need to pick something up but don't want to be going through the whole store to find it."

"That's a really good idea," Riley said, spinning around as she imagined… something. "We could have a kiosk here too, so if readers want to order something in the store they can. This could be a big income generator for us. Thanks, Sam. I do have one favor though."

"What's that?"

"Will you help me figure out how to set it up and take some new pictures of the place when we're done. We'd pay you, of course."

I nodded. "That sounds like fun. Maybe I can ask you a favor, too?"

"Anything," Riley said quickly.

"Would you be willing to save me some boxes?"

Riley laughed. "Of course. How about lunch? There's a great little sandwich place not far from here and they deliver."

"Sounds perfect. We can talk through some design ideas while we eat."

"Excellent."

~*~

I saw Brady at the gym Friday and he asked me out for Saturday night. I didn't have anything else going on so I agreed. I also really wanted to see him again. He kissed me before he went back to his office, leaving me feeling more confused than ever.

"He really likes you," Jennie said. "I've never seen him kiss anyone, and he hadn't left the office in days."

I wanted to believe her, but I still had my doubts. "What sort of meeting is he in?"

Jennie shrugged. "I'm not sure. He doesn't tell me much. It must be important though because it's taken a while. What do you say we go out for a drink later? I'd love to get to know the woman who finally snagged Mr. Wright. So many have tried and failed."

I felt like a goldfish and wasn't sure I liked it. Going out for a drink with one of Brady's employees seemed like a bad idea. "I can't tonight. I'm sorry. I've got a meeting later. I'm helping redesign a business and we're working late when the store is closed."

It was the truth, but I still felt like I was lying because I really didn't want to go out with Jennie. Sure, she seemed really nice, but I didn't think it was a good idea to become friends with her.

Jennie shrugged. "Maybe another time. Greg was telling me he really liked talking to you. He wanted the four of us to get together, but Brady never socializes with anyone. Greg and I were going to go to the concert tomorrow night in Winterville Park, but we're having dinner with his mother instead. She's been begging him to bring me over. We get along really well."

"I didn't know you and Greg were dating," I blurted, wondering why Brady hadn't told me.

"Yeah, for a few months. He's really sweet."

I nodded. "He helped me out a little when I first got here. He was nice."

"Yeah, he told me how Brady butted in so he could talk to you. Hey, you guys should go to the concert tomorrow night. It's supposed to be a great show."

Jennie blushed when I narrowed my eyes at her.

"Sorry. I heard Brady ask you out and neither of you had an idea where to go. Greg and I like to stay in some nights, but it's nice to get out and do something different too. I just figured you guys might like the concert."

I offered her a half smile and nodded. "Yeah, that's not a bad idea. I used to go all the time but haven't been yet this summer. I'll suggest it. And we'll get a drink sometime. Soon."

"I'm gonna hold you to that," Jennie said.

Twenty-One

The concert was amazing. I still couldn't believe Brady had never been to the free concerts in the park. Little by little I was dragging him out of his shell. It was fun doing different things with him, even if I'd done them before. He seemed so sheltered.

"Do you want a drink?" he leaned in close and asked above the loud music. I nodded and he kissed my cheek before jumping up. From our blanket on the grass we had a great view of the stage, but I wasn't watching the stage as Brady walked away, I could only watch him.

Just like all the other women near us.

He definitely captured the attention of women. I knew most of them were wondering what he was doing with me. Hell, I was too. I pushed thoughts of those other women out of my mind and let my attention drift back to the concert.

Brady had been attentive from the moment he'd picked me up. I wasn't sure what had changed, but he was in a good mood. He said his meetings had gone well and he just wanted to enjoy time together. I was just happy to see him, but it helped that he'd barely kept his hands off me all night.

Someone laid out a blanket next to me and I turned to smile at the newcomers but found myself unable to breathe.

"Cade?" I said breathlessly, quietly.

But he heard me.

"Sam," he scoffed. "What are you doing here?"

I couldn't breathe. His dark hair had the same recently fucked look it always had, and his dark eyes burned a whole through me, erasing my fear and replacing it with pure hatred of the man.

"It's a free country, Cade. I'm here for the concert. Just like you are." I looked past him to the tiny blonde settling onto the blanket, seemingly unaware of the tension between us. "She's cute."

Cade glanced behind himself to her and grinned. "Yeah. She a wildcat in bed, too. Almost as good as you."

I shuddered. Thinking about me and Cade together made me want to go take a shower. The fact that I hadn't slept with anyone since him made me both sad and pissed.

With every passing day I worried Brady was starting to see me the way Cade did. Was he no longer interested in me because of how I looked? I'd been losing weight, although not much. I had a long way to go before I was anywhere close to Cade's new girlfriend. Brady owned a gym, and I was fooling myself thinking he wouldn't feel the same as Cade.

"Have you lost weight?" Cade asked, eyeing my middle and letting his eyes run down my legs then back up to settle on my breasts.

"Not that it's any of your business, but yes."

"You look good. Not skinny enough yet for the lights to be on during sex, but good."

Ugh. What did I ever see in him? He was such a conceited asshole. He was hitting on me with another woman just a few feet away.

And he wasn't doing it very well.

"Yeah, well, I don't think you'll be getting another chance. No amount of darkness will hide that you're a dick."

He waggled his eyebrows at me. "You used to like my dick," he said suggestively.

I groaned. Why did I ever fall for that? Brady was so much better. Except for the fact that he didn't want to sleep with me. Cade wasn't a good lover, not even a little, but at least he wanted me. Even if it was just for sex.

Brady... I didn't know what Brady wanted. For someone who said he couldn't control himself around me he seemed to do a damn good job of keeping control. Not once had he lost it and let things go further than a little touching. Hell, he hadn't even taken his pants off yet. Nothing like bouncing from one shitty boyfriend to another to make me think I wasn't wanted.

No, that wasn't fair to Brady. He wasn't a shitty boyfriend. He was a great boyfriend. He just took things a lot slower than I'd ever gone with anyone. It wasn't bad, right?

Brady was before us, looking back and forth between me and Cade, before I responded to Cade's crude comment. "Who's this?" Brady asked with a growl.

Cade looked up at Brady and his eyes went wide before he jumped to his feet. "I'm Cade. Who are you?"

"I'm Brady, her boyfriend."

Cade looked Brady up and down then broke into a laugh. He howled, clutching his stomach and bending over as though that was the funniest thing he'd heard. Ever.

"This is a joke, right? Did you pay this guy, Sam? Is he a date for hire?"

I sat there baffled and horrified. Everyone near us turned to watch, looking at me and no doubt believing Cade's accusation. On stage the band was talking to the audience so even their music wasn't drowning out Cade's lies.

"Excuse me?" Brady asked, his eyes narrowing. He set our drinks down on the blanket and clenched his fists at his sides.

"Why would a meathead like you date a fat ass like her? Oh, wait, no I understand. You know how good she is in bed, right? She's a tiger, isn't she. Damn good fuck as long as you keep the lights off so you don't have to see all of her fat skin rolling around. And as long as you keep your hands on the good parts."

Oh. My. God. He did not just say that. In public. Hundreds of people just heard him. I looked around and saw people whispering behind their hands and snickering. They knew he was right. I wasn't special. I wasn't someone every guy wanted.

Hell, I wasn't someone any guy wanted.

When he'd first said those words to me I nearly died. It ripped my heart out to listen to the guy I thought I could have been falling for tell me he didn't want me anymore because he found someone skinnier, someone hotter, someone who didn't make him feel sick. He said he just wanted to know if the rumors were true that 'all fat chicks were good in bed.'

It never occurred to me that he only touched my breasts and between my legs when we were together, the good parts he said. He never ran his hands over my skin like he couldn't get enough of me, the way Brady did. Every touch from Cade was calculated, a careful dance to make sure he had a good time in bed disguised in giving me pleasure. Pleasure that really wasn't ever that good.

That's why I changed myself. Why I joined Dave's Gym. I didn't want to be a fat chick anymore. Cade's words haunted me. I knew they would forever. No matter how much weight I lost I would still think of myself as a fat chick. But I could try. Maybe one day I thought I could find a man who wasn't so focused on appearance, someone who cared more about what was inside than the package it came in.

"How would you know anything about her?" Brady growled, drawing my attention back to the two men in front of me. "Who are you?"

Cade glanced at me. "I see you're close, huh babe? You didn't even tell your 'boyfriend' about me," the bastard actually used air quotes. He focused his attention back on

Brady. "I'm her ex. We broke up a couple months ago. Well, I broke up with her because I met the hottie behind me," he nodded toward the blonde on the blanket. "Upgraded, you know."

Cade was laughing when Brady's fist smashed into his face. His head flew back and led his way to the ground. He landed with a soft thud, stunned but conscious. I screamed. The blonde screamed. Cade just looked pissed.

"If you know what's best for you, you'll stay on the fucking ground," Brady commanded him. "As for Sam... I don't ever want to hear of you speaking to her again. You are to stay away from her. If I find out you called her, visited her, looked at her on the street, anything. I won't stop with one punch. This woman is beautiful, inside and out, and if you're too fucking stupid to see that then I'm glad, because it means I got a shot with her. I might fuck it up, I probably will, but I will never treat a woman the way you do."

Brady glanced at me and softened just slightly before focusing his attention back on Cade. I almost laughed at the terrified expression on his face. His cheek was bruised and swelling already, but there was no blood.

"You are the sort of man who makes the rest of us look bad. You don't deserve to have a woman on your arm, and if this one," Brady nodded toward the blonde, "has half a brain she'll dump your sorry ass for being a piece of shit. But know this... you won't steal another second from us. Sam didn't tell me about you because you don't matter. You didn't matter before and you sure as fuck don't matter now. So stop trying to act like you do. Now, I suggest you leave here before I change my mind about stopping with one punch."

Cade looked at me fearfully then scrambled across his blanket. He shoved the blonde to the side so he could get the blanket balled up and grabbed the bag he'd brought. She complained that she wanted to watch the concert, but he ignored her and dragged her away. He glanced back once and Brady took a step forward, forcing Cade's eyes away and his feet to move faster.

Slowly chatter around us got louder and people started clapping and whistling. A few guys clapped Brady on the back, but he didn't look at any of them. His eyes were locked on me.

"Are you okay?" he finally asked.

I nodded, unable to speak around the massive lump in my throat and the tears stinging my eyes. I knew if I said anything I would lose it.

"Do you want to go?"

I nodded again, anxious to get away from so many prying eyes. They might be acting nice, but sharing my most humiliating moment with hundreds of strangers was not my idea of a fun evening.

Brady picked up our stuff, leaving the drinks he'd bought. I focused on getting the hell out of there. When we got to his Jeep Brady threw everything in the back while I climbed in, ashamed and shocked. For a fleeting second I wondered if I should be afraid of Brady, but I knew that was crazy. Brady wasn't dangerous, not to me. If he hadn't stood up for me I would have questioned why I was with him. Instead he took out Cade with one swing and I'd never have to deal with him again.

Brady got in the car and turned the key, cranking up the air conditioning, then turned in his seat. "Come here," he said, pulling me to him.

The center console dug into my side, but I didn't care. Brady's arms closed around me and I lost it. Everything I'd hid, all the fears I'd buried, all the shame I'd felt, all the anger I'd carried... all of it poured out.

I sobbed against his strong chest, my tears soaking through his shirt. His hands rubbed up and down my back and his heart beat a steady rhythm under my ear. I let out everything I'd been holding in for weeks. I hiccuped my breath and kept crying, unable to stop once I'd started.

Brady was my rock. He held me as close as he could. He was turned at an odd angle and I knew his back had to be killing him. I tried to pull back but he wouldn't let me, keeping my face against his chest. He had my head tucked under his chin and he kissed my hair, whispering kind words as I cried.

When I could breathe again I eased back. Brady let me but didn't let go of me. I couldn't face him. I looked down, keeping my eyes from his, unsure and afraid of what I'd find there.

"Do you want to talk about it?" he asked quietly, brushing hair back from my face. I knew he was trying to get me to look at him, but I didn't have it in me. Men never liked to talk about feelings or listen to a woman cry. He was just asking to be nice.

I shook my head, still not looking at him. "Look at me, Sam," he said.

I finally met his eyes and challenged him. "I know you don't really want to hear about it. Men hate when we cry. I'll be fine."

"I thought we'd just established that I'm not like other men. Are you afraid of me now?" he asked, sounding ashamed.

"What? No. Why would I be afraid of you?"

He cocked an eyebrow at me as though the answer were obvious.

"Okay, I thought about it for, like, a second, but no Brady. You were defending me, for some unknown reason. I know you'd never hit me."

"Good. I'd never be able to live with myself if I scared you. Now why don't you tell me about that asshole."

I shook my head again. "You really don't want to know."

"Yes, I do."

Tears burned my eyes again and I shook my head. "Maybe I don't want you to know. I don't want you to think differently of me."

"That'll never happen. Sam, I promise you. His opinion of you doesn't matter. I just want to know if I need to go kill him."

I huffed out a small laugh. "No, you don't need to kill him. He's just a jerk." I shrugged, feeling the floodgates opening back up. Tears pricked my eyes as I said, "I thought he was a good guy. He sweet talked me. We met at a wedding I was working on. He was drunk, but I didn't know it until later. We slept together and started seeing each other. We'd only ever go to his place, never out, and I had a roommate. We'd have sex and sometimes I'd spend the night, but I never realized what a jerk he was."

Tears trickled down my face and Brady kissed them away. "He doesn't deserve you, Sam. You're not the one who's wrong here, he is. He didn't know what a good woman he had. Can I ask you a question?"

I nodded.

"Did you join Dave's Gym to try to get him back?"

I bit my lip. I wouldn't lie to Brady, but I didn't want him to think less of me. "Sort of. He's right. I don't know why any man would be interested in getting up close and personal with my wobbly body. I decided I wasn't going to let anyone else make me feel like he did so I joined the gym. But it wasn't to get him back. I never wanted him back. I just wanted to make him regret what he said. I don't still want him."

"I'm pretty sure he's regretting it right about now," he said, trying to hide a smirk. Then turned serious. "I shouldn't have hit him."

"He's an asshole. He deserved it," I laughed, relaxing for the first time since Cade sat down next to me.

Brady gave me a half smile that I could tell he didn't really feel.

"Hey," I said softly. "It's no big deal. Thank you. It meant a lot to me to have you come to my defense."

Brady shrugged. "I shouldn't have lost control. All I could see was your face and I knew he was hurting you and I just wanted it to stop. I wanted him to stop so I made him. I just... I should have been able to control myself."

I rested my hand on his arm and waited until he looked at me. "Why is being in control so important to you? What are you afraid of?"

His eyes held mine and I could sense the depths that his control went. He needed it, more than anything else in his life, he needed control.

"I just need to be in control. But right now I need you. Will you come home with me tonight? Will you stay with me?"

Twenty-Two

Gulp.

This was it. The moment I'd been waiting for. The look in his eyes was unmistakable. Brady wanted sex. With me. Tonight. Holy fuck. I was freaking out.

I wanted him. That wasn't the question. But my emotions were raw. If something happened I wasn't sure I'd recover.

It was Brady. I trusted him. He wanted me. I could do it.

I nodded and Brady let out a deep breath. I sucked one in and settled back into my seat while Brady shifted into drive and tore out of the parking lot. He sped through town, weaving in and out of the light traffic, until he got to Dave's Gym. He threw the Jeep into park and scrambled out. He grabbed the stuff from the back and let us in the side door that went straight to his apartment.

Inside Lucky danced around us, nuzzling at our hands and barking. I crouched down and gave him a full body rub while Brady put things away. Brady came back and pulled me away from his dog. "Lucky can play later. Right now it's my turn," he said with a panty-melting grin. Then he turned a stern face to the dog and said, "Stay."

Lucky's butt dropped to the floor but his tail kept wagging. He looked after us with a cocked head as Brady dragged me toward his bedroom.

I'd been in his apartment but never into his bedroom. I glanced around for a second, but Brady was on me in a flash. His hands closed around me and his lips pressed against mine. His mouth was soft but firm on mine, letting me feel what he was feeling. His tongue worked my lips and darted inside when I opened for him. He tasted like his usual freshness with a hint of the Coke he'd been drinking.

"I need you, Sam. I want you. Will you let me have you?" he asked softly with our foreheads pressed together.

His breath fanned over my face. His heart was pounding beneath my palm and I knew that was it. The chance I'd been waiting for. He said he wanted me, he'd been showing me for more than a month. God knew I wanted him, too.

I just needed the courage to go through with it. Brady wasn't the sort of guy I ever imagined myself with, but I trusted him. He'd hit Cade in my defense. He was there for me. And he wanted me. He'd already seen me naked.

"Yes, Brady. I want you too."

His lips were on mine again, slowly kissing me breathless and boneless. His hands slid up and down my back, but mine stayed around his neck. I didn't know what he could handle, how he needed to keep control, and didn't want to push him. I knew if I did it would be over. He'd never forgive me for going back on that promise.

Even if I had no idea what he was so afraid of.

Brady's lips left mine and trailed down my neck. I struggled to breathe and regain some measure of sanity. Until his lips hit the edge of my neck on the way to my shoulder. That spot, that little dip just inside my collarbone, did crazy things for me. Brady paused there, I don't know if he knew what he was doing or not, but he paused there.

His tongue ran along my skin and my arms tightened around his neck. His teeth came out to play and nipped at me and my panties flooded. When he suckled my skin with open-mouthed kisses I couldn't stop the moan that fell from my lips or the bow of my body against his.

He was hard against my stomach. I wanted to touch him, to see him, to feel him. I held back, knowing how quickly other men lost it, but felt frustrated that I couldn't find a way to make the experience good for Brady without worrying about him losing control.

His hands drifted under my shirt and slid the fabric up, exposing my back to the cool room. Goosebumps covered my flesh, both from Brady and the air. He continued to feast on my neck, switching to the other side at some point, and making me forget all my concerns.

My hands fell from his neck and reached out to him. Desperate to feel him, I cupped his erection through his jeans and all my anxieties came back. He was big. Not just normal big, but huge big. I could tell by the more than a handful I got that he was a good length, but besides that he was thick. I really didn't think he'd fit.

"What's wrong?" he asked, pulling back and sensing something was going on.

"Um... I don't think I'm big enough."

"Sam, you're perfect. Please don't tell me you're fat again. That fucker was wrong. Every last bit of you is beautiful."

I smiled, grateful he was so kind, but still freaked out. "Thanks, but, um, that's not what I'm talking about. I don't think I'm big enough for you to fit. Because, um, you feel huge."

Brady looked down between us to where my hand was still holding his erection. "Oh," he mumbled. "We can stop if you want. I don't want to hurt you."

He started to pull away, disappointment reflected in his eyes. I grabbed his hand and wouldn't let him go. "We'll take it slow, just like everything else."

"Sam, I don't want to hurt you," he reiterated.

I shook my head. "You won't. I promise. We'll go slow and if it's too much we'll stop. Rumor has it babies can come out of there. I'm sure you can go in."

Brady smiled at me, but I knew we were both a little more anxious with the new revelation. My hands trembled against him, but he didn't show any fear. Brady was as controlled as ever.

His hand slid under my shirt again, his eyes locked on mine, and he pulled it up and over my head. Watching me the whole time, Brady rested his hands on me. I flinched at the contact as his hand touched my belly, the flabbiest part of me. Instead of pulling away, he glided over me, the softest hint of skin against skin.

I finally looked down and saw his lightly tanned hand against the never-seen-sun-white of my belly. Even with the lights off in his room, I could see him touching me clearly. I knew it wouldn't be long before he went to my breasts, ass, or settled between my legs. Getting to the good parts was crucial, and all that mattered to men.

"Every inch of you is a good part," he said quietly, reading my thoughts. "I'm going to worship your body tonight. Making sure you know exactly how much I want you. You're never going to doubt, ever, that I want you."

My body went up in flames at his words and the conviction in his voice. I had a lot of inches so we could easily be there all night if Brady was going to praise them all. Oh, shit, he dropped to his knees in front of me and kissed my belly.

"Brady, you don't have to."

He looked up at me, his eyes hazy and unfocused. "I want you. Every inch of you," he said between kisses.

My nipples got painfully hard and I ached between my legs, especially with him so close. His hands rested gently on my hips and he kissed my entire belly, letting his tongue get into the action and even his teeth a little bit.

I was so focused on his kisses that I didn't notice his hands working my shorts free. They dropped to the floor at my feet and I stood before him in just my red cotton bra and barely there red thong with smiley face daisies all over them. Brady leaned back on his heels and looked me over slowly. His eyes covered me like a caress, every inch of my body bursting into flames when his eyes passed over.

"I really like the daisies," he teased. "You're beautiful, Sam. Don't let anyone ever make you believe otherwise," he commanded me with conviction. Heat and desire raced through me looking at the raw need in his eyes and listening to his voice.

"Can I see you Brady?" I asked, knowing being bare was just as hard for him as it was for me.

Brady got to his feet before me and pulled me in for another kiss. His hands circled my back and his lips crushed mine. Teeth clacked together, tongues tangled, and hands explored. I ached to feel his skin under my hands and his hands all over me. He unclasped my bra while we kissed then dipped his head to pull one nipple into his mouth.

I clutched his head to me, moaning at the teasing he delivered. Between my legs ached and I moaned for him, desperate to erase all memories of Cade. Needing Brady to give me a new encounter to remember when I was lonely.

As Brady kissed me, no doubt to distract me, I tugged his t-shirt up his body, shocked to see more scars down his back. He nipped my skin and drew my attention back to us, but I couldn't un-see Brady's scarred and damaged skin.

Brady helped me get his shirt off, and I let my hands cover his body. He watched me warily, but I couldn't see his scars, just Brady. My lips followed my hands, touching, kissing, tasting Brady. His skin was hot and firm, steel wrapped in silk. He tasted as fresh as he smelled with a little hint of sweat underneath. I didn't want to stop. I didn't know if I could.

Brady pulled me up and guided me to his bed, kissing as we moved across the room. I laid down while he stripped off his pants and briefs. Holy fuck. There was no way in hell he was going to fit.

The panic must have shown on my face because Brady stopped. "We don't have to, Sam."

"I want to, Brady, really. You're gorgeous. But I'm a little scared. I've never been with anyone nearly as big as you."

He shook his head. "I don't want to have the talk of who we've been with right now, but I'm not surprised that douche from earlier has a small cock. He probably didn't even know how to use it."

I laughed at Brady's accurate assessment of Cade. He was right. Cade was barely noticeable when he was inside me, and there wasn't ever any build-up that made it better.

Wait... Why did I stay with him so long?

"I have no doubt you know what you're doing," I told him sultry, wanting to turn the night back to us, not Cade.

"Speaking of which," Brady said with a saucy grin. He slowly crawled up my body, making every pore in my body drink him in as he slid over me. I was a little disappointed that he was going to go right for the main event without any build-up, but oh well.

He settled between my legs and lowered his weight onto me gently. Keeping himself propped on his elbows he met my lips again. His erection pulsed against my core, making me desperate for him. I arched into him, and he smiled against my lips.

"Oh, honey, not yet. I'd hurt you now. But I'll be right back."

He kissed me thoroughly, pushing aside every thought in my brain except Brady, Brady, and more Brady. I moved against him, not wanting to wait any longer, and he broke away from me on a laugh.

"I feel the same way, honey. I promise. I want you more than I ever thought possible. It'll be worth the wait," he assured me as he drifted away.

His mouth led the way down my body. He dipped his tongue in my favorite spot on my neck making me moan. He floated to my breasts and offered each customized attention with licks, nips, and kisses that drove me completely insane.

He kept moving down my body, kissing my belly then dipping his tongue into my belly button. When he moved down even further he lifted my ass to slide my panties off. He kissed each of my toes when he got to the foot of the bed and slowly worked his way back up to me. When he paused at my inner thighs I started to panic.

I looked down and his eyes were on me, barely visible over my bulging belly. His eyes showed an unmistakeable desire that made me quiver in anticipation. When he ducked his head I lost sight of him, but with one swipe of his tongue against me my eyes drifted closed anyway.

His hands slid under me and tilted my hips up to him. I moaned and writhed under him, delighting in his skills. It wouldn't be long before he gave up and moved on, but I'd enjoy it while he lasted.

Except Brady was different. With every passing second he seemed more and more eager to complete his task. A thick finger joined his tongue, sliding inside me and drawing my hips to him. A second finger went in, followed by a third and before long I was aching for a release.

Brady sucked hard on me and circled his tongue around me. My breathing sped up, and my mind went black. I bucked against him and felt my body let go, flying in a delirious and satisfied haze of pleasure.

Silly me, Brady wasn't done. His fingers curled deep inside me and his mouth sucked hard on me before my first orgasm ended. Brady sent me flying into a second one, my insides burning and my whole body shattering with more power and bliss than I'd ever felt in my life.

As Brady finally let me come back to earth he slowly climbed my body, kissing his way back up until he met my lips. I could taste myself on him, something that was new and exciting to me, and turned me on even more. Need and moisture flooded me, eager for Brady.

"Brady, please," I begged, breaking our kiss.

He pulled away for a minute and reached into his nightstand. He held the foil package between his teeth and pulled it open. Desperate to get my hands on him, I took it from him and rolled it down his long, thick cock. He was shaking by the time I finished.

Brady covered me again, his kiss turning frantic. His cock nudged between my legs as he kissed me, and I wriggled to get him just right.

Breaking our kiss Brady thrust deep inside me in one smooth motion. My eyes drifted closed and my body screamed at the intrusion. Or maybe that was me.

Brady stilled, our bodies locked together. His fingers danced over my face, a gentle caress until I opened my eyes. "That's why I don't lose control. I'm sorry, honey. I never should have pushed into you like that. I'm just a meathead too stupid to be careful."

I gripped his jaw in my hand and glared at him. "Don't ever say anything like that again. You're not stupid and no one can say you are, especially you." Something flashed over his face that I couldn't identify, but I pushed on. "Besides, you feel good. I just needed a minute to get used to you. Don't hold back, Brady, please."

He shook his head. "I have to be in control. I'll hurt you. We can stop-"

"Don't you dare," I growled at him.

He grinned down at me and slowly slid out. I wrapped my legs around his waist to keep him from leaving and he laughed, his cock trembling inside me. "I said don't," I whined, knowing he could overpower me without even trying.

"Honey, I wasn't leaving. I was trying to get things going," he said, still chuckling at me.

"Oh," I said, embarrassed.

"Can I move now?" he asked, nudging at my legs clasped tightly around him.

I loosened my grip and let him slide out slowly then back in. My body adjusted to his quickly, his thickness brushing my walls just right. I angled my hips to meet his and took him in deeper.

Brady kept up his painfully slow rhythm, driving me insane. I made a noise to encourage him and he smiled down at me. "I'm just enjoying the feel of you, honey."

"You feel good, but I want a little less control, a little more crazy."

"Be careful what you wish for, baby."

I smiled up at him. Then he thrust hard and deep into me and my eyes fluttered closed. Shit, he felt good. His speed and pressure increased, and my body started to tingle. Tremors radiated from my core outward, a not-so-slow burn heating me up with each second.

"I need to see you, honey. Sam, look at me, sweetheart," Brady begged, his voice sounding strained.

I opened my eyes and saw the attempt he was making to hold on to his control. His face softened slightly, but his jaw ticked with his tension. His movements became more urgent and less restrained. I watched him and he watched me. Our bodies matched each other stroke for stroke, thrust for thrust, moan for moan.

My body coiled, tightening around him. He pumped harder, need taking over for control. He grunted and moaned above me, his eyes drifting closed for a second before he focused on me again.

With our eyes locked our bodies moved together, bringing both of us to the edge. I could see the pain in his expression from holding back. Knowing he was waiting for me, wanting to make sure I felt good before he let go, spurred me over the edge. My core locked around him sending us both into the oblivion we craved.

Brady bellowed my name as he came, jerking against me before he collapsed on top of me. The feel of his weight on me was comforting in the most amazing way. I could smell his sweat and his freshness, and it wrapped around me like a warm blanket.

Far too soon, Brady rolled off me and disappeared into the bathroom. He was back quickly and pulled the covers out from under me then crawled in with me. He covered us up and held me close, my head on his chest and his arm securely around me. I listened to his heart beat and wondered what he was thinking.

"Are you okay?" he asked in the darkness.

I wanted to tell him the truth, but I couldn't. There was no way I could admit to him that in a matter of one night I'd gone from worrying about being with him to falling hopelessly in love with him.

It scared the shit out of me to realize just how much I cared about him, how badly I wanted to hold on to him. I knew it would end once he realized someone else was a better match for him, but at that moment he was mine. And I wasn't going to do anything to jeopardize that. Even if it meant lying.

"I'm great," I whispered in the dark, admitting as much as of the truth as I could handle.

We held each other, our breathing slowing and steadying out, until Brady fell asleep. And I wondered how I would ever live without him.

Twenty-Three

The next morning Brady cooked me breakfast, egg whites with wheat toast and turkey sausage. He really made me want to be a better person, a healthier person. I still loved my cupcakes, and wasn't giving them up, but I realized I could change some things about myself without losing who I was.

Brady had work to do so we didn't spend the day together, but he told me he had fun and wanted to repeat our performance again soon, which left me feeling warm and fuzzy.

And damn good.

I invited him to girls' night Tuesday again. I'd signed all the paperwork for my new house and was hoping he would be interested in seeing it, and maybe helping me move. I had a couple weeks before I was actually going to move, but I had a lot of packing to do.

"How was your day?" I asked him when he got in my car for girls' night.

He shrugged but didn't say much. I'd learned when he was like that to let him be, so I told him about my day.

"I had the sweetest family come in today. They had friends that I worked with a few weeks ago. The kids were adorable. The little girls wore matching dresses and the boys had shirts that coordinated also. The parents were so in love it was almost sickening. I loved it though. I kept thinking about what my kids might look like, assuming I ever have kids."

"I don't want kids," Brady said abruptly.

"Really?" I asked, feeling a little hurt by his tone. "Why not?"

He shook his head. "Just don't. Never have."

"Everyone wants kids. I can't even imagine not wanting kids one day."

"Well, I don't," he said with finality.

I cringed, knowing I'd pushed him too far, but also hurt that he would speak so harshly to me.

"Are you okay?"

"I'm fine," he growled at me.

Tears stung my eyes but I refused to let them fall, blinking to clear my vision. I wouldn't let him know he was hurting me. If he was going to be an ass, I wasn't going to sit back and take it.

When we got to Bite Me! I slammed out of the car without waiting for him. I was nearly to the door when he grabbed my hand and spun me around. His lips came down on mine hard, forcing his way into my mouth as he pressed my back to the warm brick on the outside of the building. I knew everyone could see us, but I didn't care. All I cared about was resisting the jerk Brady was acting like.

Then he cupped my jaw and softened the kiss, loving my mouth instead of demanding I give in to him. I melted into him, accepting his unspoken apology, and loving him right back.

"I'm sorry," Brady whispered when he pulled back. "I've got a lot on my mind right now."

"That doesn't mean you can treat me like shit," I argued.

"I know. I shouldn't have spoken to you like that. I don't want kids, but that choice has nothing to do with you. It's all-"

"You. I know. You have a lot of secrets, Brady Wright. And a lot of excuses without actually saying anything."

He sighed heavily. "I know. It's not fair to you, Sam."

"No, it's not. Maybe one day you'll trust me enough to tell me."

"I do trust you, Sam. More than it seems."

I looked at him closely, trying to decipher his code. As usual, I had no idea what he was actually talking about. One day he'd tell me. At least I hoped so.

"Let's go see your friends before they start to worry."

I snorted. "They're not going to worry. They're going to think I'm dragging you off to bed."

His eyes darkened, the hazel color turning emerald green before my eyes. "After this, that's exactly what I'm going to do."

I grinned, hoping he was telling me the truth, then led the way inside.

Charlie handed me a plate with our cupcakes on it. Brady paid for our snack, even though Charlie protested. We joined the others at the table, me sitting next to Addi and Brady next to Mike. Addi leaned over to me, "Are you guys okay?"

I nodded. "Yeah, just a misunderstanding."

She eyed me then peered around me to Brady. He was oblivious, already in a conversation with Mike. "You sure?"

I nodded again. "I'm sure. Have you set a date yet?" I asked, turning the conversation to her instead of focusing on my confusing relationship with Brady.

"I think we finally have. We're thinking New Year's Eve."

"Really? That's so cool."

"What's cool?" Mandy asked, sitting down next to Claire, Xander on her other side next to Riley.

"They finally set a date," I said, gesturing to Addi and Joey. Joey beamed and tugged her closer.

"Ooh, when."

"New Year's Eve," Addi told everyone.

"Very sexy," Mandy said with a sly smile. "I like it. What can we do to help?"

I smiled. I seriously had the best friends ever. We were all always there for each other. Addi's wedding was only a few months away which meant she had a lot to do and not a tremendous amount of time.

"We're going to keep it small," Joey said. "Hopefully at the lodge at Winter Ridge. Family and close friends."

"It's better that way," Lexi declared. "Ours was huge and way too stressful. If I ever got married again, I'd have a tiny wedding."

"You better not be thinking about getting married again. I'll have to tie you to the bed and change your mind," Mike growled at her.

"It might be worth it then," Lexi teased.

"Get a room," Mandy crowed at them before Xander pulled her in for a kiss.

"I think everyone needs a room," Carrie said snarkily. Everyone laughed. "I think you're next, Sam. Three are already married, Addi's on the way, but Riley, Charlie, and I are nowhere near marriage. When are you up?"

I tensed immediately. After the conversation we had in the car I wasn't sure how to respond, especially with Brady sitting next to me. He didn't want kids, but I had no idea if marriage was on the table or not. And we'd only been dating a month.

Brady didn't answer, ignoring the comment entirely. I didn't know what to say, so I just joked back, "In this group you never know. You guys might all beat me down the aisle."

Everyone laughed, but I couldn't shake the feeling that I'd just pushed Brady further away.

The rest of the night I sat back and listened to my friends. Brady was constantly checking his phone, which both annoyed me and made me insanely curious. He'd never been one to be tied to his phone so I wondered what was going on.

When we finally left I asked if he was waiting for a call. All he said was, "No." No explanation, no details, nothing. I shouldn't have been surprised.

Since I'd picked him up we went back to his place. Lucky was waiting for us when we walked in. Brady told me to make myself comfortable while he walked the dog. I asked if he wanted me to come with him, but he said no. And the anxious feeling got worse.

When Brady came back in he didn't say anything to me. His eyes looked sad but determined. He unclipped Lucky's leash then reached for my hand and led me to the bedroom.

He closed the door behind us and turned me to him. His kiss was so sweet and tender it nearly brought tears to my eyes. We kissed softly, tasting each other, savoring each other. He never pulled back to look at me, just kissed me for what felt like forever.

As we kissed Brady's hands roamed my body, caressing whatever exposed skin he could reach and fluttering over my clothes. If I didn't know any better I would have thought he was trying to memorize me. I reached under his shirt and let my fingers glide over his taut muscles, doing my own search of him. I needed to feel him, to know our argument from earlier and the tension I'd felt in him was just my imagination.

Brady yanked his shirt off and let me touch him while he played with the strings tying my top together. Once he'd freed me he let the fabric float to the ground behind me. His hands cupped my breasts, rasping his thumbs over my nipples. "You're beautiful, Sam. Don't ever let anyone allow you to feel otherwise."

It felt like he was telling me something more than his words said, but I didn't know what.

And at that moment I didn't care. I just wanted Brady. My Brady.

"You, too," I said softly, knowing he needed to hear it as much as I did. We'd shared our bodies before, but the reverence in his tone and his eyes told me this time was different. He was different. We were different. It wasn't sex. It was more.

Something in my words snapped something within Brady. He kissed me fiercely, hard and demanding, but giving as much as he took. I kissed him back with equal urgency, needing to connect with him.

Our hands tore at the remaining clothes that separated us. Brady toed off his sneakers and rolled on a condom as his shorts and boxer briefs hit the floor. He reached for me and lifted me into his arms. My legs circled his waist and he slid deep into me.

Oh, dear god, he felt good. Without knowing it he was fulfilling a fantasy of mine. He surged into me, supporting the weight of both of us. He quickly worked me into a frenzy. I couldn't stop the urge to erupt around him, but I held back, wanting to feel him within me just a little longer. I needed to feel him, to grasp that this was Brady uncontrolled. This was Brady acting on desire alone. This was the Brady he didn't want me to see.

But it was part of the Brady I loved.

When his fingers dug into my hips I knew he was close. He guided my body up and down his length, his hips surging harder and deeper to hit me just right, so deep and oh so right. I felt the tightness within me, urging both of us along, and his control completely fell away. He pounded into me, almost to the point of pain, which ramped up my need for him. My body went limp as my orgasm began. I couldn't control myself. I couldn't stop my body from moving how it wanted. Brady held me, pulling my body tight against his as we both pulsed and twitched and came with matching screams of pleasure.

Brady collapsed onto the bed, pulling me on top of him. I rested my head against his chest and listened to the beat of his heart. My fingers trailed over his body. I loved seeing Brady out of control, but I knew he was going to flip out any minute.

"I'm sorry, Sam," he said softly. "I shouldn't have taken you that hard."

"I loved it. Every second. It felt so good, Brady. Perfect."

"I wasn't too hard on you."

I wiggled my hips, his erection still buried deep inside me. "Just hard enough," I teased.

Brady huffed a laugh and tightened his grip on me, but didn't say anything else. After a few minutes he got up and went to the bathroom, then came back to bed. He tugged me to him and whispered, "Will you stay with me? I need you here tonight."

I nodded, dying to ask why he needed me, but knowing he wouldn't tell me.

Brady drifted off to sleep, but I laid there wide awake. I couldn't shake the feeling that something was seriously wrong. Brady had always been quiet and intense, but there was something going on.

A few hours later Brady woke up and pulled me close. He slid inside me, still half asleep, and made love to me slowly, staring into my eyes the whole time. When he fell asleep after that time I laid there and cried, knowing without words that he was saying goodbye.

And I had no idea why.

Twenty-Four

I was so ready to relax. After a long day, and even longer week, I was thrilled to have a Friday night off and happy to spend it with Brady. He sent me a text that morning saying he wanted me to come over for dinner and spend the night. We hadn't seen each other in three days, when he'd acted so strange. I'd sensed something was going on, but like always, Brady didn't open up and tell me what was going on. I'd finally drifted off sometime around five that morning and Brady was gone when I woke up, a note saying he'd be in meetings all day.

He'd sent me text messages every day, acting like everything was okay, so I'd pushed away the thoughts I had about him pushing me away.

Until I walked into his apartment.

I could tell something wasn't right. Lucky met me at the door with a whine, wagging his tail low like he needed to go out. "Where's Brady?" I asked the dog, as though he could answer.

Lucky whined at Brady's name and I started to get really nervous.

The kitchen was empty and so was the living room. The only other place he could be was the bedroom, but the door was closed. I'd never been worried about talking to Brady, even though he never said much, but something told me whatever I found behind that door was going to change things.

And probably not for the better.

I knocked once and waited. When I didn't hear Brady's voice I twisted the knob, not knowing if I wanted it to be unlocked or locked. It turned in my hand and I opened the door.

The room was dark, but I could see Brady sitting in the corner of the room. He was tucked onto the floor like a child in time-out. One knee was raised and his elbow was anchored on his knee with his head resting on top. In his other hand glinted a bottle. One that was mostly empty.

Panic settled low in my gut. I didn't know why Brady didn't drink, but I knew he never did. It wasn't time to question why, but even a guy Brady's size couldn't put away the better half of a bottle of whiskey without it knocking him on his ass. Since Brady didn't drink, he would be even worse.

"Brady?" I said tentatively into the darkness. "What's wrong?"

"Go away, Sam," he answered, his voice harsh and his speech slurred.

"No, Brady. Talk to me. Why are you drinking?"

He stayed silent for a few minutes and I wondered if he'd passed out. I had no idea how I was going to get him into bed, or the bathroom if he was sick. Maybe Xander or some of the trainers could help me.

"You don't want to be here Sam. Just go home."

The anger and distaste in his words lanced me. He could have called me a fat bitch and I think it would have hurt less.

Okay, maybe not, but his tone hurt.

"Brady, I just want to help you. Tell me what's going on."

"Why?" he asked with clear disdain. "So you can feel bad for me? So you can hold me and tell me everything's going to be okay? Fuck that, Sam."

I moved closer to him, finally working my way into the room so I could get closer to him. Touch seemed to be big for Brady. If I could touch him maybe he'd be okay.

When I got to his side I rested my hand on his arm, but he shrugged me off. "Damn it, Sam. I said go. I don't want you here."

Ouch. I knew he was drunk and didn't mean anything he said, but he knew exactly what to say to make me feel like shit.

"Brady, I'm not leaving you like this. Please talk to me."

I tried to touch him again but he shrugged me off and stood up. He wobbled but caught himself against the wall. Another swig of the bottle vanished down his throat and fear mixed with the panic I'd been feeling. That wasn't Brady. He didn't drink. He didn't push me away.

"He's dead, Sam. My dad's fucking dead. Is that what you want to hear? He fucking died."

I was so confused. I shook my head, trying to understand what he was telling me. His dad died when he was 18, 15 years ago. Maybe it was the anniversary of his death and Brady wasn't dealing well with it.

"Is today the anniversary, Brady? Did he die 15 years ago today?"

Brady never talked about his dad. The only time he'd mentioned him was the day at my parents' house when he told them about his parents. Since then he'd never mentioned them, and I didn't ask. Now I wished I had. Maybe I'd be better prepared for drunk Brady.

"He died today, Sam. Just after noon."

Shocked didn't begin to describe how I felt. He'd lied to me. I didn't know why he told me his dad died, but it hurt that he'd lied to me.

"How? What happened?"

Brady laughed mirthlessly. His voice was full of anger when he said, "The bastard had cirrhosis. All his fucking drinking finally caught up to the son of a bitch."

Brady dropped to the bed, his arm hanging over the edge with the bottle of whiskey dangling from his fingers. I sat next to him and tried to piece together what was going on. I felt like I was the drunk one.

"He was an alcoholic? Is that why you told me he died when you were 18? You were ashamed of him?"

Brady snorted and sat up enough to take another sip from the bottle. "I told you he was dead because I left home as soon as I turned

18 to get away from that fucking asshole. Ashamed of him? No. I just never wanted to speak to him again. As far as I was concerned the bastard died then. I haven't seen him since."

I was getting more and more confused. All I'd figured out was Brady hated his father, he died that day, and Brady was drinking.

"How do you know he died today if you haven't spoken to him?"

"She called me," he growled. "He must have told her about me. She called me this afternoon and told me. She wants me to go to his funeral. Like I owe him anything."

"Who's she?"

"His wife," Brady growled like I should have known the answer.

Wait... his mom?

"I thought your mom died when you were little."

He laughed again, cruelly. "She's not my mother. My mother was the reason the bastard drowned himself for years. She was on a date with her fucking boyfriend when they got into a car accident. Both of them were killed. My father took it out on me until I got bigger than him and could fight back. Then the bastard started using props. The broken beer bottles were my favorite. A few picture frames. Once in a while he'd throw a knife at me. I got really fucking good at dodging shit."

Oh. My. God. I'd wondered since the first time I'd seen him without a shirt if it'd been at the hands of his father, but hearing the truth was a hundred times worse than I could have ever imagined. I didn't blame him one bit for hating his father. I hated the asshole, too. How could you take your anger out on a child? Fists, bottles, knives?

"Brady, I'm so sorry. I had no idea."

"Don't give me that shit, Sam. You knew. I saw it in your eyes when you looked at my scars. You've kissed them, like you could heal me, and you wanted to ask. Now you know the truth. I had a shitty childhood."

"Okay, yes. I wondered, but I never imagined it was that bad. I'm sorry you went through that, Brady."

"Whatever. She said he's been better. He quit drinking twelve years ago, got sober. They've been together ten years and said I have a sister. An eight year old sister. That he was a changed man. A good man. He wanted to see me. To apologize."

"Did you know that? Did you go see him?"

He scoffed. "Fuck no I didn't go see him. She called me Tuesday, but he didn't deserve my forgiveness. That bastard doesn't get to erase sixteen years of torture with two little words. He could have spent the rest of my life apologizing to me and I wouldn't have forgiven him. He deserved the miserable fucking death he got."

I sucked in a breath at Brady's admission. No one deserved a miserable death, not even a child abusing asshole.

Brady's eyes snapped to mine, as much as they could in his drunken state, and he snarled. "Don't get all high and mighty on me now, Sam."

I bristled at his words. He'd never made me feel like I was a snob before.

"Brady, why don't you get some rest? Give me that," I reached for the bottle in his hand, but he snatched it away before I could get to it.

"Don't bother, Sam. I'm just like him, you know. I didn't just get my name from him, but I'm unable to control myself around alcohol like him. This was the whiskey he would always drink before he beat the shit out of me. Did you know the first time he broke my nose he couldn't even take me to the hospital to get it set because he was too drunk? That's why it's still crooked. Of course the other times he broke it he was too drunk then too, but I'd learned how to set it myself. Not too well since I can't smell anything, but whatever. It's just another in the long list of things that asshole stole from me."

"Brady, you're nothing like him. Don't say that."

"Oh, but I am Sam. Sam, I am," he laughed at his joke. "I never should have pursued you. I knew I wasn't good enough for you. I'm a fucking joke and you deserve better."

My heart sunk. Brady was the most confident person I knew. He wasn't a depressed, self-bashing man. He was a kind, sweet, protective, amazing man. I hated his father just a little more for making him believe those things about himself.

"Brady, don't say that."

"Did you know I never finished high school? I just left. The day I turned 18 I left for school like normal but went to the bus station. I'd stolen cash from him and had enough for a couple of days. I took a bus to Winterville. My mom grew up here and even though I hated her for leaving me and turning him into a monster, I knew he'd never look for me here. I was at a diner getting dinner when Dave sat next to me. We started talking and he took me in."

I really thought my heart was going to break. Brady had been through so much in his life and he was screwed up. He never talked about himself, never let me in. At least I knew why, but it didn't make it easier.

"I don't care if you never finished high school. Or anything else Brady. I... I love you."

He snorted and shook his head. "No you don't. You love the idea of me. You love the strong boyfriend who can kick the ass of any jerk who is mean to you, but you don't love me. Just go, Sam. Find someone who deserves you. Find a smart guy, one who can love you back. I can't love anyone. I don't know how."

Oh, God. I turned my face away from him, not wanting him to see my tears. I covered my face with my hand, stifling the sobs that threatened to escape. He didn't mean it, he couldn't. He was just drunk. People said all sorts of things when they were drunk, whether they meant them or not. Brady couldn't mean the things he said.

Before I composed myself I heard soft snores coming from Brady. He'd passed out hard. The bottle still dangled from his fingertips but he was out cold. I wiped my eyes and eased off the edge of the bed. He wouldn't be comfortable in his jeans, but I wasn't going to risk waking him up trying to take them off. He was barefoot so I didn't have to worry about that.

I gripped the bottle and slowly worked it out of his hand. He rolled toward the middle of the bed and curled up with his hands tucked beneath his chin. He looked so small, so young. My heart broke all over again for the boy Brady was, the boy who lived in fear for so many years.

It was a lot to process, but I understood Brady a lot better having learned so much. Losing his dad was hard, even though he hated the man. It made sense why he'd pulled away from me all week too. If his step-mom had called him it explained why he was saying goodbye the other night while he made love to me.

But it wasn't goodbye. He'd be fine in the morning. We'd get through it together. Drinking was a side effect. And he wouldn't do it again.

While Brady and I were talking Lucky relieved himself on the kitchen floor. I cleaned the mess up then started on the rest of the apartment. I wasn't going to leave Brady alone, but I wasn't ready to sleep just yet. Cleaning always wore me out.

When the apartment was spotless I dumped out the rest of the whiskey and took out the trash. Lucky and I went for a quick walk, and I was happy to see he emptied his bladder and his bowels before settling in for the night.

I checked on Brady again, he was still passed out, then curled up on the couch. I wanted to cuddle up to Brady, but he was hogging the bed and I was still hurt from all the things he said to me. I knew we'd get through it, but at that moment it was painful.

When I woke up the next morning I heard Brady in the bathroom. Unsure if he'd want me to see him so sick, or if I could handle it, I stayed out. I brewed a pot of coffee and slid a few slices of bread into the toaster and waited for him to come out.

A few minutes later Brady came out and froze when he saw me. "What are you doing here?" he asked, not sounding overly thrilled to see me. He probably didn't remember anything that happened the night before and would apologize when I told him how mean he'd been.

"I came over last night. You'd been drinking."

He nodded. "I know. I also remember telling you to leave."

My heart snapped. Literally, it just cracked in half. He was sober and still wanted me to leave.

"You didn't mean that, Brady. You were drunk. I didn't want to leave you alone. I was worried about you."

"Don't Sam, just don't. I meant what I said last night. I don't want you here."

Tears stung my eyes, but I blinked them back. "Brady, you don't mean that. This isn't you. I know you're hurt, but I'm here for you. You don't have to be afraid to let me in."

He shrugged like it was no big deal. "I'm not afraid, Sam. And I'm not hurt. I just know when something is done and this is done. We're done, Sam."

"No, Brady, don't say that," I sobbed, abandoning my desire to keep from crying in front of him. "I love you."

He stared at me, his eyes cold and hard. There was no softness in him, no sign of the Brady I knew. He was the cold, unbending asshole I'd thought he was to start with.

"I don't feel the same way about you, Sam. It's over. Please go."

He turned from me, dismissing me. Tears poured down my face, but I wouldn't break down. At least not in his apartment. I'd wait until I got home.

I picked up my purse and hugged Lucky goodbye then walked to the door. I paused with my hand on the doorknob, unable to face walking away, but knowing I had no choice. I glanced back to look at him. He had his arms crossed over his chest and was staring at me without a hint of kindness. "Goodbye Brady," I said, then walked out of his life.

Twenty-Five

Before Brady my weekends were boring, long, and depressing. After Brady I knew it was only going to be worse. I knew what I could have had. I knew what was out there for me. I knew what I was missing.

My life was all of a sudden defined by my time with him. Before him I was unhappy but ignorant. I didn't know how great life could be. After Brady, it only got worse. I was no longer unaware of how beautiful life could be. And it ripped my heart to shreds.

Carrie and Riley kept me company over the weekend and talked me off the proverbial ledge. I couldn't have survived without them. They kept me fed and liquored up enough to dull the pain, although it never truly stopped. The truth was, I think I hurt more for Brady than for myself. Yeah, I missed him and wanted him back, but if he thought he couldn't love someone I felt sorry for him.

I knew he could love. I'd seen it in his eyes when he held me and felt it in his touch. If what we had wasn't love I didn't know what was. Even Carrie and Riley said they thought he loved me and were shocked when I told them he'd never said the words, and then told me he wasn't capable of love.

I ended up looking up his dad's obituary online. I told myself I hated the man, but it was hard to believe he couldn't have changed. His wife had contacted Brady, more than once apparently, to meet the man his dad had become.

Brady Richard Wright, Sr. was going to be buried Tuesday, but his wake was on Monday afternoon and evening. By the end of the weekend I knew I had to attend. I couldn't explain it, even to myself, but I had to be there. I had to see the man who'd destroyed the one I loved, and meet the woman he'd spent the rest of his life loving. Meeting Brady's sister was a draw, too.

I was nervous.

Dressed in a conservative black skirt and dark grey top, I headed to the funeral home. Like I'd hoped, it was quiet being a Monday afternoon. After a quick scan of the lot to make sure Brady wasn't there, I forced myself inside.

A greeter met me at the door and directed me toward the correct room. A woman with greying auburn hair and kind, wet eyes was standing just beyond the casket. A younger version of her, but with Brady's hazel eyes, stood next to her. A few others fell into place beyond them, people I assumed were her parents and siblings.

Brady never mentioned aunts or uncles, but then again he never mentioned his parents either. I had no idea who I might run into at the wake, but I was there for him, for a purpose. No one and nothing else mattered.

After kneeling before the man who resembled Brady in many ways, even though he always told Brady he looked like his mother,

I took my place in line. When I reached the auburn haired woman she smiled kindly at me and thanked me for coming, effectively dismissing me.

"I know Brady," I said to her, my eyes locking on hers. I saw the briefest of widening in her irises before she turned to one the of others in line and asked them to take over for her.

She led me out of the room and onto a bench in the hallway. "Is Brady coming?"

I suddenly felt bad for being there. She was dealing with enough grief and having me there would only make it worse.

"I'm sorry. Maybe I shouldn't have come."

I started to stand, but she rested her hand on my arm and said, "Please. Will you tell me about him?"

A smile crossed my lips before I could think about it. "Brady is an amazing man. He's kind and helpful and strong and independent and beautiful in every way. He's the most wonderful man I've ever met in my life," I told her honestly.

The woman nodded as though she expected to hear all those words. "He's lucky to have you in his life. Brady, Sr. told me about his son, about how he was when he was drinking. He was very ashamed and it took him years to even think about forgiving himself. I'm not sure he ever truly did."

"I'm sorry. Obviously the man you knew was very different than the one Brady knew. He told me his father died when he was 18. He never talked about him."

She nodded again. "They had a fight when Brady was 18, well, just before it. He told his father he hated him and he hoped he died. Brady, Sr. said he knew his son would leave, but he was too drunk to care. When Brady actually left he admitted he was relieved. It also forced him to face his pain over what happened with his first wife. Sixteen years was a long time to hold on to so much hatred. I know it had to be hard on Brady, but him leaving probably saved his dad's life. Well, at least gave him another fifteen years."

I wanted to be surprised by what she said, but I wasn't. Without Brady around for his dad to take out his anger, he had to deal with it. I only wish he'd dealt with it before Brady was forced to go his own way.

"Brady, Sr. wrote a letter to his son. If he's not coming today, would you bring it to him?"

I took a deep breath. It was now or never. I had a reason for going and it was time to do it. "Actually, that's why I'm here today. I have to ask you a favor. I know this isn't fair to you or your daughter, but I want to ask you to stop contacting him. In the time I've known him he's never touched alcohol, but Friday night he consumed almost a full bottle of whiskey. He's not ready to deal with all this. I don't know if or when he will be, but I wanted to ask you to give him space. He knows how to get in touch with you, and I think one day he will, but for now, I ask that you let him grieve and accept what's happened."

She regarded me carefully for a few seconds, making me feel like I was on a job interview or something. I had no delusions that she would roll over and accept my request, but when she nodded once I thought maybe she would.

"Brady's a lucky man. You obviously love him very much."

"I do," I confessed. "With every piece of my heart." Tears leaked from my eyes and trickled down my cheeks. She pulled a tissue from her pocket and handed it over.

"That's how I felt about his dad. I understand his need for space. Please tell him I'll respect his wishes and that if he ever wants to be in touch, we'd welcome him with open arms."

I shook my head, struggling to compose myself. I did what I came to do, and it was time to go. "Thank you," was all I managed before I stood and half ran from the funeral home.

Safely tucked in my car I let the tears fall. The woman I met was wonderful. Kind, welcoming, and clearly in love with Brady's dad. There was no way he was the man Brady'd known when she was with him. My heart broke for Brady that he would never know his dad without a bottle hanging around, or fear and anger. I had no claim to him anymore, but I prayed that one day he'd find someone who could push past his hurt and give him the love he deserved. The love I felt but couldn't share.

~*~

The next few weeks were the worst of my life. I wanted to believe Brady would come to his senses and call me, but he never did. He'd completely erased me from his world.

I moved on as much as I could. My friends helped me move into my new house the weekend after Brady and I broke up. It was hard getting settled in a new place by myself when I'd chosen a place imagining Brady being there with me, a home with a yard that Lucky could play in when the two of them came over to visit.

None of that would ever happen though.

I tried to go to Dave's Gym a few times, but whenever I got there I couldn't get out of my car. I'd sit in the parking lot and stare at the building that held so many memories and couldn't go inside. If I saw him I'd lose it, and if I didn't see him I'd be disappointed. It was a lose-lose for me.

One Wednesday I finally gave up. It'd been almost three weeks since I'd seen Brady, since I'd walked out his door. He wasn't coming back. I knew that without a doubt. If he'd loved me the way I thought he had he wouldn't have been able to stay away. I was hurt but had to move on with my life. I wouldn't ever forget him, but I could start to erase him from it.

It started with a phone call. "Dave's Gym, this is Jennie, how may I help you?"

"Hi Jennie, it's Sam," I said into the phone, knowing she'd know who I was.

"Oh, my God, Sam, where have you been? What's going on?" she said in a hushed voice.

"Brady and I broke up. Well, technically he broke up with me. He told me he doesn't love me and he's done with our relationship. But that's not why I'm calling. I need to cancel my membership. I can't come back there," I said over the lump in my throat.

"Oh, man. That sucks. He was so happy with you. I thought for sure you'd end up Mrs. Brady. And I don't believe that he doesn't love you. Have you talked to him? He's miserable-"

"Jennie, I can't," I interrupted her. Hearing about Brady would only hurt worse. He was the one who said he was done, who said he didn't want me. I couldn't get pulled into his orbit again. I might not ever make it out if I did. "I'm sorry. I'm not trying to be nasty to you, but it just hurts to hear about him. I wish him the best, but I can't see him or talk to him. He told me he didn't love me and kicked me out of his place. It's over."

"Damn. I'm sorry, Sam. That really sucks. I'll take care of your membership. Don't worry about it."

"Thanks Jennie. Hey, if you ever want to grab that drink, give me a call. I mean, unless it's too awkward with Brady being your boss and all..." I trailed off, wishing I didn't have to give up so much just because of Brady. I was already giving him up, it sucked that I also had to give up my gym and my new friends there.

"That would be great. I'll talk to Greg and we'll check our schedules and call you."

I smiled, feeling a little better. Greg was great and so was Jennie. I could hold on to them even though I lost Brady.

Jennie and I hung up. My smile faded quickly. Slowly but surely I would remove Brady from my world, and one day I wouldn't feel so much pain when I thought about him. As much as I hated the steps I had to take, I needed to take them.

I spent the rest of that afternoon working. My business was doing well, although I was happier than ever that I was giving up weddings. I had my last one coming up in a few weeks. It was a definite hit to my income, but things were picking up with the family portraits and business accounts. I'd taken some pictures of READ and Riley and Carrie were meeting me at work for dinner to review all the pictures and work on the website for READ.

I ran out early evening it pick up some Chinese food. We'd all discovered it was one of our guilty pleasures, and I wanted to have a good dinner for them since they were keeping me from sinking into myself most nights. Addi and the others were helping me too, but Carrie and Riley were definitely the two I'd grown closest to over the last three weeks.

Then again, seeing the happy couples just made me want to cry. I'd spent more than my fair share of time, and money, at Bite Me! with Charlie too, but she worked such crazy hours I had to go to her. Boy was I glad to have single friends. Not to mention the fact that they were awesome.

My mom called while I was carrying food back into the office. "Hi, Mom," I said, feeling the need to finally move past our fight from forever ago. I barely remembered what we'd fought about, but it didn't matter anymore. It was nice to talk to someone who loved me, even if she did it in her own way.

"Hello, Samantha. I'm surprised you answered. How are you doing?"

"Not that great, Mom. Brady and I broke up a few weeks ago. I've moved to a new house. I cut weddings from my business and am focusing on just family and business shoots. I'm sorry about our fight."

"So am I. I never should have tried to tell you how to live your life. I'm always worried about you though. That doesn't mean I can tell you what to do."

Shocked, I didn't answer for a few seconds. I dumped all the food onto the table in the back. I already had three chairs around the table, and my jaw resting squarely on top.

"Are you still there, Samantha?"

"Yeah, I... I'm just surprised is all. I never thought I'd hear you apologize."

Mom laughed quietly. "Then you haven't been listening to the messages I've left you. Heather and your father both read me the riot act after we argued. They were right, but I didn't want to admit it. I'm sorry about Brady. If you were still with him I'd apologize for treating him poorly. I did think he was a good man. He seemed to really care about you."

A lump filled my throat and tears stung my eyes. "We were both wrong about that one," I finally managed.

"I'm sorry, honey. Have your friends been there for you?"

"Yeah. Riley and Carrie, two new friends, have been hanging around a lot. They're keeping me from sitting around crying every night."

"That's good. It's hard to be alone when you're upset. You have good friends."

I nodded even though she couldn't see me. "Yeah, I'm lucky. I don't know where I'd be without them."

"You're lucky, Samantha. You have wonderful friends, a career that makes you happy, and you're a beautiful woman. I know you're hurting right now, but maybe Brady will come to his senses one day."

I sighed. "I don't think so, Mom. It's been almost three weeks and I haven't heard anything from him. I'm finally accepting that it's really over and moving forward with my life, even though I'm not happy about it."

Mom paused, making me nervous. A pause for my mother was akin to pressing the launch button on a nuclear weapon. Something bad was coming.

"I'm sorry to hear that, honey. I'm proud of you. You've shown how strong you truly are through all this and I know it's not easy. I don't make anything easy on you and I've been made to realize that lately. I'm sorry I haven't supported your choices better. You were right about your career and you were right to love Brady. I thought he was your match. I wish I'd been right."

"Me, too, Mom," I said through my tears. "Me, too."

Mom and I talked for a few more minutes before she said she had to go. Knowing I finally had her support made a huge difference. No one would ever replace Brady, but having my parents behind me, finally, would help.

I set out the containers of Chinese food and dug out some plates, utensils, and a roll of paper towels. I grabbed my computer from my desk up front and was getting it set up when I heard the bells chime on the front door of the studio.

"I'm back here. Come on back," I called out to Riley and Carrie.

Their footsteps carried through the space until I knew they were behind me. I turned with a grin, ready to tell them to sit so we could eat, and stopped breathing.

"Brady," I whispered.

Twenty-Six

"Hi, Sam," he said casually, like it was no big deal. "Can I come in?"

"No," I spurted. I couldn't have Brady in my studio. I already had too many memories of him. A new one of him telling me, all over again, that he didn't want me might break me. I couldn't let him into my studio, the one place that had remained Brady free.

I stood and walked to the side door leading to the parking lot and stepped outside. He followed me out, but looked disappointed. "Fair enough. I don't deserve anything from you after the way I treated you." He hesitated, brushing his hand over his close cut hair. I looked him over, hating myself for still wanting him after he'd hurt me so badly. He looked good, but tired. His hazel eyes were dark with bags underneath. His knuckles sported fresh scrapes. His jeans hung low on his narrow hips and his shirt stretched over his always firm chest.

Damn him. He was even wearing my favorite shirt.

He shifted his weight and I caught a hint of his fresh scent and nearly swooned. Damn, the man had power over me. It just wasn't fair.

"Are you seeing someone else, Sam? Is he on the way here?"

"What are you doing here, Brady?" I asked, ignoring his question. If he thought I could move on so quickly he was a fool. Then again, he probably had. There was nothing keeping him from being with someone new. It wasn't like he loved me and had to work to get over me.

"I wanted to tell you I'm sorry. I fucked up, Sam. I shouldn't have taken things out on you like I did, and I'm sorry."

I nodded once, willing the tears building in my eyes to stay put. I would not cry in front of him again. "Okay, thanks," I said then turned to go back inside, safely away from him before the dam broke.

"Sam, wait. That's not it. I mean, I have more I want to say to you."

I lost it. The flood of emotions was too strong. "Why, Brady? Why bother? It doesn't change anything. Thank you for the apology, but you said it's over. Nothing changes that. I can't see you."

I turned away from him again and had my hand on the doorknob when he whispered, "I love you."

Oh, shit. He did not just say that. I couldn't believe it. I knew it wasn't true. He told me he was incapable of love, and in less than three weeks there was no way that could have changed. I never thought of him as someone who would play games, but I had proof right in front of me.

My head rested against he door as tears poured down my cheeks. I couldn't look at him. "Why Brady? Why are you doing this to me?

This has been the worst few weeks of my life. Please, Brady, just leave me alone."

"I'm telling the truth, Sam. The last 19 days have been the worst of my life, too. And that includes the 16 years I lived through my dad's constant abuse. The only thing that has ever given my life meaning is you. And losing you was the most horrible thing I've been through. Please, Sam, give me a chance to talk to you. Five minutes, Sam. If I can't convince you I love you then I'll leave and never bother you again. Five minutes."

Five minutes would kill me. Hell, five seconds was torture. Hearing my name on his lips was almost too much to take. Could he be telling the truth though? If there was any chance, I owed it to myself to listen.

"Five minutes, Brady. Not one second more," I finally agreed.

Brady thanked me then jumped into his argument. "I know you met Margaret. She told me when I went to see her Sunday that she'd met you and asked where you were. She didn't know your name, but I knew it was you when she told me my girlfriend went to see her at the wake. She told me what you said about giving me time. You were right. I was so wrapped up in my own fucking head that I couldn't see straight. I couldn't see what I was missing out on or what I was letting go."

He took a deep breath. I realized I'd been holding mine and exhaled slowly, trying not to hyperventilate.

"I never should have said any of those things I said to you. I was pissed off all over again with my father. I didn't want to admit it, but I'd always hoped he would apologize for what he did. Doing it from his death bed felt too easy. Like he was just a dying old man trying to cheat his way into heaven. When I met Margaret she told me who he's been since she's known him. He's been watching me for years, just inside the shadows, and making sure I was okay."

His hand brushed over his nearly bald head again and he walked out into the parking lot. "Watching you walk out my door snapped something inside me. I was hurt that you'd actually do it. I told myself if you really loved me then you wouldn't have left me when I needed you the most."

I started to interrupt him, but he held up his hand. "Let me get this out, then you can say whatever you want." I nodded and clamped my mouth shut.

"I was an idiot. I hurt you. I meant to at the time. I wanted you to go. Having you tell me you loved me was more than I could handle right then. You're the first truly good thing that's ever happened in my life. Mixing your love with my father's hate, or my hate for him, turned everything sour in my gut, and I didn't believe it. I had to hurt you the way I was hurting."

He shook his head.

"I know. It's not fair, or right. Watching you walk out the door a part of me knew I loved you but wasn't ready to admit it. I fucking lost it when you left. I became a complete asshole to work for and work with. People started avoiding me. Greg took me aside and threatened to kick my ass if I didn't work my shit out. He told me to go home and not come back until I had my head on straight."

He took a deep breath and waited. I risked a glance at him and saw pain and shame in his eyes. "I spent a week drinking. If my dad could erase my mom with a bottle I thought maybe I could erase you. But it didn't work. Lucky whined at the door every night, waiting to go see you. I smelled you on my sheets and couldn't bring myself to wash them. I saw you every time I closed my eyes and felt you every time I closed my hands."

I'd felt the same. Brady was so ingrained in me that he was like a ghost in my house. It was like he was there, even though he never was.

"I went to see him. To his grave. I told him everything I felt, how much I hated him for what he turned me into. I yelled at him and cried and yelled some more. Margaret was there, but I didn't know it. She heard all the things I said to him and told me how sorry she was and that she knew he was sorry too, and had been for years. She gave me a letter he wrote and invited me to lunch at their house Sunday so I could meet Grace. That's when she told me about you going to see her. I knew I had to get you back."

I cocked an eyebrow at him, not speaking, but silently asking why it took three days for him to visit me. If he had to get me back on Sunday, why wait until Wednesday?

"I know, I shouldn't have taken three days to find you, but you moved. And I had to be worthy of you. I had to be someone you could be proud to be with." He took a deep breath. "I signed up for get my GED, and I threw away all the liquor I'd bought and recommitted to myself not to drink. I'm not going to be him. I'm going to be someone you don't have to be ashamed of, and I'm going to spend my life showing you how much I love you, Sam."

What? Was he serious?

I looked at him and found him studying me. Waiting. "Is it my turn to talk now?" I asked. Brady nodded. "First of all," I said angrily, "how dare you claim I wasn't proud to be with you. I love you, Brady. Not your education, not your gym, not your past, not whatever. You, every bit of you. Second, you don't know me very well at all if you think you need to prove yourself to me. And third, how dare you accuse me of being with someone else already. I've been a mess since I left your place. *You* told me to go. *You* told me you didn't want me. *You* shattered my heart. Fourth, you're not getting away with keeping me at arm's length this time. You're letting me in, all the way in, Brady. I don't want you avoiding questions, dodging answers, or changing the subject. If I ask you something, you're going to tell me the truth.

More than your words, what hurt me was knowing how much you'd kept from me. Believing you cared so little for me that you didn't even want to tell me anything. We've delved into my world, we're getting comfy in yours next."

Brady was grinning like a fool by the time I finished. I was out of breath, my chest heaving in my anger. He stalked toward me, his eyes shimmering in the light above the door. I stepped back but the door was behind me, trapping me.

"What are you doing?" I stammered. "Why are you smiling at me like that?"

Brady rested his hands on my hips and leaned in close. His lips brushed my neck and he whispered, "You said 'this time.' 'This time' like you're giving me another chance. 'This time' like you forgive me for being such an asshole. 'This time' like I'm going to be able to kiss you and love you and hold you again. 'This time' I'm not going to screw it up."

Then his mouth was on mine, demanding, taking, loving. With my back pressed against the door and Brady covering my front, I felt secure, safe, right. I kissed him back, our tongues battling for a taste, our hands roaming, our bodies aching to come together again.

A horn blared in the distance and Brady let me up for air. We both turned toward the parking lot and saw Carrie and Riley standing next to the car and smiling at us.

"It's about fucking time," Riley yelled.

"No shit!" Carrie agreed.

I pushed Brady away and started walking toward them, but they held up their hands.

"Nope. We're gone. We were never here. Drag that man inside and have your way with him. Or take him home. We'll reschedule," Carrie said with a grin.

"Yeah, what she said. And let the dog out of the car," Riley added.

"Dog?" I questioned, turning back to Brady. "You brought Lucky?"

Carrie and Riley's doors slammed shut and they pulled out of the lot like nothing had happened. I was going to need to do something nice for them. Like, really nice.

"Lucky was Plan B," Brady said as he grabbed my hand and pulled me toward his Jeep.

Lucky was on the driver's seat wagging his tail and smiling at me. I was almost as excited to see him as I was to see Brady. Almost. He whined and pawed at the door, and as soon as Brady opened it he jumped on me for some loving. I ran my hands over his soft fur and cuddled him into my neck. I'd missed him.

We all headed back toward the studio and I remembered what Brady said. "What do you mean Plan B?"

Brady grinned and pulled me close. "If you wouldn't take me back I was going to tell you how miserable Lucky was and ask for joint custody. I hoped that maybe seeing me all the time you would fall in love with me again and let me back in."

I wrapped my arms around his neck and lifted up on my toes so we were almost nose to nose. "You were never out, Brady. You were always in."

"Good, now let me in the rest of you, baby. You're already in. All the way. And once we get inside I'm going to show you," he teased me with a nibble along my neck.

Brady snapped his fingers and Lucky fell into step beside us. Brady stopped me outside the door and sealed our lips together again, his hands drifting down to cup my ass. He lifted me, pulling me into his arms. My legs instinctively wrapped around his waist and opened me up to him. He felt so good, so right with me again.

Brady carried me inside and straight to my studio, laying me down on the blankets that were scattered on the floor. He ran out for a minute and I heard the doors click locked, then he was back. "I love you, Sam. I love you so much," he said, peering into my eyes.

"I love you, Brady. I'm not letting you go again," I said sternly.

"I'm not going anywhere. I promise, baby," he whispered before slanting his lips over mine.

Then he proved to me, over and over again, just how deep inside his heart I was.

Epilogue

Riley

"This is such a cool idea, don't you think?" Carrie asked as we walked up the sidewalk. Mandy and Xander's house seemed to be the gathering place for the group, a group Carrie and I were welcomed into only a few months ago.

"Yeah, it's nice. I feel like we're a part of something with them."

"Me, too. I can't believe we've all been in the same town for so long and never ran into each other. I'm just glad Sam wandered into READ when she did."

"Yeah, she and Brady are so happy. I'm glad he finally pulled his head out of his ass and got her back."

Carrie threw her head back and laughed. My best friend was one of the most beautiful women I'd ever met. She had long, wavy brown hair that fell a few inches past her shoulders. She was curvy in a way that drew men's attention instead of made them look right past her. And her eyes... she had the most unique and amazing eyes I'd ever seen. They would have fit better on a cat, but on Carrie she just looked exotic and beautiful, not that she was exotic. She didn't know any better than I did where she got her gorgeous eyes.

Me, on the other hand, I was the complete opposite of Carrie. I had more curves than a mountain road, and not in a good way. My hair was dull and lifeless and my eyes were a boring brown color. There wasn't anything special about me.

"Xander's friend is supposed to be here. Everyone said he's really nice, and totally hot."

"He's also practically engaged," I chastised. Carrie was constantly on the lookout for a new man, even, occasionally, when she had one. Having a guy with a good recommendation meant she was that much more interested.

"Girlfriends can be eliminated," Carrie teased.

"Says the woman who wants nothing more than to become a wife and mother. You know that starts with girlfriend, right?"

Carrie waved her hand dismissively. "When it's right I won't worry about that. I'll know."

Carrie rang the doorbell and we waited. A few seconds later Mandy opened the door with a huge grin. "Hi ladies! Come in."

"It smells amazing in here," I said as we stepped inside.

"Xander's been cooking all day. He's so excited about this."

"Are we the last ones here?" Carrie asked, her eyes glancing toward the kitchen where the others were.

Mandy shook her head. "Nope. Sam and Brady aren't here yet. They're on the way though."

"Is Xander's friend here?" I asked, saving Carrie from embarrassing herself.

Mandy wrinkled her nose. "No. His bitch of a girlfriend wouldn't let him come. Something about wanting him to take her shopping."

"It is Black Friday," I said tentatively, hoping to ease the tension.

"It doesn't matter. She just doesn't like Drew coming over here. She knows we trash her the whole time and try to talk him into dumping her. But enough about her. We're here to be thankful."

Carrie and I followed Mandy through the living room to the kitchen where the others had gathered. We exchanged hugs with our other friends, grateful to have been welcomed into their world.

"Dinner's almost ready," Xander announced. "Where are Sam and Brady?"

"Probably having sex if I know Sam," Addi teased.

"Hey, I resemble that remark," Sam answered as she and Brady came into view.

"Finally! Someone who'll let themselves into the house without requiring me to answer the door," Mandy cheered.

Sam and Brady laughed and he pulled her a little closer. "We had important things to do, and no we weren't having sex. Well, we did earlier, but that's not why we're late."

"Why are you late?" Addi asked carefully, leaning into Joey.

"We had to run into the city to see my parents."

"Didn't you see your family yesterday?" Claire asked.

Sam nodded and chewed her lip. She glanced up at Brady and love passed between them. It was palpable. God, it made me so jealous. I adored Sam and Brady, but man did I want a man to look at me like that.

Not that one ever would.

"We did. But Brady promised my dad we would go see them first when we got engaged."

Sam smiled so widely I thought her cheeks were going to split in half. She waited as her news sunk in around the room. All at once everyone started talking, offering congratulations and asking questions.

"Let's eat," Sam said. "We'll answer questions over dinner, but I don't want to let Xander's amazing cooking get cold."

Everyone agreed with Sam and we all settled at whatever seats we could find. Carrie and I sat together at the breakfast bar with Addi and Joey. Sam, Brady, and Charlie pulled up stools opposite us at the breakfast bar. Claire, Aidan, Mandy, Xander, Lexi, and Mike sat at the table in the dining room.

"Okay," Mandy said, standing up and lifting her glass. "Since this is our first friends Thanksgiving, we're going to go around the room and say what we're thankful for right now and what we're hoping for during the next year. I'm going to start. Right now, I'm thankful for my friends who have become my family. For next year I'm hoping we keep our traditions going with girls' night and more get togethers like this."

"We should start calling it friends' night or something," Aidan teased Mandy. "Us guys are starting to feel like we're not wanted."

"Yeah!" the other guys cheered.

Mandy raised an eyebrow at them all and they quieted. "We'll see," she finally relented. "Who's next?"

"I am," Xander said beside her, standing. "I'm grateful for the beautiful woman by my side, for the gift of having you as my wife. And in the next year I hope the launch of XD Designs is as much of a success as our marriage."

"You're finally starting it?" Claire asked.

I had no idea what they were talking about.

"Yep. Drew and I were going to announce it tonight, but since he's not here, I'm telling everyone. We hope to be open for business by summer. We're still working, but we know if we don't take the plunge now we never will."

"What is he talking about?" I whispered to the others.

"Xander and Drew have been working together on the side to rebuild old houses, like this one. They're finally starting up their own company to do it full time," Addi explained.

"Awesome," Carrie said. "So cool."

"Yeah. They met in college and always talked about starting their own company. They're crazy talented. You should ask Mandy to see the before pictures of this place. It's amazing what they've done."

The room continued talking, everyone saying what they were grateful for and their wishes for the next year. When it was my turn I was incredibly anxious. "I'm grateful for my new friends. Life has changed with all of you in it and I couldn't be happier. And next year I'm hoping, well, I'm hoping I don't lose my job."

"What?"

"Why?"

I forced a grin I didn't feel. "My bosses are getting close to retirement. They've been handing more and more of the business over to me. I'd love to buy the store, but I don't have enough money just yet. I'm worried they're going to end up closing it down or selling off to one of the bigger stores. Not many people want small bookstores anymore."

"Wow, that sucks," Addi said. "Hopefully it all works out."

I nodded and forced a grin. I hoped she was right, but I had very little faith in that. Pam and George had started taking more and more time off work, leaving me to fill in. I loved it, but I knew it was only a matter of time before they wanted out completely. Not that I blamed them. They were in their 60's and ready to relax and enjoy life, or so they told me. I just wished they'd hold out a few more years so I could save a little more and buy READ from them.

When everyone finished telling what they were thankful for and what they wanted we all jumped back into wedding questions. "How did he ask?" "How big of a wedding?" "Have you set a date?"

At the last question Sam looked up into Brady's eyes. He leaned down and sealed their lips together in a tender kiss. Staring at each other they answered, "January 22."

"That's two months away!" "Are you crazy?" "Are you pregnant?"

Again, the last question had them pausing.

"No," Sam said definitively. "We just don't see the point in waiting."

"I don't want to wait to call this woman mine," Brady said, leaning down to capture Sam's lips again.

And I realized I'd lied. I could always find another job. What I really wanted in the next year was to have someone look at me the way Brady looked at Sam. To have someone who couldn't wait to marry me. Someone who only had eyes for me.

Someone I was sure didn't actually exist.

Read Riley's story, Plump & Pretty, now!

Acknowledgements

Thank *you*, my wonderful reader, so much for reading Sam's story. I simply adored Sam from the beginning, and I hated to hurt her, but I knew she was strong enough to survive whatever life threw at her.

I thank God every day that I am lucky enough to be here and to have such an amazing job. My husband is right there too, supporting me in my dream to become a writer. I would have given up if he weren't always there, cheering me on!

The same goes for you, my amazing reader. I love hearing from you, every time. It makes me smile to hear you loved one of my books, you can't wait for the next one, or to know you want me to tell you more about a character. I can't get enough of hearing you love my fictional family as much as I do!

To my friend, Jess, who helped inspire this series. When I first pitched this series idea at lunch one day, she jumped right on it. Without Jess, none of these books would have left my head. I miss you, Jess, and our lunches.

About the Author

Mary E. Thompson grew up loving to read, like a good little girl. Many nights she would fall asleep with the flashlight still turned on as she hid under the covers trying to finish the last few pages of a book. As an adult, the light from her ereader means she doesn't need a flashlight, but she still stays up way too late to finish a book.

When Mary's not reading she's playing with her two kids or living out her own romance novel with her hubby. She has a weakness for chocolate, especially when it's paired with peanut butter, and has been known to have a bad day just because there's no chocolate in the house.

Mary grew up in Buffalo, NY and swears she's the only local to never ski or snowboard. Soccer was always her sport, with a couple adventures in white water rafting and skydiving to keep things interesting. Mary moved to South Carolina for college but missed Buffalo every day. Yeah she thinks she's crazy, too. She somehow convinced her South Carolina born and bred hubby to return to Buffalo to raise their kids and live out their lives. He's still not sure what he was thinking.